T.A. PAGE

Gallery of Myth

First edition

ISBN: 979-8-9857577-1-2

This book was professionally typeset on Reedsy.
Find out more at reedsy.com

To everyone who showed an interest in this quixotic bundle of emotions that became a novel: thank you, thank you, thank you. (And sorry for the rants.)

I was going to give you a map of the stars to follow along with, but you know what? I lost mine ages ago. Go and get your own constellation map—and while you're at it, go stargazing.

Contents

Warning

All that is gold does not glitter,
Not all those who wander are lost;
False frost can cause a true shiver,
From a fake may arise real thought.

J.R.R. Tolkien, with adaptation

1

Start Here

February 14, 2018

Hi everyone, I'm Ashley. And I want to make this clear from the start: I'm not into nostalgia. I take pictures of plants, not people, I don't like sappy songs, and I will pass on any rose-colored days-of-yore-o-vision goggles the moment they come out. But really, sometimes when you find the things the old you wrote, they're just too funny to pass up.

For those of you who didn't read the "About" page—and really, I don't blame you—this is what's up. Recently I went through the sort of box that gets packed with high school memories and forgotten the moment college begins, and in among the old journals, I found a story I wrote a long time ago. We're talking long enough ago that the whole thing is handwritten in a series of spiral notebooks. It's not exactly worthy of the Library of Congress, but it *is* a bit cute, so I sat down and made this blog in order to put it out into the wide world, one bit at a time.

Put out the story, that is.

Let's start before I say anything *more* embarrassing, shall we?

* * *

There was a croak in the dead of night as the timber gate of the outer wall swung open. Two armored horses bearing tall, noble riders made their way out through the fields. They made it halfway down one fenceline before the larger form turned and jostled the smaller.

"How about a game of stabsies?"

"No! Why would we be playing *any* game on such an important mission?"

"You know it always makes you less nervous!"

"I'm not nervous. I just don't want to be doing this."

"But it was *your* idea to make the raid!"

"All I said was we ought to have more information about the people we're going to fight, and specifically their witch. I did *not* volunteer to leave court—and without the king knowing!"

The first form struck at the other. The horses continued down the lane at an unperturbed canter. "Terrible dodge! Weak!"

"Rude," retorted the second.

"You'd better be *glad* your father isn't coming," the first grinned. His easy—if somewhat violent—manner revealed him as Benjamin Knight, the premier longswordsman of the country, sparring partner and frequent aider and abetter of the Crown Prince.

For his part the Prince, Richard, said nothing. After all, it was true: his father wouldn't have much cause to be proud of a son who couldn't deflect an honest jab. Or, for that matter, a son who left the castle in the middle of the knight to spring upon a sleeping enemy: it was very unsporting.

The light of the moon, unusually bright and close, guided the pair away from the summer training grounds and soon to the border with their sworn enemy. Scouting parties were frequent along the border, and Prince Richard could easily direct his horse and his friend along the paths they needed to take to get to the capitol. Luckily, as they crossed through hostile territory Benjamin became focused, and as the night passed the Prince was safe from any more stabs.

They reached their target just as the night was at its peak. Leaving tired horses behind, they crept on foot through the town and the maze of walls. Looming above the ominous quiet of orderly streets, the many towers of the Blessed Queen's castle rose as though to look down noses of cultured stone.

"Guess that's what they mean by high and mighty," Benjamin muttered. Richard elbowed him, gesturing at the guard passing them by, but he had to admit—the capitol was much more impressive than its pictures had been.

Still, Richard was if nothing else an excellent studier of maps and pictures. Despite the fact that they were in a strange land for the first time, and trying to move quietly in mail to boot, they had no trouble locating the witch. Of course, that may have been because she happened to reside in the tower which oozed a noxious green smoke, but nonetheless, the mission was going remarkably well.

"Good, good," said Benjamin as he caught up with the Prince. "We're scaling it, then?"

"Of course not," Richard replied automatically. Granted,

the tower *was* on the edge of the castle complex, but if anyone was to see them—his mind raced through the possibilities. Bodily harm ranked high on the list.

"You just don't want a repeat of last time we went up The Rock."

"I thought we agreed to be quiet?"

"We *agreed* to get this done! Come on!"

"But Ben—you saw those armor-piercing arrows yesterday—"

"All you're about to see is the soles of my boots if you can't keep up!"

Richard sighed, and resigned himself to the climb. He wasn't one to believe in dumb luck, but *something* had certainly favored them this far. Maybe, he thought, the people of Blessed were too exhausted from their feasting and parties to even think about sneak attacks on their witch's tower. Maybe they were all too soundly asleep to look out their windows and see two large men clinging to the masonry like ninjas who'd failed Subtlety 101. Heartened, he climbed on.

When finally he reached the witch's window and stepped in to inky blackness, Prince Richard realized how poorly this plan had been thought out. They were now standing in the witch's quarters—where were they to go? The first thing that came to him as he scanned the room was a strange, earthy scent. The second thing was—

"Oi! Earth to Prince! Why are you always so slow?"

"Hush, Benjamin!" Richard swatted impatiently as though he could bat his retainer's voice away. "What's going on?"

"What's the plan?"

"Couldn't you have asked me that *before* dragging me out of bed?"

"You mean you don't have a plan??"

"Well," cut in the witch, "obviously the plan is to get rid of you two."

Richard and Benjamin stared at each other, wide eyes barely connecting through the shadow.

"Or maybe I'll get rid of one, and keep the other?" The unseen witch giggled. "For information, you know."

"Run!" decided Richard, a moment after the knight at his side had done just that. He tried to move, too, and immediately bumbled in to something that chinked and shattered as he hopped past on one foot.

"Get out of here!" Richard cried to Benjamin, his voice becoming commanding in its desperation as around them the voice laughed. He could hear loud thumps from the other side of the room, and the familiar sound of Benjamin cursing. To get to it he'd have to cut across the empty space he'd just abandoned — the space not illuminated by the window beyond.

"I found stairs!" yelled Benjamin. The roaring in Richard's ears increased.

He gasped as he shouted back, "Go on then!"

"Get over here!"

"No, no, no," said the witch, but not in a despairing tone. It sounded like she was playing with them. "Only one!"

Benjamin, meanwhile, sounded miles away. "Straight through, come on, it's just an old woman! What could an old witch really do to us, anyway?"

The witch cackled, and the sound seemed to come from everywhere. "You think you can see the right way to take?"

There was crashing, and swirling, and chiming, and Richard could not tell which voice was his own any more. He went headfirst into the blackness and his feet left the ground as he tried one more time to cry out to his friend—

"We agreed to get this done!"

2

Dash In

February 21, 2018

Now, a few people have told me I was a bit awkward with the first post. (Story of my life!) Really, though, I didn't mean to come on too strong. It's just, if we're being honest, and only like two people will ever read this all the way through so why not be, right? Anyway if we're being honest, I just moved and I'm tired. Not of feeling homesick or nostalgic, but of people assuming I feel that way.

Now Richard, on the other hand—but you don't know that yet, do you? Oops. I had forgotten most of the things about Richard aside from where he ends up. I guess that's the danger of a story written by a naive teenage girl: the guy ends up under-developed. I'm fixing some of that as we go along because I have to type up the story for the first time and sometimes I can't bear to type what I originally wrote without making it about 20% cooler. Or trying to, anyway. I won't be changing the plot, though, for you purists out there. Just making the characters more 3D.

With that in mind, I expanded this next intro a bit. And please, after you read it, feel free to comment. Even if you say something cutesy about "when we were kids," I promise I won't bite your head off. (This is the internet, remember? Nothing is real here. You're safe!)

* * *

"Yavalinra! Ava! What are you doing?"

"What's it look like? I'm escaping."

"You can't—that's not—get back here right now, little sister!"

Yavalinra, Princess of the Blessed Land, turned to look down upon her older brother. He stood, puffing a bit in his third-finest coat, right underneath her tree. "You're going to tear something," he insisted, gesturing to her trailing dress. It had indeed snagged on a few twigs on the way up, but Ava wasn't interested.

"Better to tear a dress than die of boredom," she retorted at once, and began apeing the ministers. "'Oh, Your Highness, what is your opinion on the cold soup?' 'Did you hear that Rann's son has taken ill?' 'Has the Queen picked a spot for the new garden?' 'I heard a noise from the witch's tower two nights ago! Isn't that *interesting?*'"

Her brother laughed as she drawled out the last syllables. "It's not fair you grew up to be such a good mimic."

"I ought to run away and join the circus, and leave the princessing to all my sisters."

"You'd get bored of that too," said the prince wisely as he settled against the large tree trunk which Ava had scaled.

"They wouldn't be interested in your thoughts on—what was it?—'human rights and civil responsibilities' there."

Ava threw a leaf at him, a frustratingly ineffective gesture. "You know exactly what it is, Van. You've heard me talk about it for years now."

"Yes, and maybe if you could restrain yourself and talk evenly about it, the court would understand your point," he returned.

"How can I talk like I don't care about it when it's so important to everyone living in our country?!"

Van laughed as her voice rose, as though she'd proved his point. Ava sighed. Her brother had the ministers and everyone else wrapped around his finger, and had since they were children; but she, now past twenty, seemed a perpetual outsider in court. He told her, "You'd better be careful at the Declaration next month."

"Of course I'll be careful. I'm always careful."

"You know what happened last ti—"

"Yes I know!" Ava looked away, hoping the leaves obscured the sudden tears in her eyes. "Now who's the boorish one, reminding me of that?"

"I just don't want you to be hurt again," her brother said softly. "I really do think your cause is just, Ava. You just have to make *them* see that. Otherwise—"

"You don't have to tell me."

He didn't, and for a moment they sat in silence.

"Tell me why it is," her brother said eventually, in a much lighter tone, "that *every* Full Moon Celebration seems to end this way?"

"Because," Ava retorted at once, "why bother looking at all those gaudy people in their shallow finery, when you can come out here and look at the moon and stars?"

"Harsh words, little sister. But you have a point." The Prince shifted against the tree trunk to grin up at her. "Sometimes I doubt you are from this land at all—and then you go and say something like that."

"I wasn't *trying* to be poetic," Ava protested, but it didn't matter.

Their conversation was cut short as the usual round of trysting ministers began to pour forth from the banquet hall. Thanks in part to her brother's aid in creating a distraction, the Princess Yavalinra was able to make an escape, returning to her room thinking,

If only everything were so easy.

3

Help!

March 1, 2018

Sorry this post is running late—only three posts in, and I'm already behind! I could give the usual excuses, like the new job being a blur of meeting people and anxiety, or the unpacking from moving that I still haven't done, or the strangely vital necessity of setting up internet in a new home or the exhaustion once said internet is up of *not* overthinking the fact that my ex congratulated me on social media. But honestly, it's because I couldn't decide where to split this next scene.

Even when it comes to decisions with no real consequences, the Indecision Monster gets me. Gah!

Well, I made the decision eventually, so here you go. At least there's now fewer days until the next post, right? And that's a good thing, because–you guessed it–you're getting a cliffhanger. Or I suppose, *another* cliffhanger. Muahaha!

* * *

Ava drifted through her room, shedding pieces of finery as she went. The heavy, beaded overskirt was the first to go, draped on a nearby chair; then the jeweled hair comb and the pins that scratched; then the necklaces and bracelets, heavy in their own way, like badges of deep responsibility. She didn't mind responsibility in general, but she *did* resent being told she was responsible for the country and then laughed at for actually thinking about the commoners.

It was a resentment she thought about a lot, and despite Van's gentle teasing, her mind raced along that well-worn track now. She tied back long silver hair—another mark of her royal blood and duty—with a ratty, well-worn scarf and climbed the stairs to her balcony.

Aside from the witch's tower, Ava's room was the highest in the castle. She had got it almost by accident, because few of her siblings wanted it, and the one who might have—Ylandria, the more jealous and petty of the sisters, in Ava's opinion—was conveniently afraid of heights. To Ava it was the one perfect place within the royal walls. She took great comfort in climbing to the open roof and watching the night sky.

"The moon is so bright tonight." Lulled by the distant chatter of the continuing Full Moon Celebration, Ava spoke to herself without thinking about it. Not thinking about much at all, she traced a familiar orbit to the wooden railing at the edge of the flat roof.

"It's almost like it's here," she laughed absentmindedly. Below her, the trees of the castle garden swayed, toddler size in comparison with her tower. They clamored upward for her attention, and she looked down and told them, "I think

I'd like that."

"Really? Well that's good, because—"

Ava whirled, reasonably certain that the voice had not come from a tree. "Who told you you could come up here?"

A moment late, the princess remembered her stance, and her weapons. From the sash at her waist she drew thin daggers attached to long strips of cloth, briefly thankful she had ditched her heavier clothing. Settling herself with daggers in hand, she waited.

But no reply came.

Richard was too stunned to speak, not least because he had managed to speak in the first place.

"Don't tell me; you've suddenly become shy?" Ava's eyes ran over the railings and the doorway, searching for the person who had spoken, expecting a boy but seeing no more than errant moon rays. "Or maybe you've remembered that of all the Royal Heirs, I'm the best with scarf blades?"

It was a lie, actually: the best was Vanderlina, the youngest, who had taken to defense training most readily. But Ava came from a family of mostly sisters, so she knew how to conceal her fear. Richard, knowing none of these things and uncertain what to do when faced with a very tall woman with a very fierce face, wavered. Around him the light walls of his prison seemed more magical than ever.

In front of—or rather just below—him, the princess sighed and straightened. She glanced around the balcony. "Look, I hate games. I know you're here. Now tell me why, and we can both go about our evening without imagining knives at our backs."

"But I really don't know why," Richard answered without thinking. He hoped that in the "real world," as he thought of everything beneath him in his current prison, his voice didn't sound as petulant as it did to his ears.

Ava's eyebrows creased. "It's kind of hard to navigate hallways, climb a bunch of stairs, open several locked doors, and then climb *another* set of stairs for good measure without knowing *why.*"

"I didn't," insisted Richard. He was still surprised she could hear him. But everyone, even in Runn, knew that the royal family of the so-called "Blessed Land" liked to think they had some connection with the sky. Judging by her hair and the fact that she had mentioned the Heirs, he figured she was one of them, and maybe their stories had some truth. But how to talk to a princess of the castle which two nights ago he had hoped to raid?

Richard cleared his throat and tried to sound more like his father. "I'm very sorry, but you see, there's been an accident, or actually, a series of them. Somehow I found myself up here, in the moon, and it's very boring up here, so I was looking around, and I just happened to hear you just now—"

"The moon."

"Right, right, well as you can see, it was obviously magic—"

"The *moon?* You really expect me to believe that? Get away from my tower, you crazy pervert!"

"I'm not though!"

"Not in the moon? Oh, heavens, I'm shocked."

"It's really not funny! You have to listen to me—"

"No, I really don't, and I don't want *you* listening to me either. Get lost!"

"But please! If you can hear me, then maybe you can help!"

4

Man in the Moon

March 7, 2018

Like a lot of other writers-who-started-writing-as-kids, I look back now and can see that my young self wrote a lot of derivative work. That one story I wrote during the fourth grade for a book-making project, that I was so proud of? Centered around a dragon just like the one in Tamora Pierce's The Immortals series. But I don't remember thinking that at the time, not even remotely. (I wish I had found *that* project, too, because that book was pretty neat!)

And yet, I'm not sure where the idea for this story came from. Moon imprisonment? I mean, sure, there are stories about a "man in the moon," and so on, but in most fantasy the idea of *banishment* does not extend that far. I suppose I was taking phrases I had heard and making them literal. And then of course there's the traveling that they do later, after—

But you guys haven't gotten to that part yet, have you? Spoiler alert!

* * *

Ava would never have admitted it, but it was something about those words—*if you can hear me, then maybe you can help*—which made her stay up there and go on listening. They were familiar to her, too familiar to let her walk away.

Richard told her his story as reasonably and as quickly as he could, as though worried that at any moment she would disappear—much as he had done, two nights before, while his friend escaped (he hoped). She seemed to recognize his description of the witch and he was almost feeling comfortable until at the end she asked his name.

"It's—um—Ae . . . Aemil? Sorry, this whole thing has me confu—"

Ava laughed. "Really, don't bother. I can tell from your accent you're from Runn. And didn't you know that only the royal family uses unique names?"

"Oh—right." Richard looked at her as he weighed his options: she was now sitting on the railing, her elbow on a wooden post, leaning her chin in her hand. Her skin was darker than his, reminding him of the tan Benjamin always seemed to have; she seemed to have some of the same natural confidence of the knight, too. "It's Richard. My name."

"Just Richard?" Ava wasn't sure where to aim her skeptical glance, but it didn't stop her from raising an eyebrow.

"Richard . . . Knight." It was true, after a fashion. Every prince or princess of Runn was trained as a knight. The fact that Richard had never been a very good one was neither here nor there.

"Knight?" Ava was laughing, and some of the old bitterness crept up in Richard.

"I don't see what's so funny about it! Anyone could get caught—"

"Yeah, but, you know, 'night'? Given where you've ended up?"

"I'm really not one for puns," Richard sniffed. His father would have laughed, but he had other worries. "And I really don't want to be up here forever!"

"Well what are you hoping I can do about it? Go talk to the witch and get her to let you out?" Ava did think about it, absently toying with the ends of her scarf. "Half the things she does, she does by accident. I bet she doesn't even know how to get you out of the moon, or wherever you really are."

"You don't even believe me?"

"Do *you* even believe you?"

"I—well, I mean, it's not like I have a lot of experience with these things, but yes! I'm actually here, aren't I?"

"You don't sound like you do." Ava sighed. "Look, I can poke around and try to find some things out. *Especially* if you're lying. But I'm not exactly a witch myself."

"Are you sure?" Richard watched the blank look on Ava's face and hastened to add, "You're the only one who's been able to hear me."

"Probably everyone else was too sane. And speaking of," Ava realized suddenly she couldn't hear the party any more, and the night was very dark— "if I was sane, I'd have been in bed a long time ago."

"Okay but wait," Richard insisted. "At least tell me your name."

"You mean you don't know? What kind of stalker are you?"

"I'm not! I told you, it was an accident!"

Ava rolled her eyes, and drew herself up to her full height.

"I am Yavalinra Ennesi, sixth heir of the Blessed Land. Skies' blessing be upon you, and *good night.*"

5

Side Pieces

March 16, 2018

Ugh. Side characters.

This might be where I fail as a writer. I just have no interest in extraneous character creation. That's the price I pay: see, I'm a story person, not a people person. That's why I work in an art gallery where I can think up stories about the art and not see people all day . . . haha.

And it's also why I don't care about extra characters—until I can come up with a story about them. The following passages from my notebooks were a bit musty and my memory of them was not good, so I had to make up some new content. That's why I am—again!—running late. For me side characters come up and at first I'm all like "who, what? No, thanks, I'm in a committed relationship" until they whip out some intrigue or a little moral of their own and then it's all "hey, catch this flight 'cause now you're in my book." Sometimes I don't even make them sit in the back.

* * *

They were drinking tea in one of several courtyards designed for the purpose, celebrating the end of one of their jobs, when they realized what was likely to be the next.

Issa gestured with her finely made ceramic cup as one of the Blessed princesses walked by. "Reckon it's that one? I can't tell them apart."

"How can you not tell them apart?" Jet, a burly man clad in black, rose in his chair to look where his companion pointed. In doing so he towered over Issa, a lean and almost unnoticeable figure.

"It's the hair," she complained, disinterested.

"It's not like they wear it all the same. Did you see the youngest princess's new bob? And Princess Lin always has perfect braids. They say it takes an entire morning just to—"

"Are we *here* for information about braids?" Issa snapped. Jet hunkered back down, his reed chair creaking. "Honestly, when the King put us together, and there you were with the axe and the hood and the big black horse, I never would have thought I'd have to put up with—"

"Black horses are very misunderstood," Jet interrupted resentfully. "You know how I feel about that."

"And I don't *want* to, that's my point."

"That's not very nice," said Jet to his tea cup. "For a bard."

"Please. Being a bard is like anything else. It's about getting things done." Issa slammed her own cup down in the manner of one more accustomed to tankards, ignoring Jet's concerned look. "So which one is it?"

"Which what?"

"You know what I mean. One of the princesses was asking

around about Runn today."

Jet smiled. "That's very neighborly."

"How can it be neighborly when we're about to have a war?" Issa hissed. Fortunately, the ferns which grew plentifully in this particular courtyard concealed her temper and her words from anyone else. The skies overhead were cloudy, and most of the other tea drinkers had already gone inside anyway.

"Maybe we'll be friends instead. There *is* a diplomat from Runn here, after–"

"We're not friends."

"But *maybe*—"

"Shut up."

As Issa sighed and frowned into the distance, Jet turned back to polishing the rings of silver he wore across his knuckles. They were starting to wear with age, and some blood had stuck to the side of one without him noticing. With tender care, he cleaned it off. The little rag he used for this purpose was in tatters by now; maybe, he thought, he could find a jeweler here in this big city—a nice person, who would sell him a new one, and talk for a while about the great versatility of rings. Someone who wouldn't mind that he and Issa had been sent by the King of Runn to find—or avenge—his son.

6

Paramnesia

(n) a distortion of memory; confusion of fact and fantasy

March 21, 2018

I decided to start doing this new thing because it's a time for new things, right? The whole blog is still new. Every once in a while I'm going to throw in a fun word. Maybe my pinterest boards full of rare word definitions will finally be of use!

I thought *paramnesia* was a good one to start with because that's basically what a lot of this story is for me. I was one of those kids who always had a fantasy conversation going on in my head—usually between fictitious characters, either ones I'd made up like Ava and Richard, or ones I'd read about and fallen in love with (here's looking at you, Schmendrick). It's honestly been interesting discovering which of my remembered conversations actually took place between Ava and Richard rather than me and any of my real friends.

But that's what blogs are about, right? Most blogs are way more interesting to the author than to the audience. I hope you are enjoying it though—it's about to get much weirder. And more fun.

* * *

After days in the moon, Richard had learned to ignore his body. After years of physical training and everyone shouting "mind your stance!" or "pick up your knees!" or "watch out for that dummy!!", he found it to be a relief.

It wasn't that he didn't have one, or that it was being held back: it was simply so ineffective that after the first day of his imprisonment, he gave up using it at all. The shifting light that the moon gave off surrounded him, and held him outside of time—he never grew tired, or hungry, or anything else. He did sometimes become bored, but that was rare, because he had discovered how to watch the world as it turned beneath him.

During the day, he could not see very much: there was too much glare. What he could see was far away, like a map on an opposite wall. But as evening came closer so he, too, was able to get nearer to land; following the rays of the moon, growing bold in the sun's absence, he could stretch his awareness. He had thought that was *all* he was doing—just looking more closely—until the night before, when the princess had somehow noticed his presence. How that had happened, Richard had no idea; he was anxious to find out if he could do it again.

Due to his anxiety more than anything else, it took him

some time to retrace the 'steps' of the night before. The sun had set some time ago by the time he reached the right tower, and the princess sat on the roof reading a book by candlelight as though she had forgotten he ever existed.

Richard hesitated. It wasn't that she was taller than him, and undoubtedly better with daggers, and all round more confident and knightly that made him afraid. It was that he didn't know what she expected him to be.

When she was reading, though, she looked nice enough. Her features were small—easily dwarfed by her book—and her eyes not so derisive. Of course Richard had noticed the silver hair before, but now he wondered if the other half of that story was true: that the Blessed royals had eyes the color of sky. As he looked he thought hers seemed grey, dark, although there in the candlelight he thought he saw some blue—

Ava snapped her book closed and used it to shield her eyes, unable to bear it any longer. "Okay, now I know you are a creep."

"I'm not a creep!" Richard jumped back, rising above the railings.

"Really? What part of showing up and *not* announcing yourself seemed least creepy to you?" As the light receded, Ava lowered her treatise, and rolled her eyes. "Don't tell me this is how *everyone* in Runn is?"

"Oh no, definitely not," Richard replied hastily. Then, collecting himself, he asked, "Did you find anything out?"

Ava wished, not for the first time, that she could narrow her eyes at something while Richard spoke. It was strangely difficult to have expressions in no particular direction. She could look at the moon, she supposed, but that was right above her, and in any case she had not been able to see any sign of a *person* in it to look at. She had tried.

Instead looking out over the scattered roofs of the castle complex and the city beyond, glowing like an ember in the night, Ava said, "Nothing particularly useful. Bess is going around acting like nothing at all has happened, just talking about some new locking spell she devised that particularly affects cheese. And no one," she added significantly, "has been reported missing from Runn."

Richard entirely missed any hint of significance. "Bess?"

"'The Witch,' to you," Ava told him. "She used to be a milkmaid. That's the rumor, anyway, but after the thing with the cows last season it's about the only rumor I believe."

Deciding he did not want to know, Richard plowed on. "But there has to be something we can do!"

"Sure," said Ava cheerfully. "You can either get used to being the Man in the Moon, or you can go and talk to Bess with your problems."

"*Talk* to a witch?" Richard hated the way the reverberation of his voice sounded, high and unkind. "But she's the one who put me here without a moment's thought!"

"Maybe it was an accident," Ava said, much more reasonably.

"I just was thinking . . . I don't know . . ." Richard flailed. Never in his career as Prince of Runn had he ever been able to convince anyone that the solution to any problem was talking to someone.

"That what, you could slice your way out with your sword?" Ava smirked, and then laughed. "You're really out of your depth, aren't you?"

"Anyone would be," Richard retorted, not a little indignant.

"Look, if it's such a bother to you, then—"

"Oh, don't get fussy, I'm only teasing. There's always a way out of spells. Don't worry, I'll help you get out of it."

Looking back later, Ava wasn't sure what had made her say it. It may have been, as she insisted to Richard, that she was bored. But more likely, she decided as she finally drifted off to sleep, it was because she was curious. *There is* something *going on here,* she decided. *If I can find out what, then maybe . . . then maybe people will listen to me for once.*

7

Intrigue Me

March 28, 2018

Well, I see y'all don't have the same reservations as I do about side characters! Maybe you were reacting more to the song I referenced in the title, but that post was definitely the most popular on the blog so far. I really can't judge, I've fallen in love with many a side character before. (Someone ought to do a study on that. Is it some twisted self-esteem thing? Or is it because the main character is so obviously taken? Or are side characters just more fun and less responsibility? Whoever did the research could have all of Tumblr as a study ground.)

Anyway you can rest assured I won't go rampaging and killing side characters just because they bore me. I've always felt like death in a novel should have an actual purpose, the way some folks say death in real life has one (even though I'm not convinced it does). Hey, I may be undiagnosedly depressed, but I'm not the kind of person who heaps torture and angst into my work just to make it more "realistic" and "gritty" . . .

Speaking of, the janitor at my new job is named Brent and I just can't stand it. Not the name—although as you can imagine I'm not a fan, but I'm also not Mr. Weeks's intended audience, so whatever—well okay, the name. I *swear* it's some sort of cover. He's *got* to be lying. He's the least Brentiest Brent ever and also he's like a hundred years old and walks around with a cigar in his pocket in a *gallery.* Where he *works.* I think he showed up one day and they asked him his name and he just took a gander at the nearest artist's card and picked something. "Uh, Brent. Sure, that's what it is." I have no idea how he got the job. Probably some of his old cronies showed up later that day and "convinced" my boss to hire him.

I mean he's a really cool guy. But like really man, what is your actual name, and how exactly did you learn what gets blood stains out of carpet?

* * *

Bertha, the witch's apprentice, never hemmed or hawed over potions. Her master, Bess, had been known to burst into song, stringing ingredients along a melody to help her remember, the way a milkmaid might croon to an unruly cow. She didn't do that much any more—not as she sank deeper and deeper into magic. Maybe that was the difference between the two: Bess had once been free of the magic, but Bertha never had. Bess had once sung and hemmed and hummed and laughed; Bertha's life had always been quiet.

Quiet, but seething, and relentlessly active. Bertha always had a place to go.

And that was why she found herself glaring at the Princess,

a woman older than her own fourteen years and yet not half as *busy* as she ought to be.

"I don't know if it's possible," Bertha repeated, with all the acid of a pubescent girl at her disposal. "You'll have to ask the Witch."

"I already did," the Princess Yavalinra said patiently. "I got her opinion, and now I'm interested in yours, Bertha. You've been studying here now for—what, three seasons?"

"Five," Bertha corrected her, though she wondered why she bothered. It wasn't as though the Sixth Princess, or in fact anyone in the castle, would remember details like that. She didn't even expect them to.

"Oh, so an even longer time!" The exclamation was an attempt to establish camaraderie. It failed. Bertha stared. "Don't you think there's something *going on?*"

Bertha shifted from foot to foot, letting the potion bottles in the box she carried clink and clatter as she made her point. "There might be if I could go actually get something done."

The Princess glanced around the courtyard beyond the staircase. She'd just come down from the witch's tower and had stopped Bertha on her way up—but even such a chance meeting could be turned into a tete-a-tete, for the tower was set into the outer wall and surrounded by an old rock garden which grew more abandoned every night. "There's no need to worry about anyone listening. And I really won't keep you; I just wanted to know if you'd noticed anything."

"Nothing," Bertha insisted. This was the Princess's second day of snooping around the tower; what had *she* noticed? Bertha wondered—for about half an instant. Then she remembered that it didn't matter anyway.

"Well, okay then. Thanks for your time, Bertha!"

Bertha paused as the Sixth Princess strode off. *Thanks?* As though her time was some sort of belonging, like the Princess was always talking about in court? As Head Witch preoccupied with impending doom, imaginary or otherwise, Bess did not bother with the court's discussions of laws and citizens; but Bertha did. And Princess Yavalinra, in her opinion, was downright weird.

"Princess Yavalinra is dangerous," agreed a voice nearby. Bertha didn't jump—she didn't want to rattle her cargo—but instead pressed against the wall of the tower as hard as she could, straining her ears.

"The Diplomat will have to be told," agreed a second voice. The people, Bertha realized, were standing on the wall along one edge of the yard. They must have heard the whole thing, including how rude she had been to royalty—

Not that it matters. Apparently royalty had bigger problems, and unlike Bess, Bertha really couldn't be persuaded to care.

8

Creativi-tea

April 4, 2018

A girl came in for the gallery's Teens Art club today and her shirt had a chain of DNA on it, but the DNA was broken at the top in this really artistic way, and I was staring at her for like ten minutes before I realized why it looked so familiar. (Yeah, her *shirt* looked familiar. Not her face. Maybe this is why I have trouble meeting people . . .)

Everyone knows that shape, right? The shape DNA makes, that goes up and twists? Double helix (I totally did not just google that!). That's such a good visual for what my mind does.

I've tried to explain it using the common metaphors—you know, an imagination like a branching path, or building a story is like setting up a scaffold—and it almost works but not really. I'm liking this DNA one more and more, though. Because when you talk about DNA, words like *imprinting* and *coding* and *sequencing* take on larger implications, and that's exactly the way they *should* feel when talking about imagination.

However, I lost the strand of whatever else I was going to say. This is delicate stuff. You think I can just spit words out onto a page and find a fully formed idea every time?

Okay, okay, I'm losing people, I get it! No more. And yeah, Bertha is an original character in the story—but she actually showed up earlier in the first version. And she was the same age and had the same attitude—you'll be seeing more of it, don't worry! I guess even as a high schooler I distrusted teens. Not too surprising, actually. As Ava is about to find out, you should never trust anyone . . . dun dun dunnn!

* * *

If it hadn't been for Mister Stuck-in-a-Moonbeam, Ava would never have accepted Diplomat Honesty's invitation. The diplomat, who insisted everyone call him by his first name, Alexander, was antisocial, grumpy, given to collecting swords, and not a little gassy—in short, a perfect example of a native of Runn. Or at least, Ava had thought so *before* she met Richard; Richard, being the second person from Runn she had ever met, rather broke the mold—at least when it came to sword collecting.

Thinking that she might finally get to the bottom of this—and that maybe the people of Runn weren't so bad, since one of them had survived this long in the moon, with nothing to punch—Ava put on her best Princess face and went to take tea with the old man.

It was after the first cup—or perhaps the second?—that she stopped listening politely to the tale of how he got his latest sword. With the third cup, she gave up trying to segue into something more relevant, and began asking blunt questions. Before the fourth cup had been poured old Alexander's face was already turning red, and Ava had a good feeling—

But after the fifth cup she didn't remember anything at all.

"Well," said Jet, dusting off his maid's uniform. "These Blessed folk sure can drink tea, can't they?"

9

Coddiwomple

(v) to travel purposefully towards a vague destination

April 11, 2018

Get it?

Believe me, before I started typing it up, this story was an even better version of coddiwompling than it is now. Maybe that's because I'm cool with coddiwompling, and I was just writing for me. They say you have to have clear goals for your characters and conflict on every page but I was just like, "meh, I know where we're going, I'm patient." Too bad all you demanding people out there on the internet aren't the same!

I kid, I kid. It really is a personal problem. Even at work sometimes I feel like I'm coddiwompling; I mean really, my *life* is coddiwompling, and I'm just hoping no one will notice. Once when I was leaving home for my first school trip to a big city, my dad told me, "just walk with purpose, look straight ahead, pretend you know where you're going, and no one will bother you." (Now that I think of it, "look straight ahead" seems like strange advice for an instructor and co-owner of a driving school to be giving out.) I feel like I have adopted that advice, given it a warm happy home, and thrown it at every freaking aspect of my life.

* * *

Richard was nothing if not systematic. When he couldn't find Yavalinra atop her tower that night, he persisted in a system of waiting: "just a few more moments," each time, until half the night went by. Finally as the sun began to shine at the edge of the world he worked up the courage to yell vaguely toward her window. When that didn't work and the confines of light around him began to strain back toward the sky, he gave one last effort and peeked inside.

"Yavalinra?"

Until this point Richard had assumed he was incorporeal—a sort of spirit, outside of the "real world." After all, he essentially moved around by flying. But even this assumption did not stop him from cringing immediately after calling the Princess's name; he doubted matters like incorporality would stop her from showing a creep who hovered right outside her window exactly what she thought of him. *I'll never convince her to keep helping me now.*

And yet, dreary as that thought was, a worse one struck him. He hadn't heard any response. Not a single peep during the whole time he'd been cowering outside her bedroom wall.

"Princess?"

Growing worried with alacrity, as was his wont—which was

finally a good thing, because as the moon shifted across the sky, he didn't have much time left—Richard straightened and looked inside, this time *really* looking. The chambers within were calm, orderly, a lovely shade of absolutely Yavalinra-less blue. Nothing, not even the bed, had been disturbed.

Oh no.

At once, Richard had a plan. He moved from tower to tower all around the palace, tallest ones first—even the witch's tower. When these proved empty of anyone but stuffy Blessed courtiers, he tried the palace walls; and from there, the town beyond. This he skimmed quickly, merely to eliminate it as a possibility. No one in their right mind would hide a princess right outside a castle and anyway, he felt more certain with every moment that he knew where she'd gone.

At first he started tracing the road that led to the border, but his plan quickly evolved. He decided it unlikely that she had left of her own accord: surely she would have told him. In that case, the people she was traveling with might not be the sort to use roads at all. Richard widened his scope—partly due to a new strategy, but also because the sun was up now, and his cage had shrunk. He was looking down upon a world crossed with rivers like veins in his hand.

Still, his vision was good, and if he had had more time, Richard would have found her. However the turning of the world waits for no man, even a spirit-man trapped in a heavenly body with a furious agenda in mind: even though he strained as hard as he could against it, soon the border and both kingdoms fell away from view. Richard had no choice but to wait until the next night.

When night returned he resumed his search immediately, hastening the moon's rays over the land. He had had time to think about it: he knew exactly where a small group of people traveling in secret would be. Or at least, he knew several places where they might be, and in the fourth place he looked, he found them.

"Curse it, Jet, d'you *have* to keep your lantern so bright?"

"You *know* I can't see very well in the dark, Issa. And what if the horse were to stumble? It might wake the lady—"

"For the *last time,* we don't care about the stupid princess's beauty sleep. And honestly if she hasn't woken up yet, do you really think she's going to? Now shut up before someone hears you, you oaf!"

"But you said first—"

"I *said* shut up!"

Richard retreated to the roof of the covered wagon, having seen enough of the two heads—one heavily armored and hooded, one wobbling on a reedy neck—and the pony. Everything about the scene confirmed his suspicions. With a sigh, he settled in to wait.

10

Double Digits

April 18, 2018

Hey, look at us! We're at double digits already!

I mean, the number 10 doesn't seem like much, but when you think about it, that is ten weeks (given the rate I blog at). I've had relationships that haven't lasted that long. Actually this also means it's been ten weeks *without* a relationship now—that's a strange thought. I guess blogging is like having a relationship with your audience, right? So this counts! Hope you don't mind that it started out as a rebound . . .

So, yeah. I get the feeling you probably don't mind, or that is, you might mind but you also have a morbid curiosity to *know*—at least, the handful of people who talk about this blog with me seem to. A lot of people have said it'd be cool if I shared more of my experiences outside of just rewriting this weird old story. (Okay maybe not a lot, since basically the people who follow this blog is like 30% old school friends, 40% random internet people who just wanted me to follow them back, and my Great-Aunt Dorothy. Hi!) Anyway I guess we've got to the point in this relationship where we're ready for the big questions.

Sooooo . . .

Or not, haha. But I will say: boy, am I beat. We just finished a big event at the gallery that I, being the new Events Coordinator, had to coordinate. "Oh we've been doing it for years," they say. "Take this year as a gimme to learn the ropes, and then you can update the program next year. It basically runs itself!" Yeah sure, all our volunteers have been doing this event for so long they could do it in their sleep, but *still.* No event actually runs itself. I defy you to find one.

I mean really I was excited about it. Kids creating art is cool. (Kids writing—well, depends on the kid . . .) But I was equally anxious about it. I've realized that my one coworker, we'll call her the Old One for now (not because she's ancient, even though she is, but because she's been here for 11.5 years, as she often reminds me), doesn't always tell me the right thing. "Oh that volunteer only wants to sit in the cozy corner and do fingerpaint with the kiddos," she'll tell me, and then I talk to the volunteer in question and find out he hates fingerpaint with a passion and thinks it's some kind of poison. (Not kidding.) Or there was the big to-do over email: "I'm not allowed to have email," she informed me, when it turns out she just doesn't want to operate a computer—she actually should have had a gallery email all along, and instead was making my predecessor (by all accounts a wonderful man, but lacking in the spine department) print every relevant email for her to read. Yeah, I nipped that in the bud—if for no other reason than to save a few trees. She acted like being taught how to email was some sort of herculean task which she had accomplished all by herself, proudly showing Brent how "I figured this thing out now, I'm really good," as she opened spam and thought she deleted everything by closing the email window. This, ladies and gentlemen, is my Tour Guide to How Things Work Here. I was not sure what to expect with this event. But it turned out well.

The realization that all is not as the Old One says, by the way, hit two or three weeks ago—right at the same time Ava should have been realizing that she, too, was being bamboozled by someone on the inside . . .

* * *

"Richard! Get down here right *now!*

"I know you can hear me, you creep!

"Maybe you'd like it better if I called you *prince?*

"Richard I swear if you don't say something this very moment then I will never, ever, speak to you ever ag—"

Ava broke off. She had been yelling at the moon; but suddenly, the light beside her window pulsed. For a moment she even thought she could see . . .

"I did try to say something," Richard said, the pathetic tone in his voice snapping Ava from wonderment back to anger immediately. "You just didn't hear me. Because of all the yelling."

"Well I'd say I have reason to yell, wouldn't you? Wouldn't you say it's reasonable to yell at someone who has lied to you, misrepresented who they are, and oh yeah, connived with common burglars to get you *kidnapped* and taken to an entirely *different country* and—gah! You'd better hope you stay up there for a long time, you coward, because if I get my hands on you—I bet you're up there on *purpose,* aren't you, while meanwhile your father is outraged and about to go to war!"

"My father?" Richard echoed miserably. He wasn't sure why, but he had somehow hoped that Ava's delivery to Runn would go much better for him: maybe she'd be thrown into a dungeon, and he could filter in through the window and console her, and somehow manage to help her escape back to her home court and—well, it didn't matter. Instead, he had found her in one of the finer rooms at the castle, and she knew about who he was now—not that he had *lied,* exactly!—and apparently she had even talked to his *father* of all people?

"Not only did you lie to *me,* you've been lying to *him,* too, haven't you!"

Richard sighed. *They* would *get along,* he thought. He could just picture Yavalinra and the King of Runn, sympathizing over how disappointing he had been to them over tankards of ale. He doubted they had tankards in the Blessed Land—he had never seen one while he was there—but he had no doubt Yavalinra would embrace the concept.

"You are going to go up there right now and talk to him, you ridiculous excuse for a—"

"Wait," cried Richard, his reverie struck down by panic. "*What?* You told him??"

"Of course I told him! He thought my mother was holding you as some kind of hostage!"

". . . And he believed you when you said she wasn't?"

Ava only missed one beat. "Not really, which is why you need to go talk to him right now and prove you are as much of a ninny as I told him you are."

Though she could not see it, Richard crossed his arms. "If

I'm that much of a *ninny,* then I don't see why I would do any such thing."

"Oh, so you do have some spine, do you? Congratulations," said Ava sarcastically. "You and your cursed identity issues are going to start a war, you know."

"You can't go blaming me for things! *Your* family is the one with a witch!"

"*My* family is obviously crazy! Yours is perfectly nice!"

"Yeah well—" Richard paused, confused. "What?"

"It's nice! It's fine! You have a mother and you still have a father and you have two adorable twin brothers and everyone puts the country first and bands together and no one's going around snitching on someone else or stealing your boyfriend and they're all really worried about *you!*"

"Um." If he could have, Richard would have sat—really as a matter of mental comfort rather than physical, but still, the urge remained. However, Ava was leaning out of her narrow window and her elbows took up most of the sill, and the nearest wall was stories above or below them, so Richard continued to hover beside the stone tower with increasing awkwardness in the dark.

"Is that why you're mad at me?" he asked her finally. Of course he had known that the King of the Blessed Land had passed away several years ago; that was the sort of information he liked to remind the other knights to take into account when planning potential maneuvers. The Queen had only become more decisive since his death, which made her more dangerous: so on and so forth. Somehow, it had never occurred to Richard that people were sad because the Blessed King had died. But as he looked at the princess, he thought he could see tears.

Ava waved a hand. "And let's not forget that you told me you were a knight. You lied to me about who you are, and there I was thinking it was actually kind of nice to—ugh. Stop shining that stupid light in my eyes, would you?"

"Sorry." Richard hesitated. "Did you see Benjamin while you were in court? He's a knight."

"An *actual* knight?" Despite herself, Ava thought. "Was he the short one, or the handsome one? I'm bad with names."

Richard shifted. "Um . . . he has black hair?"

"Oh. The handsome one, then. Yeah, he was there, and he told everyone what happened. That's probably why they listened to me, which they weren't going to do at first."

"Well that's . . . good."

"Good?" Ava scoffed. She tried to rally her feelings—it was more difficult than usual; she didn't want to admit it even to herself, but waking up that morning to find herself suddenly in a new court had been a shock. That it was an *enemy* court she didn't mind: in fact, that had been the only thing that felt familiar about it at first. The shock was gone and now she felt strangely lonely, but she couldn't decide why. "I'm still mad at you, in case you forgot."

"Listen, Princess, I'm really sorry about—everything. I didn't plan for any of this. I never thought they would attack you, or that I would get caught." Richard sighed again. "I'll go find the King and–and tell him what happened."

11

Anger Management

April 25, 2018

So, yes. Those among you who aren't blind—and even those of you who are, and are perhaps listening to someone reading this (I doubt this blog is important enough to be in braille)—seem to have noticed. Ava is angry.

Since we're being all personal and deep these days, I may as well come out and say it: I was angry, too. When I first wrote Ava, that is. But she never showed it, and neither did I. I've been retrofitting her anger in, in a way. For example, the scene last week—the one where she figures out who Richard is, and decides to give him a piece of her mind—is one that stuck in my mind. Even when I forgot which box the story notebooks were in, I remembered that scene. It was Ava particularly who I remembered. She was very calm about it, at least at first. Then her anger crescendoes into one of those classic emotional speeches that is precisely written and beautifully unrealistic, a speech in which she says exactly everything that she feels, and at the end everyone is sorry—scratch that: they aren't just sorry, they apologize in heartfelt terms, and lessons are learned, and all the anger is gone.

And folks, this is a thing about me—and I don't say this to humble-brag: it really is just a thing I think about all the time—I *need* my characters to speak realistically. I always have, even when I first wrote Ava's Perfectly Angry Scene. But I was young then and had no idea how to articulate anger. I knew how I *wanted* to, but not how it's actually done.

Okay yes, in general, Ava is just a much more fiery character now. I thought I was doing it to make her more interesting, to give her more voice—but maybe the truth is I'm still a bit angry myself. Happy now, Facebook Friends?

* * *

"You took my saber!"

"You're not allowed to have one in Shields!"

"Well you're not allowed to have *two!*"

"It doesn't say that!"

"That's because you never wrote the rules for Shields!"

"Well neither did you!"

"I'm going to write that you can't take my—"

"Hush!! Hush, right now, wee ones! This is *not* how we deal with disputes!"

The young twins Winter and Christopher glared at each other, panting, for one instant longer—and then turned to their caretaker in confusion.

"We speak calmly and explain our feelings when we are angry," the man continued firmly. His hold on the necks of their tunics was not to be disputed—the twins allowed themselves to be steered away from the training field—but his words certainly were.

Not out loud, though. Christopher and Winter could at least agree on *that.* They understood that when George had that tone in his voice, there was nothing to be said: you simply had to put your head down and eat the broccoli, or clean the mess, or whatever else it was that he expected a little Prince to do.

So they kept their knowledge to themselves. It was all very well and good for George to say that "we" don't yell in anger, but the twins had seen their father do otherwise. And their father was a king, so of course he had to be right. Of course it was right that when you were angry you yelled very loudly about it, to everyone nearby; and then you smacked down the person who made you angry.

George often didn't seem to know these things, though, despite the fact that he'd been around since either twin could remember. As the trio passed by the throne room and the King's voice boomed out the open doors, cursing the moon and witches and witchery in general, Winter stole a look at George, wondering if he might learn the error of his ways. He wouldn't, thought Christopher, but the thought was affectionate: they had a responsibility to help George, because even if his views on yelling were backward, he was a very good nurse.

12

Animorphs

May 2, 2018

You know what I love? Running around the gallery after dark. Extra especially, sliding around without shoes on that super-practical, no-nonsense Art Gallery Tile when the lights are out after closing and everyone else has gone home.

And no, it's not because I have a foot fetish or anything. It's just a special thrill—you know, like the "behind the scenes" tours that are always so popular. It makes you feel like you're part of a secret society—just you and the gallery and the art. I love it.

As you can imagine, I was the kind of kid who read books about conspiracies, like Animorphs and swallowed it up and lived it and breathed it to the point where ten-year-old me was like, "whoa, I have to stop reading these, it's freaking me out!" Like I got so scared of alien slugs I had an intervention with myself. In some ways I think I should have been a librarian, but it seems like everyone I know is on their way to being in a library these days, and I guess I figured I ought to be a bit different.

Plus, I never really got into some of the big-name book fandoms of today. Don't get me wrong—I read all the Harry Potters and I love me some comic books—but I'd never buy a "waiting for my Hogwarts letter" sticker. It just didn't hit me that way. Sometimes I feel like all of my spare love for fictional characters and universes got taken up when I was young, and that's the consequence of being an early reader. Sorry, newcomers to the literary scene: this brain is taken. Put up a "closed" sign on my heart.

Heh, heh. Sounds like something the other half of my blind date yesterday might say . . .

And now, to fictional characters I do still love, who are not involved in secret societies. Or are they? 0.o

* * *

"Are you sure he's going to show up?" asked Benjamin, shifting in the cold night air.

"Yeah, pretty sure," Ava replied carelessly. "And if not, we can always yell."

"Doesn't yelling usually scare people away?"

"Not if they're super lonely and stuck with nothing else to do."

"Ha, good one." Benjamin chuckled as he glanced around them once more. There weren't too many towers here—just guard posts: the stone platform they stood on was wide and empty save for a torch. The pages who might usually be standing guard here had gratefully taken the night off.

Just above the knight's head, Richard hovered, thinking.

Was he that predictable? In battle, being predictable was a bad thing. He turned to watch Ava, wondering if the princess was still angry.

Maybe it was her family's preoccupation with the sky—or maybe she was becoming increasingly susceptible to moon rays. Ava shielded her eyes. "You going to *say* something any time soon?"

"I just said—"

"Not you, Benjamin."

"Then who—oh!" Benjamin looked about him, flipping black hair out of his eyes. "You there, Prince?"

Richard sighed. How was it that, even standing outside in the cold on a fool's errand after meeting each other just yesterday, these two were already more normal than he could ever seem to be?

Blame it on the moon, he told himself. Even though he knew it was silly, it was becoming a mantra. "Yes, I'm here. Hello, Benjamin. Where is my father?"

"He meant to be here, of course, but—" Benjamin looked to the Princess, perhaps hoping she would put the matter gracefully.

"He was dog tired after staying up all night waiting on you to finally show up yesterday," Ava declared.

"Yeah, that." It wasn't what he had hoped for; Benjamin grinned.

"The moon doesn't move very fast, you know," Richard reminded them, and hastily added, "So what is the plan? Father said he would come up with one today."

"We tried to. Of course, it would have been better with you here," Benjamin told him loyally, before launching into an explanation.

The plan, as it was unfolded to Richard, didn't seem much like a plan so much as the way things were going to happen anyway. The Princess Yavalinra would return home, before anything terrible happened; she would tell her mother that the witch had lured her out; a campaign would be undertaken against the witch, which Ava and Richard and eventually Benjamin—who would join them later, so as not to create suspicion—could use to investigate a way to get him down. In the meantime, Richard had no doubt that his father would be shoring up all anti-witch defenses: if, indeed, there was such a thing.

Richard had many doubts.

13

Critical Fail

May 9, 2018

Guess what, folks? I started playing D&D! That's like rolling a "nat 1" on your "social status" check, right?

I really can't complain, because my modifier on that would probably be negative anyway.

Seriously though, for something that started out as a friend giving me the "you really need to get out more" lecture, bane of awkward singles' lives since the dawn of time, it went pretty well. I already wish I had chosen a different class. There's someone else playing a Divination Wizard—which I did not even know was a thing—and now it's all I can think about. Can I be a Divination Wizard in real life, please? Can I stop The Old One's bluff/deceit checks mid-roll? Can some holy spirit tell me exactly how many people are going to come into the gallery today, and when, so that I can get on with my story editing?

Har har . . . if anyone from the gallery is reading this, I

promise I'm actually a studious and attentive employee . . .

Anyway, my character is a gnome paladin because I decided that was cute. Not how you're traditionally supposed to pick a character, I know. But I already know I won't be good at the game—numbers and I are not friends—so I may as well have fun picturing a teeny tiny sword-slinging knight in shining armor, right? Besides, the DM was really nice about it. He's a pretty cool guy, believe it or not. I almost thought about going for it, but I figured that'd be kind of like dating your boss. Bleh.

. . . Not that my boss is anything but wonderful!

Before I make things any worse, let's have some more of fantasy quests, shall we?

* * *

Ava was princess enough to conceal her surprise when the knights of Runn provided her with food, tent, horse, and a swift farewell at the door. However, even after a day of riding, she still found it so amusing that she mentioned it to Richard as soon as he filtered in to her moonlit camp.

"Everyone's expected to be able to take care of themselves," he explained to her, wishing he could sit on a stump near the fire, just like she was. He was too polite to mention that even while at a distance, still hindered by the sun's setting rays, he had seen how she struggled to get the flames going. He wondered if she'd ever been *anywhere* alone.

"*Everyone?* What if—I don't know—what if Winter and Christopher decided to go on a journey?"

Richard paused. It was still strange to hear his brothers' names in the accent of the Blessed Land. "Well, we don't give them horses."

"Oh, so they have to get into trouble on their own, huh?" Ava laughed, and smiled fondly at the horse she'd been loaned. It studiously ignored the strange lady talking to nothing.

"I guess people think, the more responsibility you have, the more you should be able to handle yourself." Richard found that if he thought about it, he could indeed lower himself down and—sort of—pretend to sit. "It seems to suit you. Traveling, I mean."

She glanced in his direction, surprised. "I suppose it does. I always wanted to see more of the country."

"We're not in your country yet."

"I *know*, but what difference does that really make? Aside from it being less snowy. It's still people and trees and rocks and fields, right?"

"Of course, I was just, you see—"

"Never mind."

Ava turned back to the fire, leaning her chin in her hands. As she yawned, the cross look on her face began to ease, and Richard ventured,

"I know what you meant, Yavalinra. I just wanted to make sure you weren't lost." He didn't say, *you're definitely taking the long way there and you don't seem to have a lot of warm clothes.* And that, Richard decided, was very kind on his part.

For the second time, Ava looked and almost seemed to see him before giving up. "You're a real worrier, aren't you?" she decided with a slight smile. "Even a *kid* in the Blessed Land can navigate using the stars."

"Oh. I prefer to think of it as being strategy-oriented," Richard retorted very seriously.

"Your father *did* say you come up with the best plans," Ava admitted. "Maybe if I had a bit of that in me too, I could make better arguments in court."

"Is it true people in your court sit around all day and just talk about things?" Richard couldn't help but ask.

Ava startled the horse by laughing out loud. "Days on end, sometimes," she agreed by way of answer. "It's the worst. Nothing ever gets done. You'd probably love it."

"That's not very fair—"

"I didn't mean it like that." Ava smiled again, and yawned soon after. "I really didn't. But I should probably go to bed, before I really get snippy."

"That's fine. You need your strength. Tomorrow you'll probably—"

"Ride all day, I know." Ava looked once more to the horse, and heaved a sigh. "And right after my first night in a tent, too."

14

Selenotropism

(n) growth under moonlight

May 14, 2018

We could use a little of that around here, I'm telling you.

Because I took it upon myself to change one of our old programs at the gallery—and to run it myself, on account of wanting to see how it worked if a *normal* museum professional ran it—okay, well just a professional in general—The Old One has now taken to calling me "the *new* Events Coordinator" to everyone, regardless of whether they even want to be talking to her or not. "Hey little Jonnie, want to sign up for a class? I could do it but I guess our *new* Events Coordinator Ashley will want to." Meanwhile Little Jonnie's eyeing the postcard collection while his mother eyes the door.

I've been here now for going on six months, thanks very much. That may be *relatively* new, like if you're a glacier or a vampire, but it isn't all that new in the human world.

Oh yeah, and then to top it off this evening. After I didn't humbly beg for her help with the clean up—for heaven's sake I am a grown woman, I can pick up my own glue sticks!—she turned around on her way out like "Oh, I'm going to have to text the previous Coordinator about so-and-so who showed up and asked about him." I should probably get extra adult points for not only picking up after my own program, but for not saying *did they really bring him up or did you?* and *you probably shouldn't bother, because I get the feeling from what he told me that he retired so that he wouldn't have to talk to you any more.*

I just don't get it, folks. I don't live in such a people-centered world, where we all need to know everyone's name and what everyone's doing and how long everyone's been at their job. I don't care. Is that bad? If I have to talk to a person, I'd rather talk about their favorite work of art or song or what they think about the news. Literally I would rather talk about national news than gossip, which at this point in our nation's history is saying something.

Anyway, on to today's edition of The Story I Wrote As a Teenager, in which the characters grow more than I have apparently done . . .

* * *

This time when Richard did not find Ava on her tower, he was quicker to abandon the castle altogether. Whether this was because he had come to realize that she had certain strong habits, or because of worry she'd been ambushed on the road, it was hard to say.

He found her abruptly, closer than he'd expected, and much more peaceful. This time her camp was set up with more experience: the front of the tent wasn't pointing uphill, and the fire wasn't directly under a tree, for starters. The horse was actually tied up and even seemed to have been given a treat. And Ava herself swayed where she sat, as though listening to a song somewhere far away in a foreign land—not a half day's meandering walk from her home.

"What is it?"

Ava startled, but had learned not to look around for the source of the voice. "What?"

"What you're listening to." Richard tried pretending to sit, like he had the night before, and had some success. He told himself he could almost feel the stone beneath him as he scanned the glen around them, just in case.

"It's just an old folktune stuck in my head." Ava hesitated, realizing what—of several things—had surprised her about the question. "Not 'what is it keeping you from going the rest of the way'?"

"No."

"No?"

Richard looked at her even though she could not see him, and shrugged. "I think I know why."

For a moment they sat, listening to the fire sing, as Ava contemplated this. Finally she shifted. "Do you—Are there some times when you kind of like it? Being up there," she explained, warming to her question. "Able to watch everything, and see everything, really even go anywhere. Kind of. Without anyone to bother you."

"Sometimes," Richard admitted, the guard dropping from his voice.

"I guess you miss that girl, though?" Ava tried to keep the calculation out of her voice, but knew quite well that she probably hadn't succeeded. "What was her name? Louella?"

"What the—I mean, what—who told you about Louisa?" sputtered Richard. "It's not like there's anything actually going on, you know, like I never even—"

"Too much information," Ava interrupted, laughing. "I don't know, I think Benjamin mentioned it. So you don't miss her, huh?"

"I miss a lot of people," Richard responded defensively. Then, thinking it a necessary tactical move, he admitted, "But that's not the really hard part. Sometimes it's—it's depressing, you know, seeing but not being able to help."

Ava scoffed—more dark than derisive. "You don't have to be stuck in the moon for that to be the case."

"I guess that's true," Richard agreed, thinking of his own futile attempts to be the warrior his country wanted him to be. Sometimes he felt he simply didn't fit.

But he knew he didn't fit in the moon either, so he decided to try bringing something else up. It was nice, talking to Ava: she was quick, and she was funny; she understood; she didn't look at him like—

And yet she *was* looking at him—wasn't she?

Ava blinked. Her eyes refocused, and she lost trace of the image she had seen. But still, it haunted her, just the line of a nose, a messy head of hair. People have been haunted by much more mundane things.

"Richard," she asked, "would you say you have your father's face?"

"People do say I look like him," Richard replied—ignoring the way she phrased the question, which sounded very strange to a literal Runn mind. The ways of the Blessed were unexpectedly strange, he reminded himself.

"Hum." *Maybe because I met the king, my mind is making things up now,* Ava thought.

"I'm glad, by the way," Richard said after another pause.

"Why?"

"That—you know."

"No . . . I really don't."

"That you don't call me 'Prince,'" he explained, reluctantly. "Even though you know now."

Ava's eyes narrowed, as he had feared—but then she smiled. "Yeah, well. I can't be mad at you for being lame forever."

"I am not!"

"Then why do your family and friends say the same thing?" Ava laughed, but not maliciously.

Stirred unexpectedly into standing up for himself, Richard protested, "Just because you fit in better with them—"

It was the words unspoken which gave Ava the bigger pang. She poked the fire, levity forgotten. "What? Just because I do, doesn't mean I don't have to go back home," she answered for herself. "And it's getting late. I should go to bed."

"Hey—I didn't mean to make you upset."

Ava considered this. "I know." Then she grinned. "You're way too nice. Go back up in the sky, Prince Richard, and don't let anything down here hurt your feelings."

15

Hopeless

May 23, 2018

Why is it so difficult to find someone? There are so many people out there complaining about this very thing right now. So why hasn't someone come up with a solution yet? Why hasn't someone developed an app that tells you that the nice software developer in cute polos has horrible dental hygiene *before* you have too many drinks and let him kiss you, then have to spend an evening googling transmittable oral diseases?

I don't think it will come as any surprise to anyone that as a teen, I was a Grade A hopeless romantic. The sort who crushes on people she's never spoken to—and then devises "clever" nicknames for them with her friends, who then aid in creating elaborate schemes just to get near the unsuspecting object of affection—like a pack of safari hunters tracking some poor zebra in the savannah. Then, of course, the instant one of the zebras noticed me, I completely lost all notion of what to do. Never did pull the trigger on any of those crushes—not one. I don't think I even had a conception of what to *do* on a date in high school. Apparently, I still don't . . .

But I do have a much more heightened awareness of The Way Things Actually Work. And that is why you are now reading Ava and Richard stutter and miscommunicate, rather than some of the original text, which was much more elegant. At one point in the scene I just updated, Ava starts baring her soul about feeling inadequate, and Richard responds with the sort of passionate speech of support that ends with both parties staring, breathless and moved, at one another's lips. *This* version of Ava would probably die before anything like that could happen.

And that's the real difference. Not the language—the characters themselves. It's subtle: I didn't realize I was doing it at first, but in reality I am changing the story significantly, even though I didn't mean to. See, when Teenage Me wrote the story, she knew Ava and Richard would end up together, happy, forever. But Modern Me knows no such thing. So instead of instantly recognizing each other as kindred souls and speaking for pages with a natural vulnerability, my characters now flounder, gasping like fish out of water every time someone makes a noise.

All romantic fatalism aside, let's enjoy some of the frustrations of court, shall we?

* * *

"For skies' sake, if I can't get *power,* can I at least get 'hey Ava, where were you?'" The Princess Yavalinra stomped down hard on a fern gracefully reaching into the path before her. Its fronds were ground instantly—and loudly—into the gravel of the Meditation Garden. "Did anyone even *notice* I was gone?"

"If you aren't careful, they're all going to notice that you're back," a voice piped behind her. Ava whirled to confront her brother's gleeful face.

"Heavens forbid! *You!*" Ava glared. "Weren't you even worried?"

"Not really," he admitted with a shrug as he stepped up to walk beside her. "I figured you were just tired of everyone trying to tell you how you ought to define 'rights.'" He looked sideways at her, noticing her scowl, and surmised, "So it wasn't that, then? Well then why *did* you go?"

"I *didn't* go, I was *taken*. By agents of that stupid witch, if anyone cared to know. But no one does because Mother's new Scheduler doesn't have time to hear about anything that wasn't planned four days in advance and heralded by bloody *falling stars!*"

"Ah. Tania." The Prince nodded.

"I mean, it wasn't *that* long ago when I could just go talk to Mother! Was it? Am I going crazy?"

The distraught look on his sister's face jarred Van. "Hey, Ava, it's not all that much to get worried about, is it? You're right. We used to, sure—although you know as well as me that talking to Mother didn't always mean she'd listen. When Tania was promoted, I admit she did step in with a lot of ideas about how subjects *should* be broached, but I figure that at least now Mother's more likely to pay attention," he said, as though over-explanation might cure distress.

"Pay attention! Hardly!" Ava brushed a strand of willow out of her face with a jerking motion, reminding him of the sulky child she had often been. He smiled.

"So tell *me* then."

"Are you sure you don't want to wait until the General Assembly tomorrow? Or perhaps you'd rather discuss this via note?"

"Ava. You mentioned the witch. I thought you liked her?"

"I did! That is—" Ava hesitated. "There's something going on."

"I was getting that feeling, yeah."

"I just—" From the other side of the palace, the dinner gong rang, and Ava sighed. "I'll tell you later."

Van thought he heard her add under her breath, "This is *really* not going as planned."

16

Werds R Gud

May 30, 2018

Okay, so a couple of you have made comments about my vocabulary. You know who you are! For those of you who don't know, I don't mean the posts where I throw out new words. I mean the actual words in the story. "We can tell you're rewriting and not just transcribing because the vocabulary of the story sections is far too erudite to be that of a high school girl!"

Well let me tell you a thing, friends. I may be rewriting, but I am not rewording. I knew all those words and more when I was in high school.

It's not like I was a word nerd with five different spelling bee titles. I never went in for that sort of thing. What I did go in for, ladies and gentlemen, was Victorian literature. In a big way. The Brontes? Check. Sherlock? Yes please. Austen? Sure, as long as it's not Emma. Thackeray? For sure. Collins? All over it. Dickens? Hated him—with the kind of hate that comes from having read more than three of his works. I'm not elevating the language of what I used to write. If anything, I'm dumbing it down!

Anyway I don't say it to brag. It's actually a bit disturbing. Maybe I've already peaked and it's all downhill from there. Of course we all knew that was true of the cheerleaders and football players, but I really had hoped for more. As mentioned before, I don't go in for that "good old days" high school reunion crap.

Clearly, this is why my vocab posts are going to be important. Maybe I ought to start a whole new blog.

Not that anyone would follow it. I know you'll all just here for Richard!

* * *

Richard was confused to find Yavalinra sitting up on her tower by herself. That he was glad to see her went without question, but he did have many *other* questions, for he had expected her to be busy convincing her court of the witch's guilt well into the night.

"There's been a setback," Ava announced as soon as she noticed the balcony getting brighter. "It's named Tania."

"Is that a friend of the witch?" Richard settled, noticing Ava wasn't even in her court attire. She must have given up a long time ago. Sympathetically he added, "Did they give you trouble?"

"No trouble, just policies." Ava waved a hand sarcastically.

"What?" Distracted by this, Richard recalled something else. "How did you know when to start speaking, by the way?"

"What do you mean? In court? I never got the chance.

These things have to be *scheduled* and *dressed for* and the *musicians* called in to add drama! Ha!"

"No, I mean that's very frustrating, but you see I meant to *me*. How did you know where I was?"

Ava paused, suddenly doubting herself. But no: if she squinted, she could see that same outline, the face now familiar, maybe even more—*still probably making it up,* she decided, upset. Aloud she said only, "It was bright and I took a chance. I've been—I've been waiting all day to complain about this to someone."

Richard smiled a little at her self-deprecating chuckle. "Well, I can listen." He didn't add *it's about all I can do,* because at the moment it felt like a lot—like helping.

And so he listened to Ava's story: how she hadn't been able to enact any of their plan because the new secretary insisted the Princess, like everyone else, wait her turn to speak in a public forum. There she could explain her absence and make a case for what to do about it—*if* there was time. Most people hadn't even noticed the Princess's absence, and none were curious enough to forsake propriety and ask her about it—none except her brother, whom she dismissed impatiently as "busy."

"I think she enjoyed it, too," Ava proclaimed, suddenly talking about Tania again. "She made this snide comment about rights and how I think everyone should have them, so I shouldn't mind waiting my turn just like everyone else. And I wouldn't but this is *important!*"

"Ava, I'm really very honored—"

"How could they not notice I was *gone?*" Ava burst, interrupting Richard's glow of gratitude.

He hesitated, watching her bury her face in her hands. Not

even the stars above took notice, hidden in the clouds as they were. The world seemed so still this night he was surprised no one else seemed to have heard her. And what could he possibly say? His own father probably knew he was gone the moment before it happened. But it wasn't his place to criticize the Queen of the Blessed Land.

"You know," Richard said after a while, "what you need is a plan."

Ava sniffed. "You think everything needs a plan."

"Whether or not that's true—I mean—it's true, but it just so happens to be true right *now.* We just need to come up with a different line of attack."

"But we tried everything!"

"We can't have," Richard said, failing to keep all the desperation out of his voice. "There's got to be something else. The witch's tower—you never did get a chance to really look at it, did you?"

"I went and talked to Bertha," Ava frowned.

"Yes but that was with the witch *there.*"

"Well, Bertha *is* the witch, so—"

"I mean maybe we should try looking around when she *isn't* there."

"You want me to break into a witch's tower at night?" Ava's eyes narrowed. "Because that worked out so well for *you.*"

"If you don't want to, I can see why. I just think if you hadn't been abducted in the first place, this was the next logical step."

"Right. Breaking and entering and possibly burglary, in a den of magic. Logical." Ava sighed. "I'm in."

17

A Little Information

June 6, 2018

It's dangerous, right? It certainly goes to your head like a fine and way-too-potent wine. My life has been a series of examples of this lately.

Of course there's Ava and Richard about to creep back into what they assume on limited information is a cheese-loving witch's lair.

There's also the guy I met at a party last week who, knowing only that I am single and not that my emotions are a wrecked tangle of spaghetti, has decided he's met the love of his life. ("I'm so lucky to have met you!" "Oh dude, you have no idea . . .")

There's also the Old One, who has recently learned how to use the internet, and now uses it to satisfy her need for others to give her information. It might be the best thing I've ever done: at least she doesn't constantly interrupt my work with inane questions now. But then again, I'm going off of only two days' worth of data . . . I have this cloudy feeling that this is going to come back to bite me, *somehow*. I always have that feeling where the Old One is concerned.

There's also politics, obviously, but we won't get into that. Or religion.

I'm in a mood today. It's probably because my mom called and wants to plan a family get-together for my dad's birthday, which is fine, but I know my sister won't go, and she's the one he'll want to see. Or it might be the fact that my poor little D&D paladin broke her sword trying to attack a tree that turned out to be a rock . . . long story. D&D would make a great blog subject—but only if you could rely on your players to be constantly entertaining.

Anyway, based on what little information you have, you decide!

* * *

"Was it this one?"

"No."

A bright pink flower was pushed back.

"What about this?"

"Uh, no?"

A strangely-shaped wand was set aside.

"Okay, this then."

"What is—ew!"

A dark, cloudy object with a spider on it clattered to the floor.

Richard sighed. "Honestly, Ava, I didn't get as good a look around as you are doing. I really think it was something the witch *did*."

"But you didn't hear anything," Ava reminded him, still looking intently at the layers of shelves at the other end of the room.

"Well, no." Richard shifted. He had found he could sit on the open window sill, which made him very uncomfortable. But it helped Ava, so he agreed to it. He just hadn't expected her raid of the witch's tower to be so thorough. Or loud.

"Stop worrying," Ava called. "I can tell you are. I told you, she hardly gets up for two days after the Cheese Festival."

"I still don't understand what you are doing at a Cheese Festival that requires so much energy," muttered Richard, but he kept it to himself. They had already established that, since he came from a country which did not eat dairy as a rule, he *could* not understand.

"There's nothing else here," Ava decided meanwhile, kicking at a lower shelf full of improved milking pails. "What about a book where—"

"Ava, stop!"

Ava paused, her foot hovering above the rug. "What? I thought you said you *wanted* me to help?"

"Yes, I mean, I do, but the middle of the room—that's where *I* was when—" Richard leapt up, his pulse suddenly going too fast. "Maybe it's something there!"

But Ava was tired, and having none of it. "There's nothing here. This is where she puts her cauldron sometimes: I've seen it. It's bare." And with that she walked right across the stained, dark rug, ignoring Richard's cry of protest. On the other side she crossed her arms. "What gives? I thought you wanted to be quiet?"

"I was *worried* about you, Ava! The last thing I want is for you to get stuck up here too!"

In a moment Richard was right next to her. His voice was sincere, and the sound of it made Ava realize she wasn't actually angry at him. "I thought I could be more help," she said softly.

Richard didn't like the note of defeat in her voice and hastened to be reassuring. "But you *are* helping, Ava. You're a great help. It's not your fault there's nothing here."

"Don't you think if you had found someone who knows more about magic, then this all would have been better?"

"I—actually—not really."

"Someone else wouldn't have called you a creep." Ava knew he was very close, and she was distracted trying to pinpoint the details of his face.

"Someone else wouldn't have kept me hoping this long, though. I mean I know I can be annoying and all, but I just really don't want anything bad to happen to you, especially because I really—I really appreciate you helping." Richard returned, earnest. He leaned in—he meant to kiss her cheek; just her cheek—but she moved, tracking him, and at the last moment she realized with a start he was kissing her lips which were very warm and a little bit dry and—

With a magnificent flash of light, the world changed.

18

Ageism?

June 13, 2018

Alright so I've had a few people on the good ol' Facebook try to call me out for not liking old people. The reason, for those of you who are new, is because of the way I talk about my so-called "assistant," whom I have been calling the "Old One" because she was here before me—but also yes, she is old. Not just years-old, but this-dratted-internet-won't-work, kids-these-days-have-no-respect, in-my-day-we-made-do old.

So here's my question for YOU: Is it still ageism when it's 100% true?

Believe me, folks, I really have no problem with elders in general (hi, Great-Aunty!). Most of the older coworkers I've had have been competent, helpful people. I think that's what gets under my skin about this one: she's in denial and therefore utterly incompetent. The woman is well into the years of Bones That Don't Heal Quickly and Potential Concerns About Memory, and yet when I accidentally mentioned once that I truly, honestly just hope there's someone to look out for her—which anyone at any age should have—she all but put her fingers in her ears and shouted "la la la." She accused me of spreading rumors that she lives alone (which is true, she does, but I have never said it to anyone, because why would I? What am I supposed to do, stand in line at the grocery store saying "hey anyone, want a robbery target?") and insisted "I'm young at heart. Age is how you feel." Well that's lovely hippie dippie philosophy coming from a staunch conservative, and I actually agree, but there are LIMITS. I have so much respect for people who take care of themselves and know when to get help. I have no respect for people who assume they can assemble storage shelving alone and get mad when I mention safety precautions because "you let the janitor do it, so why can't I? I used to do it years ago, why can't I now?"

Did you hear that in there? That note of petulance? Let it also be noted that there is, at any given time, a 50% or greater chance that she is lying. She may never have built shelving: she may be confused: she may just be saying whatever comes to mind to make herself sound right. I am working with a straight-up child.

And I know I work at an art museum doing programs for kids—but I signed up for looking after kids who sign up for programs, then leave. Not one spoiled kid who follows me around all day and needs to be involved in every conversation anyone in the room is having. You want to make this about ageism? Fine. I'm ageist against children. Children who have no concept of when they are invading someone else's space or hurting someone else's feelings, and who really aren't children at all. "Children" who ought to know better—especially since education was so much richer when they were in school.

In a way, it's actually not her fault. She's just so painfully ignorant (the downside of a *little* social education—throwback to last week!). She doesn't even know what I have come to realize, which is that the rest of the staff actively avoids her. And that—not to be overly self-centered, but hey, this is *my* blog, you know—makes it so hard on me. How am I supposed to get things done when my "helper" is essentially negative help? I'm an art person, not a math person, but I know what it feels like to be starting with less than zero. And since this is an Honest Space, it's just so disappointing. That's why I get riled up. I was over the moon when I got this job, guys. This was my big break. And all it was for the first four months was cleaning up the Old One's messes. But of course no one ever told me that: I had to find it out for myself, slowly, like some sort of Lovecraftian mystery.

I mean, the job itself is still awesome. It really is. But all that, on top of everything else . . . Lay off the ageism accusations, okay? I never once have said anything mean to the Old One. I'm not handing out "send everyone over 50 to a home" pamphlets on the street corner. I'm just trying to do my job and stay sane.

* * *

The Great Hunter strode through his domain, keeping a sharp eye out for any disturbances. His club balanced perfectly in his hand; his feet moved effortlessly over timeless terrain. His eyes were as accustomed to the folding darkness and sparks of light as if they had been made for this ethereal world—as if he had always lived here.

But 'life,' to the Great Hunter, was a slippery notion. It was easier for him to think not in terms of *life* or *death,* but *struggle* or *peace.* And at that moment, his peace was interrupted by a very foreign struggle.

"What do you mean you don't even know where we are?"

"How could I know? Like I keep—"

"Ugh, *don't* give me the line about the witch again!! This happened because you did something!"

The Hunter glided closer. He could see them, two forms lying in a heap on the silver path, arguing; but of course, they had not yet seen him. This was the perfect moment to act, but he hesitated. These two forms didn't look like Intrusions; in fact one seemed to be female, and in distress . . .

"What could I possibly have done?"

"For starters, you could get *off* me. Also you know exactly what you did! We were standing there in the witch's room and you came over and somehow you—"

The damsel faltered as she looked up at the Hunter, who had pulled the other stranger off her chest as easily as though he was made of straw. Eyes wide, she finished her sentence:

"You kissed me."

19

Retrouvaille

(n): the joy of rediscovering someone after a long separation

June 20, 2018

This is a big one. It has been sitting on my Pinterest board for a while now, and I knew the moment I saw it I'd be using it in relation to this story. Help me out, folks—I'm pretty sure it is French, but am too tired right now to look it up. Tell me in the comments?

People have a tendency to think of art as just art. Same thing with books. Static objects to collect or, in the case of the school system, inflict upon others. What people miss is that so much of art and the artist's emotion are tied up together. It's a symbiotic relationship, and those aren't static at all. This story is my art right now—it's like the algae on my dead coral arms, guys. Hopefully I get it done before the climate change gets us all!

But really. Sometimes when I'm all worked up—like two weeks ago—rewriting a cute scene like Ava and Richard's kiss really makes me feel better. But then other times if I'm *too* upset then writing anything even remotely cute is impossible, and instead I go on blog-rants about old people to try to calm down. And maybe not all authors are this way, but I'd like to think at least some are. Like, whatever mood Charlotte Bronte was in that made her twist the ending of *Villette* like that—oh boy, when I read that I just wanted to time travel and snap her pen in half. And then offer her lots of chocolate and friendship and then tell her to try again.

So yeah, Great Aunty. You're safe guessing that nothing happened with the "lucky" guy. But it wasn't ever going to, so it's not like I was disappointed. Maybe I've always been a little bit of a pessimist.

In any case, speaking of rediscovering friends and all, remember that bit way back at the beginning where I said I wasn't going to include a star map? Well, I've since relented—just for you, my friends. If you want to follow along on Ava and Richard's starry adventure, and you don't have a star map of your own, check out this one here: https://bit.ly/gallerystarmap.

* * *

"So actually, I still don't understand," Richard protested. He eyed the glowy, celestial, toga-clad hunter, who steadfastly ignored him.

"What about this is hard to understand to someone who has just been in the moon for days on end?" Ava's expression became exasperated as she turned from the newcomer, who had introduced himself only as Orion. "It's more sky magic. But instead of *our* constellations it's some other world's constellations because—because mythology," she finished, shrugging amiably at Orion. Orion shrugged broad, bare shoulders back, and grinned.

"Often we get strangers from other mythologies. But they are always warlike. Never so lovely."

"Never so *alive,* you mean," Richard insisted. He pretended he didn't see Ava blushing at the star man's comment; furthermore he pretended that even if he *could* see it, he really didn't care. "We're real people. We're not *mythologies,* or fairy tales, or anything like that."

Orion straightened to his full height, which was several inches taller than both Richard and Ava. "That may be so in your time. But in the future of your world that is not so."

"You're saying that where we are, time doesn't matter." It wasn't too difficult for Ava to put together: it was common belief in the Blessed Land that the sky was timeless. And in a world where deep blue sky stretched out all around them and the only thing tangible—aside from themselves—was a floating silver path, timelessness made sense.

"That is true." Orion smiled at her. "No doubt you are a heroine told of in legend."

Richard cleared his throat.

"And this . . . your lackey?"

"More like the reason we're both up here," Ava corrected. She laughed, but still her eyes narrowed. "That curse on you backfired and *caught* me up in all of this when you—"

"Yes, well, that may be, but you see I didn't *know* that would happen." Richard sidled, looking into the deep blueness all around them. He yearned to know what it was. To know what else was out there. To know how to get home. To think about anything, in fact, other than his attempt to kiss Ava.

What was *I thinking?*

. . . That isn't how it's supposed to work . . .

With a sigh, Richard turned back to Ava and Orion. They were watching him with eerily similar expressions. *I take it back, I don't want to know the answer to this. But if she won't ask it then . . .* "So how are we going to get back home?"

20

Starry Mess

June 27, 2018

Y'all are very accepting folk, which I appreciate. When people badmouth the internet for being full of weirdos and creeps, they forget to applaud the legions who make the weirdos and creeps feel right at home. That came out poorly . . . I'm not saying creeps should feel at home, guys! What I'm saying is everybody has a posse on the internet. And I guess for me you folks are it.

And because you are so nice, you didn't give me any trouble about the fact that Richard and Ava, my fantasy characters from another universe, met with Orion, a Greek myth very much of *this* universe. You also didn't notice that I was fooling you—muahaha!

But I have a conscience, so even though it probably doesn't matter and it's all fantasy anyway, I had to come out and write it. Pretty much everything in last week's story section was stuff I made up *now*, in the present, not as a teen. I don't recall ever giving any thought to why Ava and Richard ended up on *our* Milky Way. It's not like I was unaware that other constellations existed — I went through a whole archaeo-astronomy phase (look it up!) at about the time I wrote this. Shocker! But really, I never made any attempt to explain that at all. I was just enamored with the thought of my protagonists journeying across the Milky Way, just like on the star map pinned to my ceiling.

And I can see you are too—at least those of you who talked to me or commented on facebook. The rest of you, for once, kept your snarkiness to yourself!

But I just couldn't stand it this time around. I actually put a lot of thought into *why* Ava and Richard would be here. Should I rewrite it so they come from an ancient Greek society? Eh, no romance. (Not of the kind I intended . . .) Should I make it so they came from Atlantis? Bah, too much crazy conspiracy theory overlap. Should I make them from some other society and add in all new myths? But Greek drama!!

I like the idea I came up with, about the mythologies. It's 100% true actually—in a way. I wrote a number of other stories as a high schooler, and in one the characters do reference the story of Ava and Richard as a legend. Still, I didn't want it to seem like a cheap excuse . . . so I may rework it some more as we go. What do you think?

Also as a sidenote I just have to mention how fun it was to create truly new content and then write it like my teen self—not just transcribing or editing, but creating. It's really freeing, even more than the blog. I realized any mistakes I make will just get blamed on the fact that "the author was young when she wrote it"! Har har, suckers. But now we're pretty much back to transcribing, so I have to once more ready myself to defend the original text from your attacks of "you're rewriting it too much!"

Kidding, of course. I love you all.

* * *

Ava looked between her two walking companions: one hulking, larger than life, striding along with a lighter-than-air grace; the other shrinking, careworn, and constantly looking over his shoulder. Neither had said anything in—well, she had no way of knowing, since there was technically no time where they were. Still, ever since Orion had offered to accompany them in their search to find a way home (which really, she thought, hadn't been *too* long ago), it seemed a new social code had been enforced. One Ava had not been informed of nor asked about.

"So," said Ava, who *really* didn't like social codes. At least ones that hadn't been properly thought out and debated. "Are you two just not going to talk to each other, then?"

Orion laughed, and said to her directly, "Why talk to a worm when a unicorn is present?"

Richard did not laugh but said in a similar direction, "I really don't see what there is to talk about aside from how to get home, which he obviously doesn't know . . ."

"I told you earlier." said Orion loudly and still to Ava (who was puzzling over whether Orion had actually said 'worm' or 'wyrm,' and if so what kind of dragon Richard would be, and whether or not she liked being a 'unicorn') alone, "You must get to Aquila. It will be a long journey. Since you can't go directly there. You must stay on the path. But once we get there, the gods' eagle will be able to help."

Richard rolled his eyes: there was so much for him to disagree with in Orion's statement that he felt it better not to talk at all. He had no idea who *Aquila* was, and he very much doubted it'd be a *good* journey to get to them, and the jab about not being able to go there was a painful one: Orion had chosen to investigate whether or not Ava and Richard could step off the milky path beneath their feet by pushing Richard shortly after they'd met. In a timeless sky, it had been a heart-dropping eternity before Ava pulled him back to some semblance of solid ground.

The truth of it was that no matter how foreign and superhuman and *starry* Orion looked, Richard knew his type exactly. He was, Richard had decided, precisely the same as many of the knights at Runn: knights who said things like "please allow me to accompany you!" and "a unicorn is present" as though no one had ever told them "no" and no one ever would. Richard had long ago discovered that the best thing to do with these knights was ignore them. Eventually, they would search for attention elsewhere.

"Really," said Ava, still trying to break the growing ice between them, "you should be nicer to Richard, Orion. And you ought to be grateful to Orion, Richard. After all, it was because of you that we ended up—"

"I *told* you it was an accident!"

"Well it's going to be a difficult accident to explain to your ladylove at home, don't you think?" Ava retorted primly. "I don't see why you're in such a rush."

"I told you, that isn't the situation at all," Richard muttered.

Ava pretended like she hadn't heard. It made her more angry than she wanted to be: there was something about it she didn't understand, and she wasn't sure she wanted to know what.

"I would do as you suggest, Blessed," Orion was saying. "Excuse me!" With an exaggerated leap, he left them to soar through the sky, toward a breach of light in the blue darkness.

"What do you think he's doing?" Ava asked Richard, watching the ethereal form shoot away from them.

"What he always does," said Richard stiffly. "Don't you remember? He said he gets rid of other myth intrusions. That's probably one there. He's going to be doing this the entire time. We're *never* going to get back."

"It's kind of neat though, isn't it?" Ava grinned as she watched the flash of sword and shadow of club, thinking. She hated most nicknames that other people gave her, but 'Blessed' felt special. And it *was* special, that she out of all her sisters and all the generations of royalty of the Blessed Land should be the one to travel the sky. Was it something her distant ancestors had really done, as well? Were all the myths true?

Meanwhile Richard scoffed. "Seen one duel, seen 'em all." It was too far away for him to see any strategy in the fight, so he turned to his feet. He scuffed the glowing substance beneath them, to no avail.

"I have returned!" Orion announced, landing with a triumphant air. "So many of these other myths are vicious. Nothing like *you*, Blessed."

Not when she's in a good mood, anyway, Richard didn't say. Timelessness, he decided, was going to feel *very* long.

21

Cow Tools

July 4, 2018

So someone made a great point to me last week. It's true: not everything in fantasy needs to be explained.

And this is hard for some people to get—it was certainly a revelation to me—but fantasy is *better* when not everything is explained. Because when the entire story isn't locked down by air-tight reasoning and detail, you get pockets where the reader can ooze their way in and change the makeup of the world. They can interact with it. Make it their own. Also, in my personal opinion, unexplained elements in a story make it much more relatable, because who in the real world ever knows what's going on?

Now clearly we're talking about details here, not plot points. No one likes the giant eagle swooping in at the end of the day for Reasons and making you wonder why there was a book at all. That's why I stand by my decision to "explain" how Richard and Ava got where they are. The idea of details that you *don't* explain is one I got from the internet a while ago . . . because unlike my teen self, my adult self gets all ideas good and bad from the internet. It goes like this:

Have you seen the cartoon by Gary Larson entitled "Cow Tools"? If not, go look it up. All it really was meant to be was a surreal joke about cows, because that's what everything in *Far Side* was like. But people got really stuck on these unexplained tools. They spent years writing in and theorizing what they were for. Nothing was labeled, so there was room for their own thoughts to grow. And isn't that exactly the point of stories—growing thoughts?

Now, some of you have accused me of being similarly vague about my own life. Well, duh! Truth be told I'd rather hear about *your* lives than preach about mine. But on the flip side, since you mention it . . . I used to keep a diary all the time. Gave each entry a snappy title and everything. I haven't in years and sometimes I miss it, almost as though it was a real friend.

I guess this blog is as close as I've got–not only to my teenage story, but my teenage diary too!

* * *

The next time Orion leapt away to fight a breach, he didn't leap nearly as far. The rift of light in the darkness appeared almost on top of them: Ava leapt, ready to strike back, while Richard smiled smugly because instead of his habitual heroic one-liner, Orion only had time to shout,

"This one *again?*"

And, Richard noted with satisfaction, he sounded very petulant.

Without knowing what she was doing, Ava fought side by side with Orion. It was a thrill, fighting with a partner—she had only ever known practice duels, and those with her sisters, where there was no hope of camaraderie. And now she was fighting not only with a partner, but one from the heavens as well! All at once Ava felt inspired and empowered, as though she'd been doubled and her double wasn't half bad—which was a good thing, because fighting mythology proved a confusing enterprise to say the least.

"I can't—see it," Ava shouted to Orion, but that didn't make sense, because *it* was right in front of her now, standing squarely on the wavering path, striking with a dagger at close range so bright all the stars of the heavens were in her eyes, right there at the front of her brain.

Richard leapt out of the way as Ava lashed out and Orion jumped back with his club, winding up for another attack. Like Ava, Richard had trouble seeing the newcomer directly. He noticed Orion had little such trouble—or didn't care; but Richard, who preferred to at least know what his opponent *looked* like it forced to fight, hung back until he could get a grip on the situation.

"Go back whence you came!"

"Watch the—what *is* it?"

"Blessed! To me!"

The stranger shouted, too, in a foreign language like nothing Richard had ever heard. He found if he stared at the ground—or even better, and the sky beyond them—he could catch glimpses of their adversary. He saw just briefly the blade that perplexed Ava; the determination with which the stranger met Orion's charge; and something else—

"There! I've done it!"

"Excuse you, *we've* done it," Ava corrected Orion. The two turned to each other to share an intense, breathless gaze. Promptly, they burst out laughing.

Richard scuffed toward them casually through the sudden reappearance of darkness and quiet. "Yeah, congratulations," he coughed lightly. "Good job, both of you. And Orion, you said you'd faced this one before, right? Well maybe that explains it."

"Explains what?" Ava asked, flush with victory.

"You can't have possibly—"

"Oh, you didn't notice?" Richard spoke pleasantly over Orion's brash protest. "Together you two just took down one one-armed person."

22

Why

July 11, 2018

Okay, people've been asking why I didn't write stories for a while and why I stopped writing in a diary and on top of telling me that a blog is just an online diary, y'all are in for it now.

The truth is I lost track of myself. The relationship I was in *before* the long one that broke up right before the blog—that relationship was abusive. But stop right there, before you sign me up for any "me too" movements, it wasn't physical (not most times, anyway). And it wasn't like "oh you are woman you do nothing but cook me dinner and warm up bed" type stuff. (Not overtly, but that is a bit what ended up happening.) It was the kind of abusive where sometimes you wonder if the person doing it even knows what they're up to. He was a very, very angry person. He needed someone whose sole function in life was to make him happy, since he didn't know how to do that himself.

And to be honest sometimes I think I did it to myself. The truth is I had a history of trying to make other people happy. When my older sister split at 17 (love you Selena if you ever read this, but it's true) my parents were devestated and little happy-go-lucky teenage me thought I could step up and fix it if I just did a *little* better in school, got a *few* more chores done, won *one* more award. It didn't work.

Anyway it was that relationship that broke the camel's back, I guess, and I wrote nothing at all during the two years we were together. And breaking up was a long, torturous process, and even when it was over and I was safely ensconced in a new relationship, I still didn't start writing again. Looking back I see that underneath my elation at being free, I was still just as empty as I had been before. And honestly that's why the next relationship was bound to end. He was—is—a great guy and all, but I just wasn't there.

So, now I'm alone and have nowhere else to be, so I've started writing again. Drinks, anyone?

* * *

"You—bah!" As a rule, Orion hated sputtering. He never did it—so he thought—and so he couldn't possibly be doing it now; but really what else was there to do, as he watched the new boy gloat, and pretty Blessed grow doubtful?

"What do you mean they only had one arm?" Ava asked much more articulately. Orion stepped closer, in case articulation was catching.

"He *had* both arms, but couldn't use one of them," Richard retorted matter-of-factly. "You could tell from the way his torso twisted back. And then when he moved—"

"It was a hunting accident," Orion interjected by way of admittal. Ava looked interested, as though she might ask how he knew this and let him take over the conversation, but Richard barreled on:

"And then, he moved with some difficulty. I thought at first it was the strange light, but then I realized he was actually faltering: one knee wavered more than the other. Just as if—"

"Just as if he was an old hunter. One who had practiced those moves. But in his age his body is failing him!" Orion finished triumphantly. Triumph and blank stares don't mix well, however, and he hastened to add, "I *told* you I fought him before. He just keeps coming back."

"Well who is he?" Ava asked. She had yet to straighten her clothes, which were in charming disarray.

"I never asked his *name*," Orion laughed. "We know him as Old V. He's from the same myth realm as many fierce animals. And seasoned warriors with strange boats."

"Strange boats how?"

"'Old V', because of his arm? That doesn't seem sporting," Richard said, and summarily was ignored. Orion walked on, telling Ava all about the various ships he'd met in the sky.

23

The Scale of Like

July 18, 2018

No, I don't mean in a middle school "oooooo he liiiiiiikes you" sort of way. Nor do I mean in a "how many times do I say 'like' per sentence" way, even though, as a Millennial, I do that. Okay? I am an educated person who still uses "like" as a placeholder when they talk. Would you prefer I said 'um' or 'f***' or 'eeeee!'? Well it doesn't matter. I'm going to talk about likeability.

I find likeability to be a very strange concept. Don't you? It seems like it's entirely a matter of averages—or even worse, random chance. Everyone may think you are very likeable, but then you might be very angry occasionally. That's not a likeable state, but *you* are still likeable. Aren't you? Then again everyone might *think* you are likeable but that's only because they spend only ten minutes at a time with you. The more time passes, the less likeable you become. We talk about likeability like it's a solid character trait, but it must actually be very fluid.

But anyway I'm not going to talk about the Old One, as you may have guessed I've been thinking about. I'm not going to regale you with stories about how she thought we store art according to color or how she straight up told someone today that "oh I'm adjusting very well to the New Event Coordinator, I'm a go with the flow sort of person!". And I won't talk about my absentee boss, either. (Just how many committees must one person be on?)

No, no. Instead I will talk about . . . my cats. Yes! Salt and Seal are their names, and like most cats, they are very likeable until you realize they are conning you (which might make you like them more, depending on who you are *looks pointedly at villain fanclub on internet*). Cats are in fact an excellent demonstration of the changing properties of "likeability." I always love my kitties, but how much I like them at any given moment might depend. If we think of it that way, like a sliding scale of 'like,' then it's more hopeful than thinking all your likeability has been ruined because you were angry once. Or even once a week. Once a day?

Well, uncomfortable questions aside, let's turn to someone else who has been thinking about these things . . .

* * *

Ava and Orion were deep in conversation about that one time the path they were on had turned into a spill of cornmeal—or maybe it had been beans—and how precisely one battles an intruding path. They didn't notice that they were being watched as they walked along. But Richard did.

He could feel it—he was used to the feeling. It prickled,

not pleasantly, but it didn't scare him any more. Calmly, carefully, he scanned this way and that, trying to see where it was coming from. Perhaps, he thought, this time it would be an animal, instead of a warrior; a cuddly one, looking for its home—

But the feeling passed. Richard straightened in confusion and during a lull in the conversation ahead all three travelers heard the *whump* from behind them.

"Oh, um." A skydweller like Orion, another Grecian from the look of him, cleared his throat. Richard almost groaned; but there was something in the stranger's apologetic smile that was endearing. Even on an armed half-dressed sandal-clad muscle man. "Hi!"

The newcomer listed to one side as he stood on the path, as though perhaps he was not used to standing—or he was trying to affect an aura of surprise at running into them like this. Richard was nearest to him, and could see quite clearly that this surprise was nowhere near as genuine as Orion's (for the hero had begun blustering at once). This, Richard decided, was the man who had been watching them—and furthermore he felt self-conscious about it. Richard liked him.

"But what are *you* doing here?" Orion continued, striding close enough to break Richard's thought process. "I haven't seen you in ages. I thought you'd be up there still. Mooning over that girl!"

"Andromeda," the man corrected. "Right. Are these . . . strangers?"

Ava stepped up with Friendly Mode engaged to the highest level. "Hello, yes, and we're very sorry to intrude on your beautiful home. We hadn't much choice, you see. I'm Ava, and this is Richard, and we were thrown up here by a spell gone terribly wrong; now Orion is helping us find a way to get back down."

"Oh," decided the man. "Nice to meet you, then. My name's Perseus. But then," he added, turning more toward Orion, "why didn't you ask Auriga?"

"Auriga?" Ava echoed. Richard looked on with increased interest.

"You know how he is. Always here or there and—bah!—I thought—"

"He's a charioteer," Perseus answered Ava's question politely. "*The* charioteer, actually. I could talk to him, if you want. Wouldn't you two like a lift?"

<h1 style="text-align:center">24</h1>

<h1 style="text-align:center">Monachopsis</h1>

n. The lingering, unshakable feeling of being out of place

July 25, 2018

For all its melancholy, this is a great one because it relates to the story (if Richard wasn't feeling that then I don't know who is), to me then, and to me now. Even its melancholy makes it great, because this is a perfect time of year for that.

When I wrote this story, Richard and Ava did run into troubles. They weren't *entirely* starstruck about being in the sky. And it wasn't one of those adventures where everything happens so fast that you forget about home. Maybe that's one of the things I like about the story actually: it's one of the reasons it doesn't come off as completely childish. I don't think I was ever young enough to not know what monachopsis feels like, even if I didn't have a word for it at the time.

And I don't mean to be boo-hooing for myself. It's a strange fascination really. I mean, it is sad, but it's also something I can relate to as I look back on my history. A lot of things have changed and sometimes I think the young me is gone, which makes me even sadder. It's a dark relief to realize that this out-of-placeness is something I've always felt.

Of course, I have more of a reason to feel it now. Most of you are keen, astute people who think about this blog in your spare time, searching for clues and putting them together—don't deny it! You know I moved here to work at this job. It wasn't the first time I've moved (alone), but it is the first time I've moved *permanently*. Like, when you go away to college, you know that will end someday. You'll be free to make another choice. This one—heck, I could retire from this job. I could be here on the opposite coast my entire life. Don't think I will be, but, you know, there's a scary amount of inertia there.

But the one thing combating that inertia is that boy oh boy, are the stereotypes true. You know the ones, like 'life is so laid back on the west coast,' 'everyone on the east coast acts like a jerk,' 'on the west coast you wear active wear and on the east coast it's suit and tie'. I mean, okay, not everyone here is a jerk. But I do get the persistent feeling that most of the people around me are operating on a different wavelength. And while that's not too weird, what's really weird is sometimes it takes me a while to get through to them. We've talked about it before—I am a people pleaser. I work at an art museum, for goodness' sake. I charm kids into creating pretty things. You all are seeing the *writing* me, which tends to be much angrier than *speaking* me—because in writing, anger can be funny, but in speaking, anger is just yelling. Right? Anyway

I've never had a problem establishing good relations with people—but here, everyone is kind of icy. I thought at first it was me, because of all the relationships stuff and the move and whatnot. But no. There is definitely a difference.

Anyway, enough about me. Onward!

* * *

". . . see, if you're getting pulled then you can add the strength of *two* horses, not just one."

"But what are you getting pulled *on* if you aren't in a wagon?"

"It's *like* a wagon, but way smaller. And lighter."

"Isn't that unsafe?"

"What it *is* is fast!" Perseus beamed with unconcealed delight, and both he and Richard laughed.

Ava watched them, smiling; finally Richard seemed to be getting along with someone. Though a skydweller, Perseus reminded her a lot of her older brother—with an additional fascination with speed, apparently—and she would have liked to talk to him, but he seemed more shy when she or Orion was around. Besides, Orion himself was clearly down in the dumps because his plan had been questioned, and Ava felt bad for him.

She walked beside him as they backtracked over the path to find the Charioteer. "Did you know him?" Ava asked Orion kindly. "Before, I mean."

"Before what?"

"Before you ascended to the sky?" When he was silent, she added, "I mean, you all lived on the ground at one point, right? And the myths started there and then you ended up here?"

"There is no *before*, for me," Orion said, looking away irritably.

Ava wondered. Who *were* these people? *What* were they? At home, there were plenty of myths about skydwellers–majestic, wise beings, similar to gods; people who had ascended from every day life. Orion had told her stories about hunting and grand halls; surely there was no need for those in the sky, grand as it undoubtedly could be. *So he must have been a person who ascended, right?* she thought to herself. *Otherwise, how would we be able to trust anyone here?*

Up ahead, Perseus and Richard were laughing again—this time they'd been discussing flight—and Richard came to his senses incredulously. *It's so nice to meet someone up here with a sense of humor,* he thought but was too hesitant to say. Instead he told Perseus, "I'm glad you decided to stop us."

"I couldn't help it, really," Perseus said. "It's not like we ever get visitors—aside from intrusions."

Richard saw his chance to finally ask a question that had been bothering him for some time. "Are all intrusions really that bad?"

"Bad?" Perseus seemed surprised. "Of course not. There's these two that really know how to party over near the zodiac line . . . I usually avoid the zodiac itself, they're kind of weird . . . One of the *other* zodiacs though, they have a rat and a sheep and a dragon and stuff, and they all have this crazy house, too. It's interesting to go and see them."

"You travel a lot?" For the first time, Richard felt envious of someone in the sky.

Perseus nodded, with a modest shrug. "I like to have stories I can tell to Andromeda. She's not really allowed to go anywhere."

Privately Richard decided there was definitely something *there* worth discussing, but that he probably shouldn't investigate. After a pause he looked up, ready to ask more about how interstellar travel worked—

Only to see a pristine, ethereal, shimmering example of travel from another world's distant past sitting there in front of him.

"Oh," said Richard, stopping short in front of a pawing beast. "How did we miss this the first time around?"

25

Story Time

August 1, 2018

People are the worst. And more than that, people are the weirdest.

You know those radio shows where people call up to have the DJs call their ex and find out what went wrong? Of course you don't—no one listens to the radio any more. Well, I do, since I didn't drive this car all the way across the country in order to commute to work by bus. Besides, the bus schedule here is nuts. I'd have to take like three of them plus a taxi plus an Uber plus walk under a sketchy tunnel and hitchhike on a llama.

Anyway, right now I feel like I could be a contestant on one of those shows. Not the one who signs up for it—I'd be far too mortified to ever consider such a thing; just leave me to my anxiety-riddled progressively-worse psychotic imaginings of what went wrong, thanks—but the one who gets called.

So I went on this date with this guy, right? It was nice. We saw a little league baseball game—cute. We then doubled down on "classic dates" by having a picnic, not on a beach, but near one. Then came a movie, then making meals together, then he says oh by the way I'm into little kids, then coffee—what?!?

"Yeah," he says. "But it's like, not a big deal, right, since I was honest about it and I really like you and all."

"But I work at a museum."

"Yeah?"

"A museum that runs programs for *children?*"

Smirk. "Yeah."

Oh my god, I can't believe that was the only reason he ever liked me in the first place! I mean no that's not what he said, but GAHHHH. It's like "oh he only liked me for my boobs/hair/money" but A MILLION times creepier. I mean I am usually one of those "live and let live" people that conservatives hate ("but where do you draw the LINE?") but there's the actual-legal-crime *line* for you, right there. Plus, blehhh!

If I see him in one of the galleries, I'm gonna sic Brent on him.

Sucks too. He was actually a good kisser.

What do you have to do around here, sell your soul to a minor demon for some liplocking skills?

Anyway. On to better news . . . maybe.

* * *

"What in the sky is *that?*" Ava stared at a mess of horns, fur, and unfriendly eyes.

"An appropriate exclamation, my lady!" Orion stepped

102

over to her cheerfully—then stopped in his tracks. "Oh, gods above."

"What?" Distracted from discussing the newest blade technologies with Perseus, Richard came up not far behind Orion, peering over the huge man's shoulder first at Ava then at— "Oh. I know what that is. It's a—"

"A goat!" Perseus announced triumphantly.

Ava didn't seem so sure. "A . . . goat?"

"Do you not have them, in the Blessed Land?"

"This is excellent!" Perseus cried, picking up the small, steadfastly staring goat and swinging it in his arms.

"This is horrible," muttered Orion, though probably not out of concern for the goat's welfare.

Still watching the thing watching her, Ava muttered, "Aren't they usually *hairier?*" It seemed awfully presumptuous of this half-furred farm creature to crash her interstellar journey.

"You don't understand," Perseus turned to the three disparate faces, goat in arms. "If one of his goats is here, then—"

There was a pause.

"Oh, very well then." A new form appeared, only one grudging beat behind cue. As the celestial body materialized, Ava—who was closest—recognized yet another skydweller in a toga with several *more* goats clustered at his feet. Unlike the man, who glowered and turned away, crossing his arms, the goats piled over each other to stare at the newcomers just as their brother had done.

"Hello, Auriga!" Perseus all but shouted happily, striding forward with the errant goat. "It's been too long!"

"Ah . . . Perseus." Auriga, the Charioteer, unbent enough to smile at the younger man. "Still traveling everywhere you have no business being?"

"Yeah, but nowhere near as fast as when we hooked up that team of eight to your cart." Perseus dropped the goat into the hile of hooves and horns at Auriga's feet and the two men proceeded through a series of strange hand gestures and facial expressions which made absolutely no sense to anyone else, until at the end Perseus grinned and leant back, arms wheeling—just like, Richard thought, someone on an out-of-control wagon. He broke into a grin himself as Auriga and Perseus laughed.

Ava looked at the two men guffawing, looked at Richard grinning, looked at Orion sulking, and sighed to herself. *Speed junkies. Is this what they ascended to the sky to spend their time doing?*

Despite any and all amount of secret handshakes and inside jokes, Auriga flatly refused to take Ava and Richard anywhere. When Perseus broached the subject—*finally,* Ava thought, for she quickly tired of racing stories—Auriga looked the newcomers up and down like they were made of oozing tar. "Can't have them on my chariot."

"What?" Ava stepped forward, outraged at the note of insult.

"They're not bad," Orion offered half-heartedly from the back.

Richard did his best to remain more reasonable. "Why not?"

"Not enough room," Auriga sniffed.

"But couldn't you, I don't know, I thought maybe you could set one of them up front?" Perseus asked.

"That's where Diva here sits," Auriga said, pointing at the errant goat. The goat continued staring at Ava, who said in some alarm,

"You put the *goat* 'up front'?"

"She likes the view," Auriga shrugged like this was obvious.

"Well we know why she ended up lost and alone then," Ava muttered, wondering how the goat had managed to ascend to the sky in the first place. Richard elbowed her.

Perseus cleared his throat. "Are you *sure,* Auriga? They really have to get home."

"If that's what they want then why is *he* with them?" Auriga asked, finally acknowledging Orion—who had been lurking at the back, but now stood straight, calling back,

"What's that supposed to mean?"

"Yeah," said Ava more curiously, "what's that mean?"

"Oh gods," Richard said to no one in particular, thinking, *we wanted to find a shortcut—but now we're going to be here for eons.*

26

Happy Banana Birthday

August 8, 2018

Okay, so. Let me set the scene for you.

Scene: fridge at work. Work fridge. Fridge with freezer section. Work fridge freezer section with frozen treats for children's camp. I.E., for the public. In work fridge.

We begin our action with a shot of me, the blissfully ignorant public programs coordinator, getting ready for the camp day. The sun is out, the art is shining. The museum's already hot and I want to go home so you know, normal morning. After a pirouette around the desk to check for new emails I head to the communal kitchen to check how many pints of Dots we have and I open up the work freezer to face ROT SMELLING DIRTY BLACK SLUDGE.

You know Dots. Everyone knows Dots. Dots aren't smelly. And they aren't black and they aren't sludgy. What they *are* is sold in cardboard containers which DO NOT REPEL DIRTY GROSSNESS. Instead they soak it right up. "Come right in!

Join us! Jooooin us!" Little did they know what they were getting themselves into . . .

Guys, it was the worst. I've never seen anything so slimy in a freezer. What was it, you ask? Well, I took one for the team and investigated and I can now report it was A PLASTIC BAG OF DEAD BANANAS. D-E-D dead.

And guess who brought them in? And guess who cleaned them up? NOT THE SAME PERSON.

The Old One dithered about as I detoxed the kitchen, becoming more and more defensive. "Well I brought them in for a friend." "Well *she* said she needs banana peels to fertilize her roses." "Well they were frozen solid when I brought them in!" "Well I'm going to meet her after work for my birthday party, what was I supposed to do??"

Oh I don't know, maybe KEEP YOUR GOTDAM GROSS-NESS IN A COOLER IN THE CAR OR UNDER YOUR DESK OR AT HOME AND GIVE THEM TO YOUR FRIEND ANOTHER DAY!

I can see it now. She's at her birthday party, fuming. "That *new girl* said I can't do things for my friends any more! She said I can never bring anything in from home!"

NO I DIDN'T YOU LIAR I SAID PLEASE DON'T BRING IN GROSS THINGS NOT IN A TUPPERWARE WHEN I HAVE CAMP

Ugghhhhhhhhhhh…

* * *

In the end, Auriga's word proved final. He left the party of travelers with only a nod of the head and the faint sound of bleating goats.

"He's really nice," Perseus said a bit lamely in the ensuing silence. "Normally."

Orion muttered something to the contrary, but no one paid any attention.

"It's all right, Perseus," Ava was saying. "It's not your fault he said no. Now we just need to . . . keep walking."

If Ava's consolation ended on a bitter note, Richard stepped up to smooth it over. He clapped a hand kindly on Perseus' shoulder. "You've been really kind to do this much," Richard said. "Would you—do you think you'd like to walk more of the way with us?"

"Of course he would." The trio turned to stare at Orion, whose brash tone jolted their attempts at heartwarming camaraderie. "*Wouldn't* you, Perseus?"

Ava narrowed her eyes. "Why does it sound like you're threatening him?"

"Upon my honor, I am not!" Orion winked at her, making her laugh. "Let him tell you himself!"

When Perseus faltered, Richard spoke up instead. "Well let's start walking, anyway," he decided. For one terrifying moment no one did anything—but finally Ava took the first step, and everyone fell into place behind her. Quickly Orion matched her pace, and behind the two of them—to distract himself if nothing else—Richard turned to Perseus.

"It's, um. I guess it's always this blue, everywhere?"

"Yep," said Perseus, cheerfully. "Dark blue, everywhere in the sky. Except when you're near the path, of course, which you've noticed, I guess. Sometimes I think there's something—I mean, I guess that's the other reason I like traveling. It's like I remember what things looked like when they weren't blue, even though I don't, really."

Not realizing exactly what Perseus had said, Richard asked, "What about the other skies you go to?"

"Oh, those?" Perseus thought. "They're different."

"You don't say," Richard couldn't help but comment. When he realized he'd spoken aloud he looked up at Perseus for a moment horrified—but the moment passed and both Richard and Perseus laughed.

"It's really hard to explain," Perseus admitted finally. "I guess you have to go somewhere new before you understand. You can't describe it right otherwise."

"That makes sense," Richard agreed, thinking of the contrast his own home made with this empty, sparkling place. A brief, hard stab of longing for dirt roads and towering trees hit him. He wondered, not for the first time, how long they'd really been gone.

"There is one of them that's kind of rainbow, though," said Perseus, warming to his theme. "The way the light kind of gets lighter and darker here? That's colors there."

"Sounds confusing."

"It gave me a headache," Perseus confided. "But she really liked hearing about it. Andromeda, I mean. That's what he meant, you know."

Richard, who was still trying to imagine a rainbow sky and had only barely managed to follow the track of Perseus' phrases, leant his head to one side. "Who? What?"

"Andromeda. Orion. That's what he meant." Perseus leant in, now smiling in earnest. "If we keep going, we'll go right by her."

27

Coincidence

August 15, 2018

I'd like to take a break from our regularly scheduled programming to make an announcement: there's really no such thing
as coincidence.

Humans love patterns, and you all in your pattern-loving
minds have noticed that my blog topic and story topic
sometimes align. "Oh," said Facebook last week, "even when
she goes on rants, the rants are similar to the story portion!"

Well, Facebook, did you forget that I am human too? I love
a good pattern like any of you. I do that on *purpose*. Yes, even
when I am mad about something and have to shoehorn it into
relevance, I go ahead and do that. (Never said I wasn't violent.
At times.) In fact it's concerning to me that Facebook only
sees the pattern *some* of the time, but then, I guess that's my
fault, on account of being human. Fallibility, and all.

Isn't it funny that everything comes back to that? Being
human, I mean. It's a strength and a weakness. I guess it's not

actually all that funny since we *are* human and nothing we do could be because we're *not* human because we're *not* not human—

Oh dear. I have a summer cold and I took a lot of medicine. Does it show?

* * *

"The path will go right past her. You must prepare yourself."

"But for what, exactly?"

"Anything. Everything. The ancients performed rituals. Now the very space around her is filled with evil intent."

"Uh . . . huh." Ava didn't have to eavesdrop to know that her conversation with Orion was going *very* differently from Richard's conversation with Perseus several steps back.

"It's not her fault," Orion went on graciously. "She's mixed up in things. Things too powerful for her. This square is just the latest in—"

"Let me get this straight," Ava interrupted, teasing. "You're afraid of a *square?*"

"No. Well, *yes,* but—"

"Is it because of the right angles? Would it be better or worse if it had five sides?" Ava giggled.

"You will understand," Orion insisted. "It's another intrusion. Something from an older time. There is bad magic in it."

"Well that I can believe," Ava said, calming herself. "Is there even such a thing as *good* magic?"

"I doubt it, myself," Orion agreed with an appreciative look. "It is meddling, all of it. Battles are better fought even ground."

"I'd toast to that."

For a moment Ava and Orion walked in companionable silence. Then Orion had the misfortunate thought of adding, "But were it not for magic I would not have met you."

"Yeah, well," said Ava awkwardly before laughing, "If it weren't for magic, I wouldn't have had to listen to that smarmy line!"

"It wasn't a line," Orion protested, instead of laughing along as she had expected. Ava paused: of course any courtier at home would say the same thing, *but it isn't a line, but it isn't just court manners,* so on and so forth—and normally she had no problem pointing out just how superficial they were. But she felt she might have done Orion an injustice. *Who's to say everyone else is as bad as the people at home?* she reminded herself.

But still, even if she felt bad, she had no idea what to say. "Well . . ." Ava looked around them. *Of all the times for an intrusion* not *to show up!* "Well, I guess we'll have to hold our judgment when it comes to magic."

Orion smiled. "We will, indeed."

28

Fly Me to the Moon

August 29, 2018

Some of you more calendar-oriented folks may have noticed that I missed last week. I assure you that I have a perfectly good excuse, which is that I was dead.

Lucky for you, though, that my ghost has returned from beyond the grave to finish off my work transcribing this story and keeping you all entertained!

Example A of entertainment—a conversation overheard at work:

"But like, moon travel is right around the corner."

"Oh yeah, like in five or ten years?"

"Yeah. I'd totally go."

"I'd go, but I'd wait. Like I'm not getting on the first trip up, you know? I'll wait til they get the kinks out first."

And that ladies and gentlemen is what I, Ghost Ashley, find amusing. Cautious armchair moon explorers.

* * *

Ava found herself greatly relieved when a cry went up behind them. She wheeled—minding Orion's club, already at the ready to intimidate whatever intrusion may have popped up—but saw nothing other than Perseus and Richard standing in the middle of the path.

"Orion," said Perseus accusingly. Ava looked at Richard, who shrugged.

"What? What did you see?"

"Richard told me you haven't told them anything about anyone else up here!"

Ava's heart missed a beat. *Who else is up here? What else is up here?*

"That's nonsense," said Orion. He put away his spear, but continued glowering. "I told them all the history. Ava listened well. But this one—"

"Well actually . . ." Ava paused when all eyes turned to her. She still wasn't used to such abrupt reactions when she began talking. For once, she found herself missing the time she could make sardonic comments and be safely ignored. But the truth was, even though she wanted to stand up for Orion, most of his stories had not been about the *other* beings in the sky, and after Auriga's comments, that worried her a little. Besides, as Blessed royalty she felt she had an obligation to be interested. "We could always stand to learn more."

"Especially since Perseus pointed out we have a long way to go, still," Richard said. Ava narrowed her eyes at him: though his tone was *mostly* reasonable, it still sounded rather like he was saying *so there* to Orion.

"We will get there," Orion said, with a glance at Ava.

"But we're almost there now," Perseus pointed out. "Or, we will be, I guess. And they don't know about her parents or anything."

"Her"? Andromeda. Ava couldn't decide if Perseus' constant habit of referring to Andromeda like she was the only female in existence was endearing, or annoying. And she found it hard to believe that the rest of the sky might revolve around this one woman.

That, she decided, *would just be too much like home.*

Orion crossed his arms. "So?"

"So," grinned Richard, "it's story time."

29

Hate Hate Hate

September 5, 2018

Let me just begin this blog by saying GAHHHHHHHHHHH-HHH.

Ahem.

For those of you who haven't seen *The Twelve Chairs*, go see it. Bask in the Soviet humor and let it buoy your spirits above the depths I have sunk to . . .

Okay so I was sick. I was very sick there for a while and my head felt like cotton balls dipped in mercury and my thoughts were moving at the speed of lead and this new climate definitely won one over me and *during that time* what did The Old One do?

NOTHING USEFUL THAT'S WHAT

I just can't even, folks. I really can't. I have never felt this way about anyone ever. Like I am actually a nice person. I am one of those people who the best thing others can say about is "oh she's very kind" or "oh isn't she sweet?". We've been over this. It's like a coping mechanism for me at this point to be nice to people. It is part of me. I have never-not-ever hated anyone, not my sister after she left, not my parents, not that girl in third grade who spat spitballs out her recorder at me during music class, not the first guy I broke up with who made it super awkward, not anyone. But I hate this woman!!! Like it doesn't even make sense! I can't tell if it's because she's from another generation or a very insulated upbringing or a super spoiled family or if she's going senile or if she's just straight up mean and dishonest and antagonistic and self-centered. She's so ignorant she basically exists in a bubble of stupid. And for all this trouble it's become clear she actually has no personality, that changes depending on who she's talking to, she's basically just a slithering ignoramus viper and there's no way to ever get rid of her!!!

My boss legit thinks she plots and schemes and is playing us all. Of course, my boss—much as I adore her—is always in meetings or committees of some kind, so she drastically over-estimates what The Old One can do. I honestly think that kind of scheming is beyond her. She's not even a good liar. She'll totally lie all the time, but sometimes I'm not even sure she knows she is lying. I tried to ask her about it kindly once and she bit my head off. "I don't see how you could possibly say I am dishonest! I need proof!" Then literally the next day we had this exact conversation:

Old One: "I need to copy this, if that's okay with you."

Me: "Totally fine, but didn't you copy it yesterday?"

Old One: ". . . No."

Me: ". . . I sit next to the copier. I watched you copy that yesterday."

Old One: "Oh, well sure, of course, but then I destroyed

that copy. I tore it up."

Me: "Okay, weird . . . It really doesn't matter. But remember how we talked about honesty yesterday? You just lied."

Old One had nothing to say about that. To clarify, I wasn't even out to get her or anything, like I wasn't pointing or "aha"ing or doing anything except pointing out that that was, in fact, a lie, just to see if she realizes what she is doing. And maybe also to point out that *I* know what she is doing. STOP LYING TO ME!

It's just so exhausting because it is *everything* all the time. There is nothing she won't lie about, and then lie about lying about. And at first when we worked together I was naive and nice and went along with it but now that I know I just have no patience for anything she says. It's so much more effort to a) get her on topic and b) get her to answer the specific question and then c) determine if she was making that answer up to be what she thought you wanted or what she thought would make her own vindictive point (depending on how she feels at the moment) that honestly it is 100% easier for me to make up all my own answers on the spot without any reference to her at all.

This whole thing is unsettling, folks. I can't even look her in the eye, I literally despise her that much. Is this a thing? Do other people feel this way? Do they then get over it? This morning I caught myself wishing she'd get into an accident on the way to work, and believe me, wishing harm on others is NOT my M.O. It's disturbing. Then it makes me hate her even more because she makes me feel this way.

Anyway . . . deep breaths . . .

* * *

"Um," said Perseus. "Right, story time. Uh . . . I guess if we start when I was born . . ."

Across the impromptu story time circle, Ava caught Richard's gaze and rolled her eyes. He gave her a half-tilt of the head, a sort of silent "be nice," and then focused back on Perseus.

"The story starts with *her* parents," Orion interrupted, impervious to Ava's *oh skies above don't make it worse!* look. "They're terrible."

"They really aren't . . ." Perseus sighed.

"Maybe Orion has had his own personal problems with them and is being harsh?" suggested Richard, almost hopefully, Ava thought.

But Perseus shrugged. "No, no. He's right. They're awful. I mean everyone says there's more sides to any story but—"

"They sacrificed their daughter to a sea serpent!" Orion intervened.

At the intensity in his voice, Ava felt a familiar twist in her stomach. Obviously, he felt strongly about Andromeda—the ubiquitous un-named woman—and her fate. *Just like Liam and Ylandria,* she wouldn't let herself think in so many words. It really wasn't anything like the time her jealous sister ended up with the one guy everyone in court knew Ava had a crush on. This was an entirely different situation, and moreover, that had been years ago now. Ava wondered when she would finally stop thinking about that feeling every time one of her friends mentioned another woman. *It's not like they could avoid it—*

"It's true," Perseus was saying meanwhile to Richard. "I

found her chained to a rock."

"*Chained?*"

"Skies above," Ava returned to the conversation. "Wherever you people are from was *barbaric.*"

"Not so!" insisted Orion. "Only *they* were barbaric."

"Well . . ." Perseus looked at him meaningfully.

"I defy you to—"

"I mean, there was Oedipus. And remember—remember that deal with the vultures? And then some of the things Heracles did, I think—"

"*Heracles.*" Orion ground his teeth.

"Yeah, anyway," Perseus said, reading the room, as it were— "I guess you could say it was kind of a rough time."

30

Lucida

n: the brightest star in any given constellation

September 12, 2018

You all know these people, right? Not people *named* Lucida, but people who definitely should have been. The girls who every boy in high school had a crush on, who were voted most likely to be an actual disney princess. The boys who could do no wrong and were totally oblivious of the troupe of fangirls behind their every step.

I've never been that person—I'm way too awkward, in case you were wondering. And it's not even awkward like most nerds, it's awkward like I'm watching you and figuring out what you want before I do anything too noticeable. Anyway, I like the shadows, and while I don't *dislike* these people, I find I don't trust them. I always find myself wondering about them. Is it really them? Is it just an act? Is it eating them up?

Because I think it ate my ex. The act, that is. He was that way, that "I can't believe out of everyone he chose me" sort of way. And even when you start dating that person and you realize they're acting, it doesn't make them less bright: it makes you feel special too. *Now I get to see what the world doesn't,* you think. *I'll help them shine even brighter.* Yeah. In my experience, that feeling doesn't last too long.

I know all this sounds very depressing and whatnot, but at the same time, I think everyone has a piece of this in them. Truly and cornily I really do think everyone has that part of them that shines: maybe it's an act they've perfected, maybe it's a glimpse of genuine worth. Everyone has those. Why does it show up more for some people? Is it that they can look exactly like we expect them too, and we don't notice the more hidden glimmers inside others? This is all starting to sound a bit like My Little Pony . . . but these are legitimately the things I think about, folks.

But before I go on too long, won't you join me in welcoming the newest member of our cast? (And don't worry, all this meeting people is definitely going somewhere.)

* * *

"It seems like your gods drove most of those decisions," Richard said pragmatically when Perseus was done retelling his tale.

Orion shifted. "You *were* listening!"

"Well stars forbid we end up at *their* mercy," Ava said. Yet another of those comments, she reflected in the ensuing silence, that had worked better when she was a forgotten member of court. "So anyway, I suppose you killed the dragon or whatever it was?"

"I did!" Perseus brightened. "I think. It was very fierce—"

"He turned it to a rock. It took three seconds." Orion sounded suddenly as though he might yawn.

"Oh, right, I did have Medusa's head by then—"

"What's a Medicine Head?" Richard asked with interest.

Ava reflected that this was less *story time* and more *question time,* but decided to keep her comments to herself.

"Not medicine." Orion guffawed. "Tell them about *that,* boy!"

"Right, so I guess you don't know, but there was this creature who could turn people into stone by looking at them and I had its head—"

Ava suddenly was interested too. "How could it look at people if it was dead?"

"Maybe sea monsters are particularly susceptible," Richard suggested.

Perseus, increasingly uncomfortable, said, "Okay, this is getting all out of order. You don't even know how I was carrying it and also flying around at the time—"

"You were what?"

"Was that normal?"

"You look," a voice broke in from above them, directed at Perseus but warm and clear enough to distract them all, "like you could use a little help."

31

Ultracrepidarian

*n: someone who offers criticism or judgment outside their realm
of expertise*

September 19, 2018

Well, I think we all know who we're talking about.

Because I am not an entirely unjust person (or at least, I try
not to be) I will admit that there is *one* thing the Old One is
an expert about. Knitting. All year long it's been knitting this
and knitting that and yarn falling out of overstuffed cabinets
on top of my head and there I am wearing a fuzzy orange
yarn wig when all I wanted was a stapler, not a makeover.
Honestly you'd think we work at a craft store or, you know,
a yarn store maybe.

Anyway I've been hearing about knitting since I started,
at least back in those heady spring days when I still paid
attention. (Ah, the folly of youth.) And when I say hearing

about knitting, I mean hearing about other people who knit. There's a JoAnn and a MaryBeth and a SallySue (probably) and a host of other who all have opinions, it seems, about what we do here—never mind that they only come here once a year for a certain event, or how they know about what's going on here in the first place. When I reorganized the Craft Corner in May, it was "but MaryBeth needs the light from that window to see." When I wrote up an actual roster of volunteers for the *first time*, it was "well SallySue hates it when these organizations start sending her too many emails. She likes it better when I call her." And when I started putting together this event back in August, it was good ol' JoAnn needing a particular kind of snack.

Well we just had our Back to School extravaganza to-day—complete with the Knitters, on their one annual ap-pearance—and guess what?

"Oh I love what you've done with the Craft Corner," says MaryBeth.

"Your emails were such a pleasure, how do you put the pictures in them?" gushes SallySue.

"Oh look! A new kind of cookie!" squeals JoAnn.

Either these people are all masochistic liars (birds of a feather, I suppose) or they're super nice, and furthermore, *not* the Old One's chorus of naysayers. Heck, they didn't even seem to be friends with her. I tell you, folks, it was a revelation. Hallelujah, I am not alone!

And speaking of not alone . . .

* * *

"It wasn't your cue yet," Orion grumbled.

125

Andromeda looked down on him with a confused smile. "Cue?"

"Ignore him," Ava suggested.

"Very well then." Radiantly—*because of course,* thought Ava—the newcomer turned to the rest of the group. "I happened to notice you down here, and I had the chance to get free, so I thought—why not? I hope you don't mind."

It was only then that Andromeda's shining feet took on slightly more substance, and finally touched the ground—as though she had intended to wait for their invitation. Though just as silvered as their other companions, she seemed yet more ethereal. It was obvious looking at her that in life her hair had been dark, her skin flawless, her eyes kind, and her manner entirely too shy to be shining before them the way that it did now.

As always when he saw her, Perseus reacted a moment late. "Andromeda! It's so good to see you," he enthused, springing up. "Would you like to meet everyone? Everyone, meet—"

"Andromeda?" Richard offered his hand politely, standing as well. "It's nice to finally meet you."

"'Finally?'" Andromeda repeated with a glittering blush. "I'm sorry to have kept you waiting."

In the background Perseus was still talking: "They're from below, but from a different world altogether, this is Richard, and this is—"

"Yavalinra," Ava announced herself. With a wry grin she too shook Andromeda's hand, asking, "You 'had a chance to get free'? You don't mean from that square of dubious origin, do you?"

At the tease, Orion leapt up at last. "It isn't dubious!"

"Do you even know what dubious means?"

"Oh, that," said Andromeda, not hearing Richard's verbal jab. She looked over to Perseus, her smile fragile. "No, it wasn't that; I haven't sensed it in some time. It's an arrangement Pegasus and I have—well. It's a little complicated. But please, Perseus was telling you a story, and I interrupted!"

"I wasn't really," said Perseus.

Ava wanted to roll her eyes—*could a star man* be *any more starstruck?*—but instead she sighed. Richard noticed, but said nothing, thinking of home.

32

Tea Time

September 26, 2018

Okay, okay, before you start passing out the sympathy cards, the truth is I love my work. I really do (maybe that's why it's extra frustrating to have such a coworker). Art is the best, plus most of the kids are cute—and then there's the book club.

In the first few weeks of working at the museum, I accidentally volunteered myself to be the Book Club Person. My predecessor never dealt with it at all—because, you know, people are scary—so I could have gotten by without ever even knowing about it, but I was still really new here and frankly, lonely. Book club was obviously one of those things that you force yourself to do when you'd rather stay in bed and then you go and you make a lifelong friend and your whole life turns around and they make a Hallmark movie about you because you had some human interaction. You know? So I went.

And long story short, it's adorable. Technically the group is called TAE, for Tea And Empathy, but everyone calls it TEA. There's Shaniqua, who would like to pretend she's not the leader but is, and has done the best job I've ever seen at hiding the fact that she's so Type A you half expect the rest of the alphabet to trail after her; Rose the local Chinese exchange student, who with classic gumption is trying to improve her English; Steve the token male, a true gentleman; Laura the off-and-on housewife; and Daisy, who would have been a hippie but wasn't born soon enough. When you add me, it's a pretty awkward group. But I say that with a pure heart—TEA, you know I love you! . . . Well maybe you don't because I usually eat cookies instead of contributing to the discussion, but still.

Just in case you're wondering, yes, I do read Hallmark-esque romances and cozy mysteries. And there's always a book club in those, too, preferably one that also crafts on the side and is full of great cooks. But might I remind you my life is not a cozy mystery because a) I did not leave a high-pressure job in the big city to be here, I left part-time employment and a strained relationship; b) I am not romantically interested in any of the local police officers; and c) I do not have a small dog.

I do of course have the cats, but they have far too much attitude to ever be put in a book.

***

Andromeda's presence expedited the retelling of Perseus' story. Orion filled in the remaining gaps, and—only slightly bemused—the party turned to continue on its way. For some time as they traveled, Orion left them—having seen a strange, lithe intrusion in the eastern sky—and Ava fell into the main party to find herself walking next to Andromeda—or *Herself*, as she had taken to calling her.

"It really is so nice to meet you," Andromeda confided in Ava as Richard and Perseus continued arguing about cooked meats on her other side.

"And to meet you as well," Ava murmured, picturing one of her sisters walking beside her. One of the older, prettier, courtlier ones. After hearing Perseus' story, she was certain that all these skydwellers had been human once after all. Or at least, she was *mostly* certain. They certainly seemed complicated enough to be real, and that was reassuring, because it meant they might understand her and Richard's plight.

"It may sound trite," Andromeda continued, "but I really don't get to meet many people. Although—" she caught herself. "None of us do, really."

Ava couldn't resist. "It must get boring here."

But how could I possibly say that about a realm in the Sky? Ava paused. *But of course* our *sky at home is better than this random one. It must be.*

Mistaking Ava's alarm for embarrassment, Andromeda smiled reassuringly. "Oh, it certainly would. Most of us content ourselves with playing out the old stories; or, when that fails, watching life continue below us."

"'Below'?" Before she could compose herself, Ava looked down at her feet.

"You can't see it now," Andromeda giggled. The sound was kind, and Ava caught herself smiling along. "You can't see anything from the path. But from our places—in the stars—we can."

"Like Richard could," Ava reminded herself.

"Oh! Is he a skydweller too? I had thought—"

"No, he's—it's more complicated than that." Ava resisted the urge to stick out her tongue, but barely.

"Oh, I know a lot about complicated." Andromeda stuck her own tongue out, making Ava laugh in surprise. "I know what you mean. And I have a feeling you're probably going to find out what *we* mean . . . Sorry about that."

"Can't be any worse than what we have at home," Ava remarked.

Andromeda tilted her head. "Our people have . . . a particular imagination for . . ."

"For screwing things up in intricate ways?" Ava grinned. "I think we're going to feel right at home."

33

The One (That Got Away)

October 3, 2018

This one goes out to all those perfect, dreamy moments that disappeared from my mind as soon as I woke up. All the gorgeous idols that slipped through my hands in rooms clouded with incense. All the beautifully melancholy reflections that dissipated as soon as the rude world intervened.

Oh, you thought I was talking about men?

Ha! I'm talking about ideas. Do you know that feeling—the sweet and attractive, but somehow tainted and sad, feeling—that feeling that comes when you were just a little while ago thinking through a magical idea, but now it's gone? It's like the awareness of the shape of your favorite toy as a kid, but an inability to remember its substance. And not just an inability—a reluctance to feel it out—like after you get a tooth pulled and your tongue is drawn to the hole, but you don't want to actually realize that there's an absence there, or much less feel the pain of it.

I'm feeling very poetic about this because I went on a lovely, rainy walk this afternoon and thought all sorts of thoughts, and now I've lost them. I don't know about you guys, but for me this is a familiar feeling. I get it in connection with this blog, believe it or not—things I meant to say in posts, but forgot. I even get it in echo form, reaching up from years past, when I come across a point in the story where I can remember thinking about it when I wrote it the first time . . . and I can remember it resonating or maybe starting out as something different . . . but I can't remember why any more, and now I'll never know.

It's all very strange. Maybe it would feel unsettling if I weren't so used to it; to me now, it's almost like a cozy security blanket. It's not even depressing, not even when I sigh to myself and say 'ah, well, everything leaves.'

You just can't catch 'em all, Ash.

* * *

As the group continued, Orion still absent, a peace settled between them. They walked on, in pairs and in whole, talking and smiling—even laughing.

Ahead, a form coalesced on the path—just for a moment—then another, then again. Straining to see, the two visitors could hardly understand. But Andromeda and Perseus knew the shape well, and their shared glance was a warm one.

The form ahead shimmered, too large to be a person, even a warrior. It moved like water, in ripples and eddies. It seemed to fold back on itself, in and out again, flexing like a strange paper craft until finally Richard realized—*wings.* It has wings, he thought, and turned to share the revelation with Ava at the same moment she turned to him having realized that it moved so gracefully because it was *gliding.*

It picked up speed, not gliding but soaring, nearing and yet refusing to take shape. They stood still, in a dream, watching it come.

Ava found herself wishing she could touch it, doubting it could be even the slightest bit corporeal. Richard still struggled to make out the details of its glimmering starlight, details that flashed and hid from his eyes. Knowing better, Perseus and Andromeda sat back, and tilted up their heads.

When it was upon them it was higher than they thought. Though still on the path, it was yet high overhead, mingling with the stars. It shadowed them, shed light on them, and in an instant it was gone.

Richard recovered first. "What?"

"Don't worry," Perseus grinned.

"Pegasus," Andromeda explained.

Ava closed her mouth, and smiled. She was, she realized with a twinge of star-struck awe, now thinking of Andromeda and Perseus not just as 'real' or as humans, but as friends.

34

D&D Interlude

October 10, 2018

The party goes from walking through a lovely fantasy forest to climbing a mountainside, and the grumbling begins. Who ate the last goodberry? Whose turn is it *really* to ride the carthorse? And whose idea was it to accept a job looking into a shrine at the top of the highest peak in the land? These questions and more will never be answered, because at that moment, a growling is heard.

Party rolls perception

"Guys I think I heard something!" proclaims the wizard excitedly.

The ranger is preoccupied in looking at her shoe. Should she have gone for the lizard gut lacing instead? That merchant back in Typical Town talked too fast.

"I'm pretty sure it's an owlbear. We should hide," says the rogue.

The paladin was busy thinking about her next meal. "What's

an owlbear?"

"You're about to find out!" cries the rest of the cowardly party, having ducked behind a nearby boulder. The paladin shrugs, turns, and finds herself face to elbow with a very angry, very sharply beaked creature.

"Oh," she says, her gnome voice barely audible over the creature's snort. "Are you an owlbear? Well what do you have to say for yourself?"

Owlbear roars.

"That's nice. Do you climb this mountain often? Do we have a long way to go, do you know? Because this armor is heavy. Have you ever worn armor? You might not know, but it's much heavier than it looks."

rolls persuasion

Owlbear cocks its head to the side, as though considering what wearing armor might be like.

"Still very useful though. You might like it if you tried it. Only, you have to make sure the smithy doesn't cheat you, you know. I found that out the hard way."

rolls persuasion again

Owlbear begins sniffing the paladin's armor, moving closer. Party shrieks from behind rock.

"It's not as bad as it looks," says the paladin proudly. "My master helped me fix it up. It's the best armor there is! . . . But it *is* very heavy. If you can carry this, you can carry anything, my master said."

rolls persuasion once more

Owlbear scoops up gnome paladin. Puts her on its back. Turns to look at hidden party. Then begins meandering up trail.

"Um . . . wait up?" calls the ranger.

"This is great," says the paladin. "And if you come back to town with us, I'll help you commission a set of armor all your own!"

And that, ladies and gentlemen, is how with three simple 20s I earned my paladin an owlbear mount.

* * *

"I think I see something ahead," said Richard, after a peaceful stretch of walking.

"I already took care of the intrusion," Orion announced. He turned to Ava. "You would not believe it. It was a giant—"

"I think he might be right though," Perseus said, looking to Andromeda. "Do you see it too?"

"I do. But doesn't it look like one of us?"

"It does!"

Ava extracted herself from the ruins of Orion's story. "If by 'us' you mean one of *you*?" she asked Andromeda with a grin.

Andromeda blushed. "Oh, I did, I'm sorry. I forgot you were any different!"

Ava faltered. *Wait. If we become too much like them, will we still be able to get home?*

Only Richard remained focused. "Are there skydwellers up here you don't get along with?"

"Not if they know what's good for them!"

"Well, I mean," said Perseus, casting a look at Orion, "there *is* the bear. And the dragon. And sometimes Taurus goes on these terrible rampages—"

But Ava was distracted yet again. "A *dragon*?"

"Yes," shuddered Andromeda.

"Hardly!" scoffed Orion.

137

". . . Definitely," affirmed Perseus.

Richard looked around the group, thought about the shadowy shapes ahead, and felt deep in his bones how necessary it was to get home in one piece. He made his decision. "We need," he announced, "a plan."

35

Spice and Skittles

October 17, 2018

You know some things on my list of Ads That Work? Most candies, but that's just because I have no self control when it comes to sweets. But also Old Spice. Remember those commercials? Oh. my.

So yes, okay, when I met a guy at Applebees (long sad story involving D&D and a disturbing love of appetizers) and he smelled like Old Spice I did, in fact, give him my number. Let the following story serve as a warning to you, my friends! Advertising can work on a smart, competent person just as easily as on a troglodyte one step away from homelessness.

My people sense is not as good as my word sense (in case you hadn't noticed). I made it all the way through dinner with the guy, and then back to his house. I know, I know—I had my misgivings about it. But it's my favorite time of year, I'd had some delicious hard cider, I was feeling okay, so I thought—why not? Let's try it! Plus, he really did smell nice.

Flash forward to me sitting *alone* in his home because he realized upon getting in that he'd left his phone somewhere. At first he thought it was in his car and said he'd be back in a moment, but as you'll see that was clearly incorrect, because I was waiting in his dingy apartment cave for a good ten minutes before I got bored of playing nice. I'd exhausted all other options—putting on lip gloss, fussing over my hair, quelling sudden anxiety—so I went and checked out the window. Not a car in sight.

That's right, Mr Good Smelling Genius left me alone in his home. So while he was back at the bar checking for that all-important little gadget box, *I* decided to check out his house. I had skipped dessert and was regretting it—especially if I'd have to wait before finally walking out on him. His apartment was so cold, I could practically feel the wing calories burning off. So I opened up some cabinets—because why waste a huffy exit on an empty stomach and apartment? Oh no, I was going to be fed, and I was going to deliver a parting shot before never seeing him again.

And I can hear you saying I was being harsh. But really, the guy left me *alone*. In his *house*. I wasn't half as offended as I was just disgusted by the stupidity.

Well guess what Brains had in his cabinets? Not quite nothing. There were quite a few dust bunnies. Delicious, no doubt, but I required more sustenance. So I turned to the fridge.

It opened with a squeak and there to greet me was a six pack and a costco-sized bag of skittles.

Skittles? I thought.

I opened the bag. I don't know—I thought there was a balanced meal hiding in there, maybe? I never said I was brainy either! But no, it was in fact a bunch of half-frozen little sugar lumps, just as advertised.

At that point, I had no words. I cackled. I was still cackling when he came back. Needless to say, neither of us was too sad about parting ways that evening.

* * *

"A plan," said Perseus. "Good idea. So . . . what is it going to be?"

"Well, we have to keep advancing," Richard considered. "And there's really no hope of cover."

"What do you take us for? Cowards?"

"It'd be preferable not to fight," Richard said, speaking over Orion. At least Perseus and Andromeda still regarded him raptly. Ava seemed amused by something. "Ahem, that is, not if we don't have to. So, our best bet is to make our numbers seem bigger than they are, and hope to intimidate the other party—"

"See," said Ava quietly to Orion. "We're hoping *they* are cowards."

"They probably are," said Orion stoutly.

"—and with luck they'll be gone before we get close enough for them to see otherwise," Richard finished.

"Great," agreed Perseus. "So how will we do that?"

"First things first," Richard decided. "We need to get in a line."

36

Dramatize Anything

October 24, 2018

Pro tip from the Old One: If you want to make anything in your life seem just that much more important, refer it to it as "that whole episode". Bonus points for a wave of the hand and a shake of the head. I.E.:

"Remember when we lost the colored pencils so I used markers instead?"

"Oh! *That* whole episode." Shakes head, begins preparing colored-pencils-are-just-never-where-you-need-them-not-at-all-like-it-used-to-be borderline conspiracy speech.

Or:

"Oh, it's raining."

"Not like that one time five years ago when we got that storm. I'll never forget *that* whole episode." ExtraSpecial-Bonus Points: hand to forehead, walk away.

* * *

Perhaps more cautiously than confidently, as had been the plan, the group of travelers strode forward along the path. They were arranged in particular order, with Richard to one side, then Perseus, then Orion, then Ava and Andromeda on the far end. Richard hadn't wanted to put Orion in the middle, but he *was* the largest and most impressive. Perseus of course hadn't wanted to be separated from Andromeda, but Ava had assured him they'd be safe and he couldn't find it in him to contradict a lady—especially a lady so forcefully spoken. In fact, no one was too happy about the arrangement, except Orion himself.

As they walked, arms out, trying to look large and glowy and scary, the flashes on the path ahead intensified. If he tilted his head away from Perseus' glimmer and squinted, Richard thought he could make out two shapes—which wasn't bad, he thought, against their five. He was just starting to feel hopeful when the sound crept up on them.

Loud and sharp, the voices were almost enough to make the intrepid party turn back. With each step they grew clearer and more menacing:

"They said it was here!"

"They could have been wrong?"

"Are you calling me a liar?"

"I wasn't, but now that you bring it up . . ."

"FIRST YOU LOST IT AND NOW YOU ACCUSE ME?"

"Nevermind?"

"I CAN'T BELIEVE I HAVE STAYED WITH YOU FOR SO LONG!"

"Ah." Beside Ava, Andromeda stopped, and let her hands slide off her hips. "It's just my parents."

37

Halloween

October 31, 2018

This is Halloween! This is Halloween! Halloween! Halloween!

The kids I had art with today were practically chanting that the entire time. Little gremlins, all of them, and totally adorable. We made characters from spooky stories such as Winnie the Pooh and set up a fashion model runway so the kids could show off their costumes. Our volunteer Marco did a surprisingly good job announcing them!

Honestly this has been the Week of Halloween. Like Christmas, I'm edging up to Twelve Days of Spook and I love it. We had the haunted house one-shot in D&D, plus the obligatory friends-drag-me-to-party-where-I-met-no-one (probably why it went so well), and the museum events—plural!—plus I made a day out of decorating my apartment and watching classic horror movies. Because why not?

I considered making the blog spooky too, to celebrate, but honestly Cassiopeia and Cepheus are spooky enough, not to mention just as dangerous to Richard's hopes of getting home as a vampire or chainsaw-wielding zombie might be. And this is the very day you'll get to meet them. Look at that! Masterful planning. It's almost like I sat down with a calendar and . . . don't hold your breath. I didn't.

Enjoy!

* * *

"Those are your *parents?*" Richard hissed across the group. He *could* make out two shapes, and they *did* seem humanoid, but still . . .

"*YOU NEVER LISTEN TO ME! YOU ALWAYS MESS THINGS UP!*"

"Yeah," Perseus said, accompanying Andromeda's silent nod. "That sounds like them."

"The Queen?" Orion sounded incredulous, and Ava turned to look up at him, asking,

"You know them too?"

But no one had a chance to answer, nor to make any further plans. One of the glowing shapes had noticed them as they stood conferring, stretched across the path.

"Oh look," said the weaker voice. "They're here . . ."

Andromeda sighed audibly. When Perseus broke formation to stand beside her, Richard didn't complain. He felt a bit like hiding behind someone else himself.

Immediately, the yelling stopped. There was a bit of a stand off, as the flickering forms ahead seemed to wait—as though they expected the visitors to approach first. *That does seem like royals,* Ava thought, squaring her shoulders. She was glad when Orion took the first step. With each movement closer, the path felt more and more like a courtly receiving hall—though the angry yells still rang bright in her ears.

"Orion, is that you?"

"It is," said he, bowing. "And—"

"Oh, come, you know we don't stand on ceremony here." The stronger voice, now sweet and alluring, belonged to someone Ava could only assume was the Queen. As she stepped forward and embraced Orion, her head barely rose to his shoulder, her piled and bejeweled hair tickling his cheek. Star glimmer wafted around her fine features like perfume, slipping in and out of the many folds of her draped dress.

"And you are?" The Queen did not step away from Orion before addressing Ava, who was closest. At the same moment Andromeda and Perseus finally willed themselves to catch up, and the King—who had faded into the background entirely—announced them with a strangled,

"Daughter!"

"Oh." The Queen turned. It was only a very small moment before she smiled widely, but Ava noticed the delay with narrowed eyes.

Perseus, too, was welcomed with open arms, and he stammered his way through introductions. Watching, Richard wondered sympathetically if it had been as clear in the court of Runn when he himself hadn't wanted to be there. This King, Cepheus, seemed nice enough; but the Queen, Cassiopeia, reminded Richard of all the worst stories he'd heard about the reigning queen of the Blessed Land. He shifted a little closer to Perseus and Andromeda. Cassiopeia turned the instant introductions were done, saying,

"What a pity you had to come at a time like this!"

"We're sorry to have interrupted you," Andromeda returned, watching her father.

"I mean, we really couldn't have helped it," Perseus muttered over her shoulder.

"We're actually in a hurry to get ho–" Ava started to say.

"You didn't interrupt anything," Cassiopeia beamed as she interrupted. Then, assured of their attention, she gave a dramatic sigh. "You are all friends, so I can tell you. There has been another sighting of my lost crown."

38

Philophobia

n: the intense fear of falling in, or being in, love

November 7, 2018

I know as well as anyone the dangers of diagnosing any of your problems—medical, mental, or otherwise—using the internet. (Looking at you, Mr Oh-that's-a-symptom-of-depression Tumblr!) But still . . . you know that feeling where you relate to some of your vocabulary words on an emotional level?

Maybe you don't. Maybe this is why I'm destined to be alone. *dramatic sigh*

For real though. Maybe it's a little bit of way-too-early-Christmas blues, or maybe it's something about this point in my story (weird to think my past life is influencing my present life so much). I told you all before that I've always been a hopeless romantic, but y'all don't realize, there's a sad dark emphasis on the *hopeless* part.

I only say this because I know Great Aunty is too busy planning this year's Thanksgiving Extravaganza to be reading right now. Sometimes I really think I'm broken. And sometimes, I think it's my family's fault. Not that they're bad or that they meant to . . . but that almost makes it worse. I personally would never have a child, because a) you're bound to mess them up somehow, and b) they're going to be absolutely heartbroken when you divorce/work too much/move/get sick/die. And let's face it, you're going to do at least two of those things, probably repeatedly (well, except dying. Unless you're a vampire or something. Monsters have family problems too).

And yeah whatever, that's life and it's an important part of growing up and toughening up and blahblahblah. That's cool dude. But why would I inflict on someone else what I haven't even figured out myself?

* * *

"And *how* did you lose a—"

Richard kicked Ava before she could finish her question, hoping no one saw the movement behind Orion's huge legs. "A sighting, you say?"

"Yes. By the Earthdwellers." Cassiopeia's dark eyes gleamed for a moment. "Say, aren't our new guests earthdwellers? Or am I mistaken?"

"'Earthdwellers'?"

"'Earth'?"

"They are," affirmed Orion.

"But," Perseus hastened to add, "they're from another—"

"How wonderful," Cassiopeia said, rising from where she'd reclined on what Ava could only assume was star magic. "Perhaps it is not a pity you have joined us after all! *You* can be the ones to find what has been lost!"

"Hold on," Ava protested, too loudly to be shushed by a kick to the shin. "By 'Earthdweller' you mean the people who remember your myths, right? The people who look up at your sky? You can *hear* them?"

"Did I say that?" Cassiopeia looked bemused.

Richard watched the color rise in Ava's face, and resigned himself to the incoming argument. He spoke first. "How was it you realized they had seen the crown?"

"Oh, that." Cassiopeia laughed, and turned to her husband. "I'm afraid I don't have the head for these little details. Dear, explain it for them."

"U-um," said Cepheus. He still stood several steps back from everyone else. "Our stories are still known below, of course. As such, they continue to talk about us, and recount our tales. When something new or of particular note is added, we naturally become aware—"

"You see we really don't hear them at all," Cassiopeia interrupted. "My, can you imagine how loud that would be?"

"Indeed!" said Ava, in not at all the calm tones Richard had used. "How strange! And how strange to assume a pair of strangers would know anything at all about your crown, least of all where it is or how to find it. Why don't you try looking where *you* last lost it?"

"Blessed—" Orion tried to whisper.

"Are you trying to say you don't want to help me?" said Cassiopeia, hurt. "Even though all your friends do?"

"What I'm saying is we can hardly help ourselves," Ava

laughed harshly. "If you had asked anything about us at all, you might have known we're already *on* a mission. We don't need another little fetch-quest to keep us busy."

"Little?" sniffed Cassiopeia.

"What she thought," Cepheus hastened to explain, "is that, since you are earthdwellers, you might be able to see differently than we skydwellers; you might be able to succeed where—"

"I am *not* an earthdweller," Ava proclaimed.

"But Blessed—"

"What?" she whirled on Orion so fast Richard, standing behind him, winced. "*You* know as well as I do. We're not from the world below your sky. We've already been over this. And I don't appreciate any assumptions made about who I am or what I'm going to do!"

39

Radio Silence

November 14, 2018

Radio silence is what we have in the gallery right now, because the local stations can't stop playing pre-Thanksgiving Christmas music, and I'm not having it.

Also I made the Old One angry by inadvertently suggesting she doesn't always remember everything she says, so she's not talking to me.

Radio silence is also what we had when I posted the blog to facebook last week, and don't think I didn't notice. Look, guys, I wasn't trying to depress anyone. I started out going for funny, actually—we know where that ended up. That's the problem with my comedy: it gets too close to the truth sometimes. Have you seen the post, "I Was Trying to Be Funny But It Came Out As Really Mean"? Those moments give me cold sweats when I'm in bed feeding the anxiety monst—I mean, trying to go to sleep.

Anyway, back on track. I didn't mean to shock y'all into not commenting or anything. Heck, even if it's a comment to try to depress me right back, bring it at me. But that's the thing about that sad stuff, guys. It's not *all* there is. (It *is* always there, but you know, sometimes in the background. Okay, I was trying to be uplifting . . . clearly I need to start trying to be *depressing* . . .)

Radio silence isn't how it always is, either. I dread the day the Old One wants to talk again, but I welcome your comments.

Just, you know. So you know.

* * *

Richard watched the faces around them. Andromeda was staring at the ground; Perseus looked supremely uncomfortable. Orion, for once, looked torn; Cepheus was trying to hide again. It was, Richard decided, too awkward to bear. He poked his head out around Orion's shoulder, and suggested,

"Ava, let's at least consider it?"

Cassiopeia pounced at once. "Oh if you *would* listen, it would lighten my heart so! You have no idea."

"The trouble," said Cepheus in the background helpfully, "is we can't see it."

Richard could see Ava swelling, getting ready to tell them all *exactly* what she thought about looking for an invisible crown when she already had a giant godly bird to be looking for, and for once was grateful for Cassiopeia's interruptions.

"Of course we can see it, don't be silly," she waved a hand at her husband. "But if it's somehow in a form that the *earthdwellers* can see, then it would be beneath our notice, naturally."

"So you can't see it," Ava pointed out acidicly. "And what are we supposed to do? Sit here with spyglasses? And when we *do* see it, if we do, what are we supposed to do then? It's not like we can go and get it. We can't leave the path!"

"My, what a negative thinker," Cassiopeia said sadly. "I'll never have my crown back!"

"If you can't get it you could ask Canis," Cepheus said, his voice echoing as though he was getting farther and farther away. Just in case.

"Canis?" Richard asked Perseus.

"Oh, he's the best hunting dog." For the first time in the encounter, Perseus smiled. "There was one time he—"

Not to be outdone, Orion threw his weight in. "You forget the time he—"

Andromeda coughed, her eyes on Ava. Though her voice was small, all the men heard it clearly. "He's back the way we came. Opposite Aquila."

"Oh yeah," said Perseus. "Quite far, actually."

"Oh, wonderful," said Cassiopeia. "You know exactly how to get to him, then?"

Ava burst. "As if you don't! You *live* here! Find your own damn crown. I am so done with this—I am done with this conversation!"

"Well," said Cassiopeia brightly in the silence, as everyone else watched Ava storm off. "With the four of you, I think you could still do it, don't you?"

40

Thanks One and All

November 21, 2018

It's a Thanksgiving miracle. I really mean it. Thank you, thank you, thank you to everyone who commented on facebook last time—even if it was just an emoticon.

And thanks to all you lurkers who keep reading and never commenting here, too. It may be creepy, but hey, that's what writing is about, right? I'm just glad to know you're there on the other end.

Thank you to all of you, and I hope you stuff your faces to your stomach's content this weekend.

* * *

"Sooo." Scuffing his feet as he walked along, Richard wandered over to where Ava sat on the edge of the path. "That didn't go well."

"And you're the one they sent to clean things up?" Ava

scoffed. She tossed her head, not needing to look to know that the constellations were huddled just out of earshot, pretending not to watch.

"Look, Ava . . . Would you at least come back from the edge a little bit?"

"I'm not that near to the edge," she retorted. The milky substance that made up the path floated around her bent knees and she ignored it. Richard sat behind her, where the starry light had a little more substance.

"Is there a *reason* you're being so difficult?"

"Yeah, and it's whatever reason Her Highness has for being such a *bi*—"

Richard cut her off. "I mean aside from that."

"What do you mean 'aside from that'?" Ava turned finally, and took a good look at the expression on Richard's face. "Oh, skies above. You're going to do it, aren't you? You're going to delay us getting home so you can run errands for that self-centered harpy?"

"Look, I don't think you're being fai—"

Ava leapt up, gaining steam once more. "You *heard* what Andromeda and Perseus said about her. And you heard her just now! How could you possibly want to help someone like that? *Especially* when it means staying up here longer! I thought you were the one who didn't want to be here in the first place. Who *knows* how long we've been gone?"

Though he rose, too, Richard was silent for a moment. "Ava, that's . . . that's kind of my point. Who knows how long we've been here? It might have been—it could have been a long time, like a *really* long time. Maybe they've even stopped looking."

"They're never going to stop looking for the crown prince of Runn," Ava retorted—not without bitterness. She didn't say what was really worrying her: *what if the longer we stay here running errands and being privy to petty fights, the harder it becomes to go home?*

"But Ava," Richard protested, "there's a chance we could really do some good here. Haven't you noticed they all seem to have bad memories? I mean come on, Orion has told you the same story like three times. Even Perseus couldn't quite remember the last time he'd seen Andromeda. Maybe a quest like this *is* something they can't do alone."

"As if finding a trinket will make the Queen suddenly a good person!" Ava snorted. In fact she hadn't noticed Orion's repetition, or thought anything of it, and that needled her too. "Admit it, Richard. Talking about their memories and petty problems like it actually matters—you feel sorry for them."

"You don't?"

"Of course I don't!" Ava stomped the ground, which swirled unsatisfactorily around her feet. "I feel sorry for *us,* stuck up here with no way to know what's happening at home, and you should too!"

"I don't think you do," Richard said, crossing his arms. "I think you just feel sorry for *you.* After all, it must be pretty depressing to come up here and realize all those gods in the sky you thought were so awesome are just a bunch of ordinary people just like they have at home."

This was one step too far, and it wasn't even true. Ava lashed out. "Meanwhile all *you* can think about is finally having the chance to play hero, like you never could at home!"

"Fine!" Breathing heavily, Richard fought his impulse to run away as fast as he could. "Think what you want, Ava. Sit here and stew, for all I care. *I'm* going to help the people who have been helping us. While you're all alone up here, you might try thinking a little bit about *gratitude*!"

As soon as he finished the word and not one instant later, he whirled on his heel and was gone.

41

Cars on a Cable

November 28, 2018

Remember that song, "Breathe (2 AM)," that was super popular a while—okay maybe more than a while, I may or may not have been in high school then—ago? And remember the last verse, that goes,

And I feel like I'm naked in front of the crowd,

'Cause these words are my diary screaming out loud

And I know that you'll use them however you want to

Then of course the chorus comes in and she basically says well it doesn't matter, I have to do it because that's what I do. That is my answer to the curious inquiries about all the confessions and drama in recent posts. And go listen to that song again, because it says all that much more poetically than I just did, and it's much better than some other modern songs by the same title which one could (and necessarily did) name.

Granted, blog writing is much less glamorous or important than songwriting. And I didn't start out *intending* to write a blog. Okay clearly I set up the site and it's not like I thought I was getting myself into a netflix subscription and then was bamboozled and like 'oh, guess I have a blog now?' instead. When I set this up I thought of it more as telling a story. A *previous,* past, already-told story, now brought out of a dusty storage box. Not the daily stories of my life, which everyone can agree are pretty pathetic.

Really this could have just been a page or two of star story and a few sentences' worth of intro—or less. It could have been *just* story. But all y'all had to go and ask questions, and now we're *here.*

I'm not a religious person (I had no luck being a people pleaser, what luck would I have being a supernatural-being pleaser?) and I don't believe in fate, per se. All those people who say we have no free will because the neurons and chemicals inside us are dictating our every move confuse me. What are the neurons and chemicals inside me, if not *me?* Damn right they're dictating what I do, and they're me, so *I* am. That's what I say. So really it *is* my fault we're here. But I'm okay with that—after all, I really don't see how else it could have gone.

Speaking of going . . .

* * *

Gratitude.

"A princess never forgets to say thank you," she could hear her mother saying.

Then her sister, sneering. "I did you a *favor,* you know. The least you could do is say thank you."

"Thank you," her brother had said. *He* was always good at

thank-yous. "For still being here."

Ava bent her head into her knees. She was sitting at the edge again, alone again and painfully aware of it even though she didn't want to care. The slow steps of the others receding into the blue distance fell heavily in her already-loud mind.

What *was* everyone doing at home? Ava wondered, even though in wondering she realized she really hadn't thought about it much at all. She had been *glad* not to think about it—not to have to worry about what others were saying, doing, or thinking. It had been a relief.

Ava wiped away the escaped tear and tried to think about something else. The skydwellers—*aside* from Cassiopeia. Did she care what they were thinking? The sinking anxiety at the back of her mind reminded her that she did. Of course she did: they were part of the vaunted sky, and more than that, her friends. *If only someone would distract me from it,* she thought, *before it grows.*

And, *could they really have left me alone?*

The emptiness of space pressed around her. This land—supposedly so perfect and bright! It was unbearable. Maybe the sky *was* different at home, Ava decided, but at this rate she'd never get there. She let her frustration fuel her, goading her to her feet, and turned—to do what, she had no idea—

To stop, as it turned out.

"I was waiting for you," Andromeda smiled shyly as she rose too. She had been so quiet, sitting there in the middle of the path, that Ava had not noticed her. "I hope you don't mind?"

Ava said nothing.

"I just couldn't bear to leave you here. But if you'd rather—I can go—"

Realizing the mistake she was about to make, Ava cleared

her throat. "It's fine. I'm coming."

"That's great!" Andromeda's face held no trace of mockery, though Ava looked carefully. They fell into step with startling ease.

"I was only trying to help, you know," Ava said suddenly. "I mean, I know it wasn't help. But she was so mean to you."

Andromeda smiled. "And you are very loyal. I knew that all along. That is why," she said sweetly, "I waited."

42

Metanoia

*n: a transformation, or complete change of mind;
often associated with repentance, conversion, or other spiritual
journey*

December 5, 2018

This came up in TEA (the mis-named book club) and I like it, especially in a 'spiritual journey' context. I hardly have to explain how it's relevant to the story, do I?

I've always been fascinated by changes of mind and heart. I think that's what interests me so much about love. My personal experience is it never *really* changes anything, but it's so commonly used as a tool to create/explain beast-to-beauty transformations in stories that I can't help but believe it has that potential. Not to make a whole new person, but to make a whole new world (sorry, disney).

Man, of all the Disney songs to encroach upon, too. Aladdin

isn't even my favorite movie. It's better than the Little Mermaid at least, so good thing I didn't say anything about being *part of* someone's world.

Anyway, is it weird that I like that part about love especially? I've just always been obsessed with change. I've always thought of change as a good thing, too. It wasn't until The Break Up (which was almost a year ago now; I wonder when the capital letters wear off?) that I realized that however much I honor change, I'm actually bone-shakingly terrified of it, too.

Just a bundle of contradictions wrapped up in reading glasses, that's me!

Back to our more interesting quest:

* * *

As the women walked up to the waiting group, Perseus beamed. "You're coming, then?"

"I guess," Ava said, not entirely graciously. "Are you really going? Why are you all doing this?"

The impromptu circle shifted nervously as their hosts looked at each other. Finally Andromeda said, "My . . . Cassiopeia has been known to call upon Draco from time to time."

"Don't tell me," Richard realized. "That's the dragon."

"A really bad one," said Perseus.

"I've fought worse," Orion told Ava. "But . . . there's no need to do so again."

"So, basically, you're all wusses." But as she said it Ava smiled, and relief washed over the group as they left the topic behind them.

"Exactly how do we look for the crown?" Richard asked them all.

Orion shrugged. "Carefully."

"Can someone describe it for us?" Ava asked, lifting an eyebrow at Orion beside her. It took some moments of shifting and umming before she recognized the truth. "Oh, skies above. None of you even know what it looks like?"

Perseus scratched his head. "I haven't seen it since . . ."

"It's been some time," Andromeda agreed. "I'm sorry, Ava."

"So how are we supposed to know it's *hers* and not someone *else's* crown?" Ava glared around the little council, but no one had any answers.

"I guess that'll be the sort of thing we know when we see it," Richard said, ignoring Ava's displeasure. "So we'll just keep an eye out, then. Maybe it would be wise to do the first part of the search *while* we go call on Canis?"

"Two birds, one stone!" Perseus grinned.

"Let us not waste time, then," Orion agreed.

"I don't suppose you need any rest before we begin?" Andromeda asked of Ava and Richard. Ava was in no state to admit to needing anything, and Richard was bemused. It was stranger every time he thought of it, this complete disregard for any hunger, exhaustion, or even foot soreness—a feeling he'd once known well.

"I suppose we're off," he said, turning back the way they'd come. He hated to admit it, but Ava was right: it *was* disheartening.

"Get along," said Orion cheerfully, as without any further consideration or hassle, he went.

43

Strategic Incompetence

December 12, 2018

Some of you may be ignorant of this term, and for that, I commend you. I myself didn't realize it was a thing until I came across it while scrolling through Pinterest a few days ago—but I was very familiar with the concept already.

The Old One is a pro at it.

Regarding holiday cheer: "But I have no idea where the decorations go. The *Coordinator* used to do that every year."

Regarding Excel: "I'm afraid to touch it, so I didn't even look. I'm sure I'll get in there and delete everything by accident."

Regarding any decision at all: "Oh I don't know, I'm just a paeon. I leave the decision-making to the *Coordinator*!"

That's her new thing, you see. *The Coordinator.* Like he's still right around the corner and I'm just a glorified secretary, which sometimes I think I must be, because *she* is incapable of doing any actual secretarial work!

To be fair I'm honestly not sure if she's doing it on purpose or not. She *is* miraculously incompetent. Naturally she blames it all on her late mother, who spoiled her (in her own words); because of course, no one ever learned new habits and got over themselves after having been spoiled. No, now she is content to go through life having others do her work for her while she gossips, and then when anyone asks she's all, "Welcome to *my* gallery! Let me introduce you to *my* volunteers!"

Ugh. Gag me with a spoon made entirely of kids' macaroni art, please.

* * *

Somehow, without any of the skydwellers planning it—at least as far as Ava could tell—as the party fell into walking once more, Perseus, Andromeda, and Orion suddenly seemed to have something very interesting to discuss, and she was left alone with Richard at the back.

They walked for what seemed like a very long time in silence. Richard turned his head this way and that, ostensibly looking for errant jewels. For her part, Ava grew more and more impatient waiting for him to speak.

"What is it, then," she burst finally. "You're too much of a coward to talk to me now?"

"That isn't fair," he protested immediately. "I just didn't know—"

"Didn't know what?" To his surprise, Ava seemed to soften a little. She laughed as she went on, "That I was too much of a baby to want to speak first?"

"I wouldn't have put it like that," Richard ventured cautiously.

"Of course you wouldn't." It sounded a little like she was still frustrated with him. "You're *too* kind, you know."

Richard looked down at the path, moving slowly underneath their feet. "I know," he said miserably. *Kind* was something princesses, queens, and occasionally kings were praised for; it wasn't something princes were supposed to be. "But I can't help it."

"Yeah. I guess you can't." It was Ava's turn to look up, and doing so gave her a sudden sense of deja vu—even though there was very little to see. "Remember when you were in the moon, literally trapped with no way out, and you wanted to talk about *my* problems?"

"And now we're both trapped."

"That's not what I meant." Ava turned as though she might cuff his shoulder, then thought better of it. More quietly, she asked, "So what about that girl in Runn? Think she's still waiting for you?"

Shifting uncomfortably, as though struck with sudden worry that "earthdwellers" could hear what happened in the sky, Richard muttered. "I told you already. Probably not. I've been gone longer than you have, after all."

"You really didn't tell me anything about her," Ava corrected him—then grinned. "You probably never even spoke to her, did you? It's just like you knights of Runn to—"

"Ava *please!*"

Ava stopped, blinking at Richard in surprise.

"At least," Richard resumed as he started walking again, "I didn't tell her the same four stories about hunting over and over. *Endlessly.*"

"Hey—that is *not* all Orion talks about," Ava protested when she realized what Richard was referring to. "Don't be mad at me just because I happen to get along with someone up here."

"I do too!"

"Sure, but not enough to—" Ava paused and shook her head. "I don't want to talk to you about this. They put us back here hoping we'd make up, not argue some more!"

"Fine," Richard agreed.

"Fine," said Ava, not to be outdone.

"Are you alright back there, then?" Andromeda called over her shoulder, smiling.

"We're *fine!*"

44

Gallery Cheer

December 19, 2018

I know things have been heavy lately. So, to counteract that—and in honor of the season—on this, our first snow day, I present to you an offering of art-themed merriment: a collection of the silliest things heard in the museum through-out the year.

points to a photo of panthers
   "Is this your only picture of bears?"

"So you actually get paid to work here?"

"How much does this painting cost?"

hastily closes windows of porn on public art station com-puter
   "It's for, um, research . . . Say, do I know you? We should

get coffee sometime!"

"But why *doesn't* the museum have a fireworks display for Independence Day?"

'sneaks' a sex-help text among the art books for sale
   "They're never going to know, they don't notice what goes on here!"

They're never going to know . . . ha! Famous last words.

* * *

Richard avoided Andromeda's sympathetic gaze like the plague as he caught up with the others. Ava saw this and was glad for it, because she knew *she* could act like nothing happened—but, she decided, Richard was obviously a horrendous actor. *Just another reason he never fit in at court.*

The group shifted and resettled as though everything was normal, Ava talking to Orion and Andromeda alternately, Richard and Perseus making each other laugh over things no one else quite understood. It was impossible to say where precisely they had been before, or how far they had gone. The path flickered on and on, as did the stars and the darkness above them. It was—though no one would say it, for fear of alienating the others—rather boring.

Or maybe, thought Richard, the skydwellers simply didn't have a concept of 'boring' any more.

He relaxed more and more as they went on, still trying to keep an eye out for the crown. But the trouble about such an easy journey was that its ease became deceptive: he found himself snap suddenly out of conversation with Perseus from time to time with the sudden realization that he was still walking, and he hadn't been looking anywhere at all.

Ahead, Ava was not much better. In a flash she'd remember what they were doing, and become indignant about it all over again; she'd then renew her decision to help Andromeda; then she'd say something to Orion, and he'd say something back, somehow oblivious . . . he was a simple, lively friend, but the more they walked, the more she suspected that what Richard had said was right. For anything aside from the myths about his deeds, he had a strangely short-term memory. They all did.

And thus uncertain of its progress, the quest continued on.

45

The Twelve Constellations of Christmas

December 26, 2018

Okay, yes, in addition to being light-hearted, last week's blog was a tiny cop-out. But the reason is now revealed: I was working on *this* week's blog!

I think you'll catch on to the idea pretty quickly. Because we all live who knows where, under who knows what sky, I couldn't go with "winter constellations" per se. Instead, I chose my favorites. Enjoy!

Go to this link to see what I mean: https://bit.ly/xmasblog45.

* * *

"It's really not bad," Richard insisted. "Especially if you add redbark."

Perseus continued laughing at him. "What, you stick a

whole stick of some red tree into your drink of old moss in order to make it better?"

"It's not just *any* red tree!" Richard protested, laughing too. "It has this kind of nutty taste, and"—ignoring his friend's comment— "it looks like—like—"

Richard paused. He'd been looking around in desperation—a very desperate desperation, since there was nothing anything *remotely* like a tree around them, much less a red one—and even in his merriment, his eyes had caught something.

A glimmer.

"Like what?" Perseus asked, stopping beside him. He looked in the direction Richard stared, but saw nothing. "Hey. What are you doing? Looking for one of your trees?"

"The crown," Richard murmured.

"What was that?" The trio ahead had realized they weren't following, and Ava called back to them.

"The crown!" Richard repeated, louder this time. "I think I found it!

"And," he added privately to Perseus as they rushed over, "we *can't* tell them I spotted it because we were talking about alcohol!"

46

Resolution

January 2, 2019

First of all, no, I'm not making resolutions, and I'm certainly not posting them online for you all to pick apart and nag me about the whole year. To me, New Year's isn't so much about making resolutions as it is about taking a step back and putting things into perspective.

And I have to admit . . . this year, the picture isn't pretty. It's been rough, and thanks to me oversharing every time I'm behind a computer, you all know it. I've been single and unhappy about it for most of the year, plus I moved to a new place, started a new job, and realized none of that was quite as cool as I thought it'd be.

But if we're talking about disappointments, the biggest one has been in myself. Looking back at this year—heck, just looking back at this blog—it's hard *not* to see that I'm a whole lot angrier than I thought I was. I'm not sure what to do about that. I can't just *resolve* to not be angry. Right? All that anger has to go somewhere. Honestly what I've been doing for years is resolving not to be angry, and look where it got me! Ranting about stupid old ladies to strangers online. Not something I ever pictured in my future, believe me.

I know the anger can be funny, and because of that, it doesn't seem so bad to most of you. At least that's the feeling I get. But to me when I stop and think about it, it is actually unsettling. We've talked about how much I like change, but . . . changing from being the nice girl I was isn't the change I wanted. I wanted to be tougher and more independent, sure; more confident, definitely; more *certain,* if I could manage it; but not more angry. No one *wants* to be angry.

Well, I dunno. Who knows what I can do about it, but at least I know about it, right? Now on to our favorite people, who actually *are* doing something.

* * *

In an instant the group was swarming, elbows flying and chins jutting as they all tried to get a look.

"Where? Where did you see it?"

"Is that it there?"

"Just past the—uh—the really bright one?"

"Is it that bright one or the less bright one?"

"Stop shoving!"

"How bright is 'really bright'?"

"I don't see anything." Orion stepped back, and eyed Richard, still stuck in the middle of the star-searching herd. "Are you *sure* you saw it?"

"Yes! . . . Probably?"

"Then what did it look like?"

“. . . A crown?”

“This is ridiculous!”

“No!”

Just as Orion thundered, Andromeda’s clear voice rang out. The confusion increased beyond possibility and somehow one fact buried inside it settled into them, like the eye of a hurricane: in the hazy mist at the edge of the path, Ava’s foot had slipped.

“Ava, hold on,” Perseus called, leaping to action. He tried to steady Andromeda, who was holding tightly to Ava’s arm, guiding her back to solid ground. Richard rushed the two steps forward to see what was happening, unaware in his haste that Andromeda was standing only *one* step ahead of him—and a heart-dropping jumble followed.

47

Apocalypse 2020

January 9, 2019

Apocalypses are on everyone's minds. And in the dead of winter, who can blame them? I literally just watched this city shut down because of a foot or two of snow—just imagine what a zombie or alien invasion could do. And yes, I am going to make fun of this, because yes, even though we've had so many traumatizing historical events within living memory—from scary wars to y2k—there's one way to go about worrying about apocalypses, and then there's another. If someone made a venn diagram of "People who worry only about unlikely things" and "People with very strange priorities," *guess who* would be in the middle.

My predecessor and current coworker are responsible for the following hordes:

—copy paper
—three-ring binders
—staples

—(not staplers)

—expired band aids

—business size envelopes

—crappy pens

—that we don't even use in the office

—outdated business cards

—half-used bottles of glue.

So don't worry, y'all. If there's an office supply catastrophe, just come to the art museum—we've got your life-threatening glue needs covered!

I just don't even get it. My boss says they were always worried they wouldn't get funding the next time round and that's why they'd order twice what they needed. I know we always talk about 'oh old people lived through the depression, now they're damaged,' or whatever, but is that generation even around any more? I think the Old One just missed it. So she'll have to come up with some other excuse—not that that'll be difficult for her.

It's just like, what did they think, everyone was out to get them? Did they have no faith whatsoever?

But you know, I've decided I don't really want to talk about the Old One here any more. All it does is get me worked up, and she's honestly not worth thinking about outside of work. Even at work I have better things to do. Namely, decide where to keep our three boxes of staples that *isn't* right under the front desk.

Now to endings in a different world . . .

* * *

Ava disappeared over the edge, and to Richard the world

went entirely silent. He couldn't move. He couldn't see. He couldn't make any decisions, hear anything . . .

In which case, why did it feel like he could hear barking?

For Ava the situation moved much more quickly, and with far less confusion. One moment she was falling. The next moment she wasn't. Instead, she found herself riding a shape that coalesced as they moved, up and onto the path once more.

There was an instant in which no one said anything–in which it became clear that rather than losing one member, they had gained one. Or more accurately–as the barking increased–two.

"Canis!" cried Orion, turning not to the large, rangy dog which had rescued Ava, but to a smaller ball of fluff and feet that leapt around his ankles.

"Well that was . . ." Richard surveyed Perseus, Andromeda, and Ava–and the newest members of the party. "Easy. Ava, are you okay?"

"I'm fine," Ava said, concealing the fact that she'd only just recovered her breath. She gave the large dog now sitting beside her a friendly pat.

Andromeda, collecting herself as well, beamed. "Wonderful. How frightening that was! What excellent timing!" She went over to pet the dog too.

"Meet Canis," Perseus grinned to Richard. "Major, and Minor" – still occupied with Orion, who was cooing at it like a mother hen– "both hunting dogs."

"With excellent senses of timing," Richard noticed.

"So we have the dog, it looks like," Ava grinned as Canis Major woofed. "So what about the crown? Where was it, anyway?"

"Uh—" Richard looked back, but in the confusion he had completely lost track of anything resembling a crown.

48

Epanorthosis

n: the quick replacement of one word with another, usually more emphatic or correct;
a rethinking of one's word choice midway through a sentence

January 16, 2019

The most common example of this on the internet is *thousands, no, millions!* Which I feel like sums up the early perception of the internet pretty well.

So many of our really fun words relate back to words and word use. Onomatopoeia, for example. Palindrome. Alliteration. And on and on . . .

But I didn't throw this word up here just to get lost thinking about writing. No! In fact, it is relevant to the story today . . . see if you can catch it!

Also, can you catch what exactly the thing in question was?

* * *

"Don't say you've lost it!" Now sitting on the ground with the smaller hunting dog in his lap, Orion piped up. "We had a plan. To send the dogs after it!"

"Well, *dog*," muttered Perseus, looking askance at the fuzzy barking teddy bear.

"I'm aware of what the plan was," Richard snapped. "Just give me a moment. It was right . . . right . . . "

He flailed helplessly, his hands seeking to gesture to something he couldn't find.

"Maybe it isn't there any more," Andromeda said. She meant it to be placating, comforting even, and shrank back when everyone else looked at her in surprise.

Ava was the first to catch on, taking up her friend's side. "Oh, of course! Like the way an intrusion comes and goes."

Canis woofed.

"I don't know of any *crown* intrusions—at least, I don't think so," Perseus said slowly. "What did it look like, Richard?"

Ava rolled her eyes at Andromeda, saying light-heartedly, "We should have established that *before* we all tried to look."

Richard ignored them, focusing. "It had a bright center, and two sides that curved out. The light of them seemed to have colors. They—no, it—"

"How many stars was it?" Orion interrupted.

"They blended together," Richard replied defensively. "In fact I . . . I think it was just one." When he turned and saw Andromeda and Perseus just as hesitant as Orion to believe him, he sighed. "That's not it, is it?"

"The crown has six," Orion said confidently.

Under her breath, Andromeda murmured, "I thought it was

five?"

"Star count is important around here," Perseus explained to Ava and Richard with a shrug. "It couldn't be just one."

"So it must have been a mis— an intrusion," Ava concluded, looking at Richard.

"But of what?" Andromeda wondered.

Perseus shrugged again, scratching his head. "We probably won't ever know, at this rate."

"Good riddance!" said Orion, still scratching Canis Minor's ears.

Richard didn't look at anyone–not immediately. Here was everything, perfectly laid out: the hunting dogs, all the party members, an easy solution. But once again he had overlooked something.

"Well," he said with an effort. He didn't want his new friends to see him even *more* disheartened, even though he was starting to wonder if he'd *ever* get home. "Now what?"

49

Gifts We Really Need

January 23, 2019

Forget the electric toothbrush that tells you when to switch sides, or the socks that cradle your feet. Here is a running list, too late for Christmas but now you know for next year!, of magical items we need to have in the real world:

—any sort of container that magically refills itself. With anything.

—a car spatula: it extends out the front of your vehicle to remove any problems in your way

—a ring of bird talking: not for talking to birds, but making you sound like a bird to everyone else every time you open your mouth

—a handmill that constantly grinds salt (so people will stop feeling they have to perform the job)

—a 'find your dreams' potion that literally takes you to the dream world

Oh also, yes, I was trying to be coy and ask y'all to identify the intrusion. It was an intrusion of science—an actual galaxy! Isn't that cute? Look at high school me making commentary on modern society (whether I meant to or no, I don't remember now).

* * *

"What we need is some sort of crown detection device," Andromeda joked. At her side, Canis Major was tall enough that she patted the dog's head as they slowly walked back the way they'd come.

"What we need is a better description of what it looked like," Perseus added with a sympathetic glance at Richard.

"It can not have gone far," Orion said. Now carrying Canis Minor, he lagged at the back of the group. Ava couldn't help but chuckle to herself.

"Hopefully we'll see it on the way back," she said. "Or closer to that area."

It was redundant—they'd already made the decision and begun walking back, dogs happily along for the ride—but no one could seem to stop making such comments, often with careful glances at the unusually quiet Richard.

"It's fine," said he, completely aware of what they were doing but not entirely sure how to tell them to stop. *It's not the first time I've made a costly mistake. At least this was only* almost *costly.* "I'm sure we'll find it."

"It could even be that shine up ahead," Andromeda remarked encouragingly.

Canis Major barked.

Ava hesitated. She *did* see the glow, up and to the left, but . . . "I thought you all weren't supposed to be able to see it?"

"Maybe sometimes we can," said Perseus.

Ava looked back to exchange a look with Richard, but he was distracted—his face not exasperated or amused, but scared.

A *boom* reached their ears and Perseus stopped. "I think we need a plan."

"Another one?" Ava looked ahead once more, and found she agreed with him. Whatever it was, it was coming closer.

Behind them Orion dropped Canis Minor. "Beware!"

50

Gifts We Really Love

January 30, 2019

I started thinking about this because we got into a discussion during TEA about fanfic. The common, easy opinion is to look down on it. And sure, some of it is crap, especially since we have the internet now and we get exposed to every Jack or Jill's Great Romantic Novel. But aside from author skill, where do you really draw the line? If *fanfic* is any text that deals with ideas someone else created, then honestly, even the snobbiest of us are reading it and watching it all the time. My own story is a fanfic of the night sky.

I guess my bottom line is not where the ideas came from but the author's skill in developing them and conveying them. Not to say I have any of that. But I sure do love it when someone else can put a new twist on something I already like.

And don't we all? Don't we all enjoy the reboots and the retellings and the steamy (though unlikely) love scenes?

. . . Those of us who don't feel an innate, born-ofinadequacy desire to rip everything apart, that is.

But this is the season of love and I'm not supposed to diss people; I'm supposed to be spreading affirmation and enjoyment.

And speaking of fan fic and things I love:

* * *

The bright blaze descended upon the path, making twice the amount of noise Richard had expected. Granted, his senses were still a bit wobbly after Ava's fall and the appearance of the two dogs—but even so, he thought—

Yes. As it had been with Canis, so it was with this new intrusion. There were *two* of them.

"What is it?" Ava was calling back from the front, standing on guard in front of Andromeda.

"They," corrected Perseus, joining her.

Canis Major barked. Canis Minor cowered behind Orion.

"Curse those good-for-nothing twins!" Orion said meanwhile, pushing past Richard. "They *always* let them through."

"Now is hardly the time—" but Andromeda didn't get to finish her lesson on etiquette. She reached Richard and managed to shield him just before the two huge figures crashed down, stardust and sparkles scattering like ash and debris.

In the wake of an explosion of dark, purplish color, battle began. The newcomers loomed, larger than Orion, fighting with axes which those lifted high over bearded heads. Unwilling—or possibly unable, Ava couldn't tell—to leave each others' sides, they were instantly surrounded by Ava, Perseus, a snarling Canis, and Orion. Andromeda and Richard stayed back, doing their best to yell helpful hints.

"Watch out for his arm! No—the other one!"

"Get him in the shin!"

"I think they're armored!"

"Hey—ow!"

"What are they, lumberjacks?"

"We—are—the Great Twins!" roared one of the apparitions, nearly missing Ava's head with his ax blade.

"We—guard—the Passage!" cried the other, landing a blow on Orion.

"Try to separate them!" Ava yelled, darting behind one towering warrior's back. Orion was too busy nursing his thigh; Perseus and Canis leapt in.

Forced to take a staggering step back, the first twin roared and swung wildly. The second kicked at Canis, trying a little harder not to hit his brother.

"It's working," Richard called, catching on to the plan immediately. The stranger's movements seemed obviously weaker to him. "Press them back!"

As one Perseus and Ava turned on the tottering giant, Perseus's sword flashing and beaming. Though it could not reach skin through the elaborate armor, it did make the large man retreat.

"Lugalirra!" he cried out.

"Come on," Richard urged Andromeda. "Let's pull him."

"Pull him?" Andromeda hesitated. But Richard had already run up, his hands seeking any purchase on the second giant. For an instant he was alone, vulnerable, and then all at once a form came to his side and muscled arms yanked the twin back.

"Need help?" Orion grinned triumphantly at Richard as the

giant crashed to one side. Both twins hit the path at the same time and seemed to fall straight through it, disappearing in a swirl of dark light.

But just before they did so, the heavy boot of one caught Perseus hard on the chest, and he vanished too.

51

Bot Love

February 6, 2019

Historically, this is the season to talk about people we love. Or to think about them, send them cards, buy them gifts, take them out, take them home, and so on. But now, we can: take online quizzes to end our wondering if they're suitable, and track their online activity to know exactly who they're thinking of; send them ecards; pick something off their amazon list and direct it to their door without ever leaving home; and, I just heard, we can even hire a service which will take them out on that first date *for* us.

Now you know me. I'm not one to hate on modernity. In fact I'm all for it. Let me order groceries, catch up on the necessary home gossip, be entertained, pay bills, secure my house, and pick a mate all without leaving my bed! I'm all for it. Sometimes the real world sucks.

No, what interests me is that *more* people than just me (and all y'all already hooked in to the internet) feel that way. The fact that there is a viable market for these things just goes to show you that the more people there are on the planet, the more we find that we really don't like anyone at all. We might love the idea of people–sometimes–but we love being alone and pulling strings from behind a screen much better.

And again this sounds like the common old people refrain, but I don't think it's all bad. "blah blah blah social skills," but honestly, you can learn so much more about a person through typing with them. Because they feel safer. Safer! Everyone is terrifying, that's my Valentines Season lesson for you.

* * *

"Perseus!" Andromeda shot herself into the middle of the swirling lights and mayhem.

"Andromeda!" Ava leapt to hold her out of harm's way.

"Ava!" Richard and Orion collided as they ran forward, their feet slipping through the shadows where they twins' feet used to be.

Andromeda stood upright while everyone else, in various states of falling down, seethed around her. "There's nothing!"

"Of course not!" said Orion helpfully.

"It'll be fine," said Ava, a little desperately.

"Nothing? Are you sure?" Richard asked. "What usually happens when one of you–erm–"

"Nothing happens!" Orion insisted, disentangling his legs from Richard's.

"What do you *mean* nothing—"

"Hey guys!" Perseus materialized just behind them. "I'm back."

52

Love Cubed

February 13, 2019

Wahoo! Pop the champagne and chocolate truffles! Break out the party music! Put on your best dress!

And NO, this is not for Valentine's Day. Don't even ask me about that red-headed devil I met at that stupid fair, or the anniversary of the Break Up, or anything else guy related.

Unless it has to do with Richard, Orion, or Perseus because can you believe it folks? It's been a whole year!! We've made it roughly halfway through the story and y'all have stayed here and I haven't given up, which was pretty likely at the outset, let me tell you. I'm really more shocked than anything else. This is crazy!

Here's to another year. I told myself I wouldn't do yet a *third* blog about love in a row but it's gotta be said, I love this project. It has been with me through some hard times and–sniffle–you all have been so encouraging. Even when you don't mean to be.

So thanks again, and love to all!

* * *

"You're back!" Andromeda announced needlessly to Perseus, probably stepping on Ava as she went to fling her arms around him. "I was worried!" she continued—also needlessly.

"Yeah, I ended up back up there," Perseus shrugged, blushing at the attention. "But then I thought you guys were probably still down here so I came back."

"You remembered us?"

Ava elbowed Richard as she finally managed to stand up. "You sound surprised," she hissed at him.

"Well she didn't seem to remember that he could just come back, did she?" he whispered back.

"Maybe she hadn't seen it happen—"

Their argument was drowned out by the sound of Orion's laughter as he, too, rose, and strode forward to take control of the scattered group. "We're together again! And we routed that infernal intrusion!"

"Yes, well done." Andromeda turned to smile at Ava. When Perseus agreed, Ava blushed.

"I mean, we all fought. Or gave directions," she said, looking at Richard.

"But it was your idea that weakened them! You carried the day!" Orion said, clapping one large hand on her shoulder.

"In a manner of speaking," Richard attempted to joke. No one noticed too much, but Canis Major did come over and lick him. Canis Minor, too, emerged from wherever it had been hiding.

"Still it wasn't just me," Ava was saying. "It was all of us.

That was really . . . I mean, we work together really well, I think."

Richard smiled at the surprise in her voice, and realized that he was a bit surprised himself. "We're lucky you're here," he told the group at large—even Orion, who still stood very close to Ava.

"*We* are lucky you came," Andromeda beamed back.

"Definitely," agreed Perseus. "Right, then. I guess we keep going?"

53

Epeolatry

n: the worship of words

February 20, 2019

You folks aren't surprised to see this here, are you? I didn't think so. Words are the best. They're like the ultimate listeners—they help you express yourself.

I don't get to use all of the words I would like to in a day-to-day context. Most guys when you meet them are not impressed if you trot out "indignant" or "heuristic". You would think that at work I use more words, but the truth is most of the time at work I'm talking to children (or their haggard parents). That's fun in its own way because I get to explain the words.

Kids are excellent language learners. Everyone knows that by now, what with the Rosetta Stone "learn like a native child" and "I'm too old to learn a language" thoughts out there. But kids are fun because they have no shame. If they don't know a word they'll just throw together some other words and see if it sticks. Examples:

(speaking of me): "let's go see the paint queen!"

(of the water fountain): "I need to go to the inside waterfall."

(of snacks, to another child): "You can't have that thing that makes crumbs in here!"

I guess when I first wrote this story I never thought of *why* Ava and Richard could talk to all the constellations. We'll just have to go with Magic, I suppose.

Word Magic.

* * *

With the ease of routine they fell into place and resumed walking. Canis Minor, apparently elated with their survival, frisked up and down the rows as Ava turned to Orion, smiling.

"I take it you knew the dogs before?"

"Yes," said Orion. "They're good dogs."

"I don't suppose you know the stories behind them?"

Orion hesitated. "Canis Major is fast. Very fast! He's won countless races. Canis Minor is . . . cute."

Ava burst out laughing. "Well, that is certainly true!"

"You think our people had strange reasons. For believing in myths?"

"Not any more than anyone else," Ava said, laying her hand on his arm to console what was a suspicious look on his part. "And I think it's okay, too, if you don't remember the exact reasons why. It's clear you appreciate the dogs for who they are."

Orion turned to watch Canis Minor again, brooding. "I

didn't think of it until you came," he said finally.

"I hope our being here hasn't made things any worse for you," Ava realized with sudden guilt and sincerity.

"No. You couldn't make anything worse." Orion looked at her again, carefully. "It is good to have someone to talk to. Someone who does not judge."

"Any time," Ava smiled, blushing, ignoring the voice in her head that reminded her that sometimes she could be *very* judgy. But not, she decided, when it came to her friends. And that made it okay, right?

54

Circles

February 27, 2019

I doubt many of you are Pogo readers, so you may never have come across the little poem that's been on my mind lately. It goes like this:

He drew a circle to shut me out,
Heretic, rebel, a thing to flout.
But Love and I had the wit to win,
And drew a circle to take him in.

Museums are a great example of this, I think. And sure, of course I would say that, because I'm working at one. But really, think about it—we provide so many services to people from all levels of society and we run programs to encourage them even more. All while naysayers are at the back talking about how museums are doomed and we have to stay Within Budget and on, and on, and on.

What really got me thinking about this is my own gallery's preparations for Maker Day. In the kids' section I'm running a number of tinkering activities, and the adult sections are on board too. It's going to be a veritable maker fair and I know what you're thinking—what's a hall of art doing participating in an event that has to do with STEM? (That's Science, Tech, Engineering, and Math for those of you who are uninitiated. Basically all the things the collective We has decided kids need to learn more of.) The answer is everything, muahaha! The college recruiters and robot makers and k'nex marketers may have forgotten us, but we put this event together on our own, for everyone.

But will people know that, or remember that when it comes time to vote about things museum-related? No. And on one level it's cool. At least I got the chance to inspire the kids. But on the other hand, people kind of suck.

* * *

"Come on, keep up!" Perseus called back to Ava and Orion, seeing how Richard's gaze drifted.

"Are you keeping your eye out for the crown?" Andromeda called too, more lightly.

Ava's blush said enough.

"It's all right," said Richard, turning his eyes forward again. "I'm keeping watch. Isn't that right, Canis?"

Canis Major, who had apparently taken to him, woofed and continued trotting at his side.

"Though I still don't know what I'm looking for," Richard confided to Perseus, and to Andromeda on his other side. One could not really say anything to one without saying it to the other.

"At least you are looking," Andromeda said.

Perseus nodded. "And even if we haven't seen what we are looking for yet, we've seen lots of other good things."

"A journey blind is no journey at all!" Andromeda added.

"Hum." Richard considered the quote—for it sounded very much like some old wisdom, though he had never heard it. "I guess you're righ—oh look, it's the goat fellow."

"Auriga," Perseus said, looking ahead on the path. "Oh, and he's got Ophiuchus with him!"

The trio plus dog ran up to the two figures, silhouetted in the darkness. As they came closer Richard could hear the familiar bleating of goats.

"Auriga!" Richard hailed the man, grinning. "Good to see you again!"

"And you." Auriga turned to Richard, his eyes stony in the starlight. "And who have you got with you?"

55

Murder Most Deserved

March 6, 2019

Consider this a Part Two to "Gifts We Really Love" last month. Because I have no run out of things to say about fanfic just yet.

I'm coming at it from the other side this week, though. Not "fanfic, oh how unoriginal," but "originality, oh how unattainable." As someone who works with art day in and day out, originality is just about dead, folks. And that isn't a bad thing.

Look, I know every budding author wants to write the *New* novel, and every nascent artist wants to create *The* picture, and every start up business owner or inventor wants to solve *Basic* problems. But honestly, people have been around for millennia now. Do you really think your idea has never been thought before? And even if it hasn't, can you really say it wasn't based off anything else? Let me answer that for you: you can't. Because you live in a society and your society has a culture and you live and breathe *within* that culture—even if, according to Them, you are actually an Outsider.

It bugs me when people can't recognize this. Not only when it's young artists or authors being down on themselves, but also when it's audiences being uncritical. To this day I can't stand the *Eragon* series, because it reminded me too much of Lord of the Rings, and no one else seemed to see that. Likewise, all YA dystopia fic leaves me cold. You're never going to do it better than George Orwell, and I wish we could take a moment to appreciate that before buying more anti-corrupt-government-warrior merchandise.

But that's my inner elitist showing, isn't it? The truth is I don't begrudge people liking those books. At least kids are reading, and quite honestly who cares about "originality" when the important thing, the warnings and lessons of those stories, is being passed on to a new generation. That is hands down the most important part. Also giving kids heroes and getting them attached to characters outside their narrow worlds.

I sound like an old bitty now though, so I better stop. Moral of post, don't be afraid to create. Or to ask, or to wonder.

* * *

Eventually Perseus managed to explain the situation—again—to Auriga and his silent, snake-carrying friend. He failed to get them a ride on Auriga's chariot, again. But, Ava thought as she eyed Ophiuchus, that probably was for the best. There seemed to be a lot of skydwellers with strange animal companions in the neighborhood, and she wasn't sure how many more it'd be safe to meet.

They resumed walking and the sky around them settled once more, as though nothing had happened. Richard decided it was high time Andromeda and Perseus got some quality time alone, and slipped back to walk beside Ava.

"You don't need to belabor it," Ava told him. "I noticed, okay?"

"Noticed what?"

"The memory thing."

"Oh." Richard glanced around, relieved to see Orion busy talking to Canis Minor again. "I wasn't going to belabor it, exactly. I was just thinking, maybe it has to do with when they go back to their positions—"

"—but it didn't when Perseus went back," Ava pointed out, entirely unconcerned that they might be overheard. "He remembered us *while* he was there, if we can believe what he said."

"And why shouldn't we?" Richard paused, letting go of his indignation.

In the pause, Ava tipped her head, musing. "I wonder what it's like when they go 'back.' They say they can see things below. Maybe it's like your moon prison?"

"I hope not." Richard shuddered.

"But they don't even notice the time passing. Would it really be . . ."

"We're not going to find out," Richard said with unnecessary force. "My *point* was, with all the inconstancy and the intrusions and the fighting, how can we be sure Orion's idea will get us home? We're basically going to be an intrusion in our own sky. What if they forget everything as soon as they intrude and—"

"Do you always worry this much?" Ava interrupted. A part

of her buried deep in her chest was too afraid to admit she worried about things like this too.

"Ava these are real questions! Aren't you *thinking* about this?"

"Of course I am," she snapped back. Richard realized too late he had implied she wasn't inclined to think at all. "But I had forgotten how *unsettled* you people of Runn get about change."

Just because we don't worship a sky that is always changing doesn't mean we can't adapt, Richard might have said in reply. But at that very moment, Canis Major let out a bark of triumph, and darted off into the distance.

56

Destination Inspiration

March 13, 2019

Some of you made fun of me for being a hypocrite—in the best way possible, I suppose, although I'm not sure being a hypocrite is ever good. I really do appreciate having conversations about the story though. You folks are the best.

It's true—I don't know of any other stories where the Milky Way is a path in the sky and you meet constellations. But even so, this story can't be entirely "original," because I used plenty of other myths when I wrote it—and now in revising it, I'm using plenty more. Sometimes it feels more like an anthology than anything else!

And before you ask again, the answer is no. I really have no idea where I got this idea from. I can say that it snowballed from a small spark and became more and more complex as time goes on—but you could say the same for just about any idea, I think.

Remember those old party places you could go to, Destination Imagination? I was in to that as a kid. Even did the improv competitions and everything. The whole premise is they give you the stuff and you come up with great ideas from it. But inspiration doesn't always work that way. You could have the coolest building blocks ever and create nothing better than a dilapidated outhouse. Conversely, you could have nothing but scrap wood and old sponges and you could make something amazing.

It's one of the truly intangible things about being alive.

And speaking of intangible . . .

* * *

"Has he got it?"

"Did he find it?"

"Is it out there?"

The group clustered around the edge Canis Major had so recently vacated—everyone careful to stay a step or two back from the edge. Finally Ava asked the question that cut through the babble:

"But would Canis know the crown if he saw it?"

"Of course!" Orion watched the starry streak in the sky with confidence.

"Erm . . ." said Andromeda.

"Did we describe it to him?" Perseus wondered reasonably.

Ava grimaced. "You didn't even describe it to *us!*"

". . . Would he have understood us describing it? I mean, do they really understand human speech?" Richard looked up at Orion curiously. The hunter scoffed and seemed to redden slightly as he looked down at Canis Minor, who was happily doing nothing more helpful than being underfoot.

"The animals up here *are* exceptional," Andromeda remarked with a diplomatic cough.

Ava remained unconvinced. Having lost sight of Canis Major's movements, she too eyed the group of mythical beings. "Are they really *that* exceptional though?"

"Well, of course it would vary," said Perseus, "depending on their myth, you know. Some of them aren't even animals—not really. They say that once upon a time Ursa—"

"Stories later," Orion decided. "Canis Major returns!"

And indeed, with gleeful yaps, Canis Minor confirmed the point. All a once the bundle of light Ava and Richard had strained to see was upon them and everyone went down in a warm, furry heap.

57

Food

March 20, 2019

We interrupt the regularly scheduled programming to bring you this important bulletin: living in a big city means access to excellent FOOD!

Of course living in a big city means a lot of other things too, like confusing streets and grumpy people and public transit that sounds like old mine carts being chased by dinosaurs. But all the different wonderful groups of people who live in cities bring all their wonderful foods with them and that variety makes it all worth it.

And no I don't mean variety like "italian meatball" vs "philly cheesesteak" hot pockets.

If you're wondering, this ode to food is because on of my friends—currently my best friend, as she can attest—brought fresh empanadas to D&D the other day and I STILL CAN'T GET OVER how delicious they were.

I guess I should go make dinner . . .

* * *

"Does he have it?" The question was once again on everyone's lips. Many hands reached out, searching, and finally someone pried the thing from Canis Major's jaws. The warm, fuzzy thing.

Richard, resident almost-crown spotter, was the first to catch on. "Oh."

"It's just Lepus," said Perseus. He held the creature, a large rabbit, in both hands as though it was stuffed with radioactive slime. Lepus contemplated him calmly.

"Lupus?" Ava, pinned under Andromeda's hip, struggled to right herself and make sense of what had happened.

"Oh, I'm very sorry," Andromeda moved.

"Not lupus. Lepus!" Orion emerged from the back of the group and held out his hands as though to give the frozen rabbit a hug. The dogs barked encouragingly, and Perseus handed it over. Richard watched in exasperation—what *was* this guy, an animal lover or a hunter? Couldn't he pick one role and be done?—which quickly turned to shock and horror as Orion grasped Lepus by the scruff and hurled it ears and all out into the void.

"No good to eat in this form," Orion explained succinctly to Ava.

"It's fine," she said weakly. "We're never hungry anyway."

"It's not *fine,* I mean where is the rabbit and where *was* the rabbit and doesn't being flung through space kind of—"

Richard gave up. No one was listening to him as they stood and brushed nonexistent star dust from themselves, fixing their clothes. Orion showered affection on a preening Canis Major. Perseus and Andromeda laughed.

Let's just add it to the list, shall we? Richard sighed. His father had always told him that list-keeping was his worst habit. And judging by her look as they set off yet again, Ava would have agreed.

58

The Ides of Love

March 27, 2019

I dunno, folks. I don't really like this time of year—when the calendar says it ought to be spring but it feels like winter still, and everything seems very far away: the holidays were over a long time ago, and summer's only barely on the horizon. It's supposed to be all colorful and grow-y but instead everything's grey and dripping with last week's dingy snow melt.

It probably doesn't help that I got a message from The Ex the other day. Several messages, actually. And it was super cool and he's off on a great spring adventure in an exotic place and yay for him and . . . if one were to summarize the conversation into meme form, it went like this:

Him: Here I am in Excellent Art Museum at Romantic Foreign Capital and this painting made me think of you!

Me (to self): You went to Romantic Foreign Capital?

Also Me: Okay, who's the broad who went with him?

Also Also Me: Do I keep talking and asking questions or do I stop? HELP

Also Also Also Me: . . . If we get back together does this mean we could go to Romantic Foreign Capital? *begins complex algebra computing chances he stills likes me based on time of message, length of message, word choice in message, painting choice, painting time period, museum location, color of socks, response time, phase of moon*

Me, sleep deprived the next day: *never responds to message*

Maybe if I paid more attention to social media, the trip (and subsequent museum visit and message) wouldn't have taken me by surprise. But also if I paid more attention to social media, I'd have been dying over that trip for the past few weeks, instead of just, you know, the rest of my life.

Oh, fine . . . It's not as bad as all that . . . but it's weird and the weather is weird and everything is weird and doesn't turn out the way you expect. Sometimes.

* * *

Without fully understanding how the journey had happened, Ava, Richard, and friends found themselves once more in front of Cassiopeia—and still empty-handed. Unless a small dog counted. Which apparently, according to this particular queen, it did not.

"You were tasked with finding—finding—"

"Your crown," suggested Cepheus from his customary position several steps behind Cassiopeia.

"I need no help! You were tasked with finding a *crown,* and you come back with these *animals?*"

There was a silence. Canis Major tilted his head to one side. "I think they're rather nice," Andromeda couldn't help but say, very quietly. "We could still look—"

"You! I need no input from *you*. Why, it was most likely *your*—"

"Actually, Andromeda's right," interrupted Ava. She stepped forward, pushing past a mute Orion and a stricken Perseus. She had had *enough* of inconstant royalty, and where Richard had managed to stymie her before, she was determined now to succeed. "They *are* lovely dogs, far better than whatever crown you lost—which, by the way, we never had any proof was yours. You never even told us what it was, so for all we know, Canis Minor here *could* be your crown. Although personally, I think Canis Minor deserves better. So if you really 'need no help', why don't you find the blasted crown on your own—try doing something yourself for a change!"

Here Ava paused. It became clear that her definition of success was different from everyone else's. Suddenly there seemed to be a strange amount of room on the path, as everyone shrank back.

Cassiopeia, her starry eyes narrowed into lasers and her long hair flowing back as though hoping to escape, walked very slowly toward Ava. "You *dare* to insinuate that MY CROWN is not my own?"

"I honestly don't think it's a very daring insinuation," Ava retorted. She crossed her arms and refused to move another inch. She knew from years of dealing with sisters that each step backward she took would only fuel Cassiopeia's fire. "I wouldn't call your behavior very royal, would you?"

Seems to me it's very *royal,* Richard thought, sighing to himself as the mythological queen threw back her head and began what could only be some sort of terrible summons. *I don't see how we should have expected anything else.*

59

Sciamachy

n: a sham fight; conflict with an imaginary adversary; fighting a shadow

April 3, 2019

Oh, the layers upon layers of this word. Especially in this context.

I had originally planned it because of the upcoming fight. But as I was transcribing last week it occurred to me that it also, in a way, suits Ava's own fight. She gets into this argument with Cassiopeia each time they meet and it's

1. Not about Cassiopeia but instead about Ava's own shadows
2. At the same time not about Ava, but about the injustice done to Andromeda, which Ava feels more deeply than she wanted to

3. Essentially a 'tilt at windmills' (to borrow from another excellent word/definition)—that is to say, a sham or pointless endeavor—because Cassiopeia is an imaginary adversary who will never change, *and*
4. No one else is going to leap in and have that fight too. Except when a dragon gets involved.

So anyway, I nerded a little. Just a little. Onward!

* * *

It descended all at once, sending the dogs scurrying for cover. The sky became a whirl of sparkles as Cepheus stumbled back, Orion drew his club, Richard tried to shield his eyes while simultaneously see what was going on, and Andromeda and Perseus clung to each other. Everyone was yelling, but none of it made any sense to anyone else. Only Cassiopeia remained unmoved, watching Ava in hungry anticipation of the moment the dragon's jaws would close over her head.

And the dragon in question *did* have jaws large enough to do so. Its twisting body stretched and looped, as long as the path itself, with massive fins and spikes flailing in every which direction as the beast took first one swipe, then another at the offending party.

It doesn't know which of us to attack. Ava experienced this revelation as a blade of guilt running through her stomach. Crouched behind a coil of the dragon's tail, she watched her friends dodge and fall underneath its fangs. Orion struck the white-edged scales and hurtled backward when a leg knocked out both of his own.

"Run!" Ava yelled to her friends.

"Run!" they yelled back.

Cassiopeia's wild laughter made it hard to think. Ava dodged through the folds of the dragon's sinewy body, trying to get closer, to understand what they had meant.

"Get out of here!" she cried, catching a glimpse of Andromeda, who struck the creature's hide with an unfortunately less-than-lethal sandal.

"*You* get out of here!" Perseus replied, leaping to look at her over the dragon's spiked back.

"What—" Ava swallowed. If he was angry at her, well, he had every right to be.

Just then Richard appeared at her feet. He had dove under the beast's belly, only to be smashed to the ground as it writhed away from Canis Major's teeth. "Ergh," he said at first, unhelpfully. Ava's guilt grew. "He means get out of here," Richard continued as he stood shakily. "To both of us. They mean to draw it off."

"But they can't—"

"Look." Richard actually grabbed her shoulder and turned her round, so she could see where Canis Minor was yapping at the monster's head, leading it farther down the path.

"But we can't—"

"Listen." Richard shook her. "I know how you feel. But this isn't lethal to them. If they get hit they just go back. If we get hit we're *never* getting back. So run!"

Ava thought for just a moment longer. It made sense. And though she hated to turn away from her friends, the agony in Cassiopeia's voice as they got away, running past her and into the darkness, lightened her burden for just a moment.

60

Dress Rehearsal

April 10, 2019

Never experienced death very close before. Now distant book club member is gone—irrationally touched. In the saddest way, this is kind of like what fiction should do to us, good fiction. Everything else seems petty and there is only sympathy but it is also strange . . . the world is fragile in a way fictional worlds are not. You can always go there in your mind and it's the same . . . but in the real world there is a difference. It is always different now. And if you think about it, the world is doing this all the time. This is change. . . . it's hard to imagine losing your partner . . . not because it's tough to do, but because it hurts so much . . . a personal rehearsal of loss.

So I actually wasn't going to write about this. Not this week, given where we're at in the story. It seemed like too much. But then I didn't know what to write instead because I don't want to pretend to be happy or funny . . . I'm not sure it would work too well anyway. I'm a bit like Richard in that respect.

So I was just staring at this blank blog and to give myself a kick start I typed up my notes from earlier today. And I think I'm going to leave them. This is as au natural as it gets, folks. There you have it: my head. One of our more sporadic book club members passed away last night and I heard about it today through Rose—who is very good friends with his widow—and I went and sat down to have lunch and wrote that up there instead.

He was a very good guy, and so are a lot of people, in retrospect. Funny how something sad makes us think of happy things that are somewhere else—in the past, or the future.

I'm not sure what my thoughts on all this are, but I've found it moving.

* * *

Ava followed blindly, leaving Richard to make the decisions—but that was much easier than he might have anticipated. The darkness around them cleared as soon as they had run out of earshot of the fight. Whether this was because the dragon had given up, or because the sky was in some sympathy with their plight, he could not tell.

So much for their escape: but what came after was much, much harder than either would have guessed.

The group of five regrouped in the blue inkiness, Richard still panting, Orion still puffed up and proud. The dogs had run off, leading Draco on a merry chase. Finally, Richard and Ava were free to make progress, having bypassed the gatekeeping Queen Cassiopeia. But their feeling of triumph was marred when Andromeda admitted she could not travel any farther.

Ava tried asking her about it, tried figuring out *why*—"Is it *her?* Or is it something about the deal you made with Pegasus-whatsit?"

But it was no use. Andromeda only smiled sadly. "It is, Ava. That's all."

"I'll go back with her," Perseus said. Ava hardly paid attention, but Richard stepped up to shake hands—and was pulled into a hug. "I'll miss you," said the constellation.

"We both will miss you," said Andromeda, luminescent even as she grew fainter.

"Wait—but—we—" Ava stumbled forward and caught herself. "I—thank you."

"Yes, thank you both," Richard agreed, his hand on Ava's shoulder.

"We'll remember you," Ava promised, chagrined to find a tear in her eye. As the two forms continued to fade, she repeated, "We'll remember."

61

Gallery Hollaback

April 17, 2019

I thought we could all use some humor, so welcome to part two of the popular winter blog, funny things that people say and do in their local art museum:

holding a wax crayon "I think this marker is broken."

"You guys should provide a dating service based on the art people make!"
   Me: believe me honey, you don't want to know what people draw here.

Coworker: "If ONE MORE PERSON pays for admission in COINS then I SWEAR I'LL—"

Teenaged patron, to me: "I need help finding a painting."
   Me: "In the kids' section?"

Teenager: "It's for, a, uh, cousin. So, you here with your family?"

Me: "I work here. I did bring my boyfriend in today though!"

Teenager: ". . . bye!"

What patron says: "Oh look, legos! Just like we have at home!"

What patron means: "Excellent, now we can destroy these innocent toys with impunity because they can't make us clean up!"

Legos: *cower in fear*

Brent: *lurking behind the bookcase with a broom* "Oh they think I can't make them clean up?"

Patron 1: "Did you know the museum has a cat?"

Paron 2: "The museum does not have a cat."

Patron 1: "Are you sure? Because you are *puurrrr*fect!"

And speaking of strange animal sightings . . .

* * *

Richard walked on in a daze as Orion distracted Ava with talk. The sky around them was just as changeable and dark as before, and yet it seemed colder now, the silver sparkles more icy. Looking out from the path, he seemed to see specters moving in the shadows; echoes of the dragon's movement.

But I'm just being ridiculous, Richard reminded himself. *I shouldn't be down. If Ben were here, would he be down? Of course not. This is what we planned from the start. It's working.*

For once, the fact that a plan of his was *working* was only a slight consolation to Richard.

He continued looking up, as though the physical act would lift his thoughts. He realized that in the stars above them, he could trace a sinuous line—more than likely, he thought, the dragon's constellation. The sight was too distant to make him shudder, but it did fill him with that familiar, nervous calculation. It wouldn't come down again, he assured himself; the right variables weren't present. It hadn't been called; they had nothing of interest for it; they were a smaller group;

But there.

Something *did* move.

Richard tried to watch it carefully but the shadow was *huge* and just in eyeing the edges of it his lungs expanded and he couldn't help but leap forward and— "Ava!"

She turned with a slight smile, making room for him. "It's fine, Richard. Weren't you listening?"

"Uh." With a sideways glance at Orion, Richard admitted what his father had warned him never to do. "No, I wasn't, sorry."

This time, though, she laughed. "It's all right. It's not coming down. It's a large bear, can you tell? It's Ursa Major."

"Oh." As Ava watched to see why he sounded sadder than ever, Richard explained, "Perseus mentioned it."

62

Zemblanity

n: an unpleasant discovery or surprise; the opposite of serendipity

April 24, 2019

Kind of like that teenager's failed attempt to pick me up, chronicled in the post last week! Really, I didn't mean to talk about that, but then Facebook got Great Aunt Shirley all in a tizzy. So let me clarify before moving on: NO, I do not have a boyfriend. Why would I hide anything from you? Clearly I lied to the poor kid. It was a test, and a pretty effective one too.

What I *actually* had in mind for this word was . . . well, not as lighthearted. First of all, though, this word has a neat story. A guy created it to be the opposite of serendipity—because every word needs a pair, right?

Call me Curator Ross.

Seriously, though. I'm not the type to go around drawing

yin-yangs on everything, but I like zemblanity and serendip-ity. I guess it's not so much because of any sense of balance as it is because I saw this word on my feed and thought, "finally! A way to express it!". There's always two ways to see something, you know? Two, at least. Which you choose is up to you: language is just here to give you the option.

* * *

"Look." Ava stopped and turned to Richard. "I know you're going to miss him. But we have to keep going and paying attention."

"I *was* paying attention," Richard protested.

Ava cast a glance at Orion, who was doing his best to fade away. "Really? Then how come you didn't hear Orion explain about the bear?"

"Well what did you expect me to do?" Richard was suddenly very tired of hearing about Orion. Or hearing Orion at all. Or the way his conversations with Ava always seemed to become fights. "Just keep walking along like nothing happened, like you? And *eavesdropping* at the same time?"

"It isn't eavesdropping, you're part of this group too!" Ava reminded him, her voice growing hot. "But if you think we're too *insensitive* for you and you'd rather not be here, then—"

"Then what? You'll just leave me here, right? Because leaving people is so easy for you!"

Richard turned away, half unaware of what he'd said. But to Ava, it was a gut-plummeting discovery. Her face shifted from open-mouthed anger to frozen calm.

"It looks to me like you're the one who left first," she said. "And that's fine. That's exactly what I expected you to do all along."

Richard heard but didn't compute, and did not turn around. He stepped away again, trying to clear his head, hide the tears. And as he did so, Ava turned and followed Orion out of sight.

63

May Day

May 1, 2019

Happy May Day, everyone! Just when you think nature has nothing to do with humans any more, and we've conquered all semblance of seasonal observances—what with our air conditioning, indoor heating, greenhouse plants, winter vacations, and international trade—not to mention that indoors, sedentary lifestyle oldtimers love to talk about—then along comes May Day and . . .

And, to be honest, most folks have no idea why we celebrate it or even how to, aside from the fact that it may or may not involve a pole. (The number of children who spoke about "poles" to me today was frankly embarrassing. I could never work at a fire station.)

For those who would like to know, though, I put together a collection of art pieces on the topic earlier. The art was for the kids' gallery and therefore mostly just more poles and flowers, to be honest—but in the process I did some googling!

If you take the more traditional view, May Day is indeed a celebration of the beginning of summer, with roots back in Roman times (because everything in the West has roots in Roman, or even better Grecian, times). Then the Catholics came along and wanted to pretend it had nothing to do with nature or naturalistic deities, so they associated it with the Virgin Mary and went right on partying.

Now during the 1800s, May 1st was designated International Workers Day by a bunch of Socialists and Communists. That's right folks, despite the fervor of current politics, we've lived with socialists and communists in our midst for more than a century now! All flippancy aside, it was a meaningful gesture connected with the Haymarket Affair, which you should look up.

All this to give you some perspective and to remind you that, terrible as the Bloodhound Gang is, they were right: humans are only mammals.

And speaking of anthropomorphic animals . . .

* * *

"You were completely right."

"I don't want to talk about it."

"Of course. But I got the same sense of him. Always hanging back—"

"Did you not hear me?"

"I did! I'm just saying. You can never trust a coward."

"Oh for skies' sake. Just be quiet for once, would you, Orion?"

Feeling teary and not unlike a coward herself, Ava didn't look at Orion after snapping at him. She kept her chin stubbornly pointed forward.

I shouldn't have pushed him. He clearly feels for the skydwellers as if they were human. And if I'm honest, I do too! Why else would we be following them and helping them? He was being reasonable. He's always reasonable. The reasonable thing is to keep going . . .

Any moment now Richard would catch up with them and be just as annoying as always, she knew. It wasn't like he could get *lost*. And she *knew* she had been right about everything; Orion didn't have to tell her about that. But even if she *was* right, she hadn't meant to—

"Hello?"

"I said be quiet and let me think!"

"But Blessed," Orion protested, sulkily, "that wasn't me."

"What?" Ava whipped around, only to see no one behind them. Just a vast, drifting shimmer of shadows.

"Hello?"

Ava turned around once more and found all at once there was a large bird in front of her—a large bird that had *not* been there a moment ago.

"Who are you?" Orion asked.

"Do you not know?" Ava hissed at Orion before she considered the creature. A human-sized, hovering swan, it was gorgeous—all star creatures were naturally beautiful, of course (if you liked bright, effervescent, sparkly things)—but this had a special grace.

"My name is Leda," the swan said in a musical voice.

"Nice to meet you," Ava said, because even if it wasn't, she needed someone new to talk to. "My name's Ava."

The swan's wingtips brushed over Ava's extended hands as it responded to her greeting. It shimmered—a ripple of light—then tilted its beaked head to look into her face.

"Hello, Ava," said the swan in a very different, in fact far more *masculine,* voice. "I'm Cygnus."

64

X-Ray Vision

May 8, 2019

No, this post isn't going to be about comic book characters—because I STILL HAVE NOT RECOVERED OKAY—but instead about super powers. Because obviously those are very different things!

I feel like X-Ray vision is one of those super powers that gets less and less love as time goes on. Like people used to think it was novel and neat but now people would rather have the power of flight or chance or invisibility or pretty much anything else. And on one hand I get it. I'd rather manipulate probability than look at everybody's organs, or worse, their underclothing.

But on the other hand, I think X-ray vision on people's *minds* would be interesting. Not to see their thoughts (because mind reading is scary, and not for invasion of privacy reasons, but because people are weird) but to see their intentions. Kind of like reading auras. Like they'd show up with a big "pants on fire" emoji if they were lying, or you could see a line connecting them to who they really love. That's one of those things I've always liked picturing.

Anyway. That's my random muse for the week. Enjoy!

* * *

"You're—what?" Ava faltered, but the swan seemed to smile at her.

"You're from the world below, aren't you. Do you know a friend of mine—"

"It's always this way," Orion whispered helpfully to Ava. More loudly he said, "No, Cygnus. The world is wide."

"But my name is—"

"We know you," Orion interrupted, not without kindness. "But we have to go. Ava is in a hurry."

As if with a choreographed movement, the swan swiveled its gaze back to Ava's. "Then you should leave. Do not let me stop you."

"Wait," Ava said, shelving her questions, "if you see someone else come this way, tell him we were here, won't you?"

"Gladly," said the swan. "I'll tell him which way you go."

"Which way we—" Ava peered around the swan's curled wings to see that the path did, indeed, sift itself into two branches. A moment of panic struck—what if they took the wrong path by mistake?—and passed.

"That's great." Orion reached back and took Ava's hand, leading her toward the left fork. "Look after yourself, Cygnus."

At something—perhaps the friendliness of the tone—the swan shimmered again. "I will!"

"What?" She was just past the swan when Ava realized its voice had changed again. *I wasn't* making that up. Coming to a stop, she tugged on Orion's hand. "What's going on? Why are we in a hurry?" Her voice became more demanding as she realized that the world behind her was growing darker, the spark floating past her eyes more colorful. They changed her vision—for an instant it was as though she could see *through* the world; as though she was apart from it, and everything was revealed, in lines of red and gold and purple and—

"Orion?" This time Ava yanked hard on his hand. He shifted immediately back into place, resuming the shape she knew.

"Crane," he said, looking behind her.

"*What?*"

Ava was by this point so frustrated that when she turned to see an entirely new bird standing behind her, her first impulse was to strike it at once. The only thing that stopped her was that same strange trick of vision, that made the crane look both see-through and technicolor. Afraid of touching it, Ava stumbled back. Orion stepped up beside her, his club in hand.

"But it hasn't done anything," Ava heard herself say.

"It's an intrusion," Orion muttered.

"Is *that* why everything here has been strange?"

"Strange?" Orion cast her an impatient glance. "Do not worry, Blessed. Just run. I will catch up."

"No," Ava said, because she was tired and Orion was starting to look concerningly colorful again. She grabbed his elbow and tugged, hard. "We're both getting out of here. *Now.*"

65

Lalochezia

n: the use of foul language to relieve emotional stress or pain

May 15, 2019

Neat that there's a word for that, am I right?

I work in a place that's a) public, b) kid-friendly, and c) full of little old ladies so of course we try our best not to *actually* swear. But I wonder if all those stand-ins give the same relief. In my year+ at the museum (but of course I'm still "the new girl," not that I wanted to talk about HER), I have heard:

Cheese-and-rice, cheese-and-crackers, gosh, darn, shoot, dangit, goodness, goodness gracious, blast, ba—-asketball, jiminy, cricket, jiminy cricket, criiiikey, ffffffun!, oo, aff, aaack, and my personal favorite, aieeeee!

But when we're not open and therefore not obliged to sound like Johnny Quest villains, you best believe all the *actual* swear words come out. I've learned a few of those, too, in my time here. Probably even more than the fake swear words. But I'm not going to tell you, because we only discuss good things here.

Ha. Ha. That or I am lazy . . .

* * *

When Richard came to the fork in the path, it was empty.

Granted, he wasn't looking around too hard—he had settled into a resentful comfortableness with being alone. Ava thought he was going to wander off, did she? Well, in retrospect, it probably wasn't good that he had been walking away at that moment. But she *was* very insensitive, and should have noticed he wasn't abandoning anyone on purpose. He *never* left men in the field. Unlike, of course, Ava, who with every moment of absence was just cementing his point.

Richard's comfort, cold as it was, vanished the moment he realized there was a stranger standing beside him, also looking into the void between the two paths.

"Hello," the giant swan said.

"Wow," said Richard. "You can talk?"

"And you can reason!" The swan responded, its wings stretching as though in an avian clap.

Richard laughed despite himself. "I'm sorry, that was stupid. I'm just really distracted. My name's Richard, you probably noticed I'm not from here. Who are you?"

The swan, stately and unalarming, answered, "My name is Cygnus. You are from Below, correct?"

"Yes." Richard was interrupted before he could add any more—

"I was once, too, you know. I have a friend down there."

"You do?"

"He's gone now."

"Erm—yeah, I would imagine so. I mean—I'm really sorry to hear that," Richard said, and he meant it. The memory of watching his family from behind the moon's rays hit him with a force that shook his already fragile state of mind.

"It's okay. That's why I'm up here."

"Oh," said Richard, as though this made sense. The bird was starting to sound a bit like Orion to him, and he didn't want to feel any more sympathetic to it than he already did. "Since you've been here, have you noticed another person—two other people go by?"

The swan shimmered again, and cocked its head at him. "I did."

Richard paused: the swan's voice sounded different. "You aren't an intrusion, are you?"

"Me? Oh gods, no," said the swan, with a feminine giggle. "My name's Leda."

"But you just said—" the *first* version of the swan hadn't responded well to stupid questions, and Richard hesitated, thinking. "There's more than one myth with a swan in it, isn't there?"

"You know, I bet there is," the swan agreed pleasantly. "They're so pretty, don't you think?"

Richard bit his lip. "Sure. You said you saw someone go past, right? Do you remember which way they went?"

"Remember?" The swan swung its long neck back and forth, then looked back at him, eyes wide. "I think I do. I think it was right. That sounds right. Yes, I know I'm right. Isn't that funny?"

Richard laughed politely, and—not without some doubts

hidden in his chest—strode down the rightmost path.

239

66

SQUIRREL!

May 22, 2019

All y'all might not be nerds like me and follow writing prompt blogs online. Sometimes when I am bored they are good for an escape. One of my favorite ones is something along the lines of, 'write from the perspective of a first-person narrator who just showed up to a story in progress and has no clue what is going on.'

And guess what? I just did that in real life!

Well, it wasn't *me* exactly. (Although gotta say, moving and switching jobs *is* kinda like that.) The DM for my D&D group was out a week or two back and had his friend step in for him, but the notes he left were very vague apparently. Stuff like "xx's character appears to be a conspiracy theorist" and "not sure Squirrel realizes her owlbear can't talk."

Squirrel is, in case you were wondering, the nickname that my character has grown into. (And yes, she still rides an owlbear. See previous post for details.) As she's developed I have put all of her points and feats and so on into nature-y things rather than anything resembling intelligence or social skills, so she's ended up—hate to say it, but my friend pointed it out and it's true—a bit like the Old One in nature. Just an actually cute, actually well-meaning Old One and not a stupid-evil hobgoblin.

As a result all the guest DM's villains ended up being Squirrel's friends, all the real party members were exasperated by the owlbear's pontifications on life, and the beholder was taken care of in two rounds with a magic flask, a pretty flower, and a series of very good rolls.

Throwback to the lalochezia post—remember what that word means?—guess what that poor DM's new favorite fake curse word is . . .

It was a riot, but I really do feel sorry for him. Life is confusing enough already without D&D throwing you for a loop . . . and plus, he was pretty cute.

* * *

The farther he traveled, the less certain the world became. Richard found this was always the case; usually he was fortunate enough to have Benjamin—or, of late, Ava—around to counteract that by force of sheer confidence. But now that was no longer the case.

The trouble, he decided, wasn't that he was lost. There was only one way to go, and even if it was the wrong way after all, he still knew exactly where he was. One point in the sky was hardly any different than another, as far as he was concerned, and it was literally no sweat for him to move to another point if need be.

No; the trouble was that the more he thought, the more he had no idea what was going on. And it wasn't something he could blame on the amorphous darkness around him, either—although it did fill him with a homesickness which probably was not helping. This sort of uncertainty was familiar to Richard. It happened all the time at home: he'd argue with someone because he'd finally had enough and gone and snapped, only to then spend the next few days rethinking the argument from so many different angles that he ended up taking back all his words and accusing only himself.

It wasn't productive: he knew that. But it was the cost of having an analytical mind, and sometimes it seemed analysis was all he had to offer Runn—or anyone within it. Or without it.

Richard sighed and squinted at the points of light around him. It seemed like ages since he'd talked to any skydweller; of course at the time he most wanted to be distracted, they finally were not going to bother him.

If I'm going to be alone, he thought, *I should at least be able to figure things out.* But this loneliness was different, something he referred to now as 'moon loneliness' in his thoughts. It didn't matter that he had a secondary plan—to retrace his steps and find Perseus once more—in case the current one failed. It didn't matter that he could see where his conversation with Ava went wrong. *What good does it really do to have everything figured out if everyone is so far away?*

67

Beach Requiem

May 29, 2019

Like millions of other Americans, I celebrated the day when we're supposed to be remembering all our fallen camarades by relaxing on a beach. "America's Most Solemn Holiday?" Ha!

. . . Sorry, Civil War ghosts.

You know what's funny? My awareness of the Civil War before I moved out here to the east coast was about a two on a scale of one to This Is ALL The History And We Need To Talk About This At Every Opportunity. Don't get me wrong—I'm on board with reevaluating statues and monuments and discussing the civil rights movement heroes. It's the "General So And So slept here for two hours!" and "a confederate soldier once looked at a woman here!" that keeps catching me by surprise. Does *everyone* here have all the battles of the Civil War memorized? Speaking for myself and my west coast camarades, things we could say about the Civil War include a) it was messy and b) people died.

But that's the neat thing about travel. (Yes, I am determined to write about travel, not war.) There really is no substitute because even if you're an avid armchair explorer there are things you just can't imagine are important until you meet someone from a different part of the world. Everyone knows about different customs and forms of politeness and checkered pasts. But things like war interpretations? Milk in bags? Trains that stop at nowhere? Beaches covered in arcades? You just won't understand the complexity of being faced with these on a normal day when you thought all you had to worry about was frizzy hair and where to eat until you actually do it.

And so please, by all means, do. I think it ought to be mandatory, personally. You can be the sweetest person ever but you're still not reaching your potential of open-mindedness until you've traveled.

For some people it backfires though, and they get even more close-minded. Tell us *more* about your problems, Ava . . .

* * *

"And that one over there. You can barely see it. See the head? The neck? It's a Camelopardalis. You might not have heard of them. It is a fierce creature. The coat of a leopard, the head of a camel, the—"

Ava sighed. "You *know* none of those animal names mean anything to me."

". . . Ah, yes. You come from a land of snow. I remember. But perhaps you have lizards. There is a little one just there—"

"And you battled it and cut off its tail," Ava interrupted again. "Yes. I heard. But no, I still don't know what a lizard is."

Unruffled by her weary tone, Orion chuckled. "It is so strange to think. You come from an entirely different world."

"Yeah," agreed Ava, and she took it as a sign of how weary she was that her voice dipped into melancholy. "Apparently there's a lot of them out there." *How* she was ever going to find the right one to return to was a niggling worry, one that had become worse since Richard and his dependable—even if silly—plans had disappeared.

"That you came here is perfect," Orion declared abruptly. "You have changed my way of thinking. About outsiders. And about everything."

"People don't change," Ava responded on autopilot before she'd processed Orion's meaning.

"It is easier for us."

". . . What do you mean? What 'us'?"

Orion waved a hand, indicating himself, the stars. Ava's eyes narrowed as the mantras in her head–*they're the same as us, they understand, this is all happening for a reason*–faltered and fell away.

68

Don't Look Back

June 5, 2019

Well I come back fresh from vacation and guess what I hear? The Exalted Sister is spending *her* vacation at home.

It's not even summer camp season just yet and everything is falling apart, guys. I need you to distract me. It's fine, of course. Everything is fine. But like . . . wtf?

Have you ever had a family member do something so out of character that you wonder if you even know them any more? My sister did that oh, say, ten years ago now. And now she's decided for a reprisal? A reversal reprisal, no less. I mean, whose idea was it that she should stay with Mom and Dad? Usually she stays on at whatever college she's chosen and waitresses over the summer. What is even going on?

But it's not like it is my problem. I won't be there—though you can be sure I will be hearing about it. I just had to vent about it to somebody, and it looks like you're it. No one here quite gets the family thing at home. I've talked a lot about the benefits of travel but . . . yes, okay, that is a downside. And of course it's the subject everyone asks about.

Funny that this should be happening in my life while we're at the "things fall apart" section of the book, too. My life is starting to feel more like fiction than reality—not something I ever thought I would have minded, but then, I always pictured myself in a fantasy, not in a daytime drama. I started out purposefully choosing blog topics to match the story and now I feel like someone Above is purposefully directing my life.

Bleh, I'm in a weird mood.

* * *

Richard looked up all at once to see a person sitting on the path—not ahead of him, but off to one side. It seemed to be a man, clothed like Perseus and Orion—but it was difficult to tell, because the man was hunched over, facing the edge of the path. In fact he was so close that the edges clouded around him, and a sudden premonitory sound filled Richard's mind.

"Hey," Richard called, starting toward the stranger. "You have to be careful!"

But the man didn't respond. He leant farther into the shadow. The sound intensified.

"Wait!" Richard shouted. The moment he was close enough, he put a hand on the man's shoulder.

At once, the sound ceased. Two unfocused, deep eyes turned up to Richard's. "Why?"

"Um." Richard faltered, his eyes straying. An unfamiliar instrument lay in the man's lap. The swirls of stardust were receding. "Oh. Were you playing that noise?"

The stranger's lips twitched—in offense or amusement, Richard couldn't tell. But his eyes became more focused as he answered, "Most people think it music."

"Right, sorry." Richard stepped back. "And it, it's what made the path move? I kind of thought—"

The strange man kept looking at him, but the sentence was never finished. Richard looked away, only more embarrassed to realize that his state of mind was getting the better of him.

"Many things happen when you play music," remarked the musician finally. "It is the only time I truly speak."

"Oh. Well—"

"It is the way the universe speaks back to me," the man continued, unperturbed. "It told me you were coming."

Richard wondered if he should start edging away—but something made him hesitate. " . . . It did?"

"Yes." The man stood, unstooping to a height far greater than Richard's. And after a moment, he grinned. "Your footfalls nearly threw off my time."

69

Gone Forever

June 12, 2019

Okay, one more irrelevant Ashley Life Post, and then I'll get back to more interesting stuff.

I feel bad, first of all. Which is not news enough to merit a post, but bear with me. There's actually good news but I don't feel good, hence the bad, if you catch my drift. Apparently one summer night around the fire pit in the backyard was enough for my mom, dad, and sister to all open their hearts to one another and heal grievances and move forward with lives full of family love.

I have heard about this event now approximately one million times from about six different people, which is funny when you think only three were involved. And it just keeps filling my head with that same foreboding music Richard was hearing last week. I know I shouldn't and everyone hates a naysayer but come on people, help me out. Does one heart-to-heart ever fix anything? Yeah we see it on My Little Pony all the time and I love the idea of it, I really do, but . . . have you ever seen it work? If you have, post it below.

Bottom line, I should be happy. They're over there singing a happy tune in chorus but instead I've got the same old song stuck in my head. Maybe what I ought to do is go out dancing . . . clearly that is the best response to all these terrible music metaphors.

And then my one bad mood won't be forever immortalized on the internet . . .

* * *

"You aren't a deity, and you aren't a human who's ascended, either," Ava said, crossing her arms. "Not at all, are you? You're just shaped like one. You're a shadow."

"I am a skydweller," said Orion simply. "And also a man."

The strange fixations, the battles, the memories swirled around Ava, mingling with her own injured assumptions. She stamped her foot. "You can't be both!"

"Don't be ridiculous. Of course I can."

"Don't *tell* me I'm being ridiculous!" Ava's voice rose. "*You're* the never who never explained! You never explained anything—not any of you! You let us think you're our friends. And now Richard is out there sulking because he thinks he lost someone important but you were all just fantasies and–and *magic* in the first place!"

Orion sputtered. "You are talking nonsense. There is no difference."

"There is to *me!* All of you, you have no memories and you come and go and you talk about belief and have the same problems over and over. Like you've been cursed. Like you're *stuck.* You're just—you're just *myths*! How can I know you were right about us getting home, or that you even want to help us? How can I know anything you have said is real?"

"Everything I have said is real!"

"Nothing you *are* is real!" Ava had a moment of awareness of herself screaming, of her loneliness bearing down. But it was too late. "I am sick to death of you and everything in this place! I am going *home!*"

70

Whelve

v: to hide something by burying it deeply

June 19, 2019

And that is, of course, what we are doing with our emotions. Shove 'em down there and wait until they don't exist any more, am I right?

Well actually I meant this in a more *past* sense than a present or future sense. Clearly it's what Ava has done, even though I didn't know this word when I wrote the story originally (although I did apparently know the word *premonitory*, did you guys catch that a week or two ago? That must have been the year my grandparents gave me a vocabulary builder for Christmas).

Incidentally, people make fun of me for referring to Ava, Richard, Orion, etc more like people with agency than like puppets. I dunno how real writers do it, but that is legit how I see them, folks. I mean, I'm not crazy—I don't think they're alive/real (yeesh Ava, let's not get into that argument again)—but after initially thinking them up I kinda . . . let them go. It's like planting mystery seeds. They're mine for sure and they wouldn't be alive without me, but I can't predict the ways in which they'll grow.

My metaphor game is on fire lately, y'all.

* * *

Ava's feet pounded the path as she ran away. But the feeling was probably the most unsatisfying of her life, because her furred boots made absolutely no sound on the unreal mist beneath her.

And it didn't help, either, that she had no idea where she was going or if she would ever get there. She wasn't one to get torn up over existential questions, but she was very aware of that voice in her head that was laughing at her, mocking her lack of self-control.

That voice had always been there, and she had always thought it sounded like her sisters. Not one of them in particular—though it was true, some were worse than others. But the worst part of court life was that it blended everyone into faceless groups and put a mask over their individualities. Ava wasn't good at masks and she hated derision. But she still carried this voice around with her wherever she went—even, it turned out, into fantasy realms.

What did you really expect to happen?

Now look what you've done. Make one run away, and run from the other yourself. Congratulations.

This is why he never would have really loved you.

This is why you have problems.

Ava shuddered as she finally collapsed to a stop. That voice—she had never paid so much attention to it before.

It didn't sound like her sisters, or her mother, or the court.

It didn't sound like a curse or a witch or an old story.

It sounded like herself.

71

Musically Yours

June 26, 2019

You know, the one thing we've never talked about is music. I can't believe our relationship has come this far and I haven't brought it up! Seriously though folks, the whole "so what's your favorite song/album/artist?" line of questioning is the one series of first date questions I really believe in. I don't need to know your favorite color or which kind of pizza you like best. But I *will* be picking apart your "three songs that define me" answers, so be ready!

Was talking to a guy recently—actually an old friend—online and I asked him that question, the 'three songs' one. He said he wasn't that into music. I had known this guy since high school and always had a thing for him and everything was coming together for a summer trip (him coming out here; what, you think I'm fool enough to go home right now?) but I KID YOU NOT, I got that answer and it absolutely killed everything for me. Now I think of it, I'm pretty sure I haven't messaged him back in a day or two . . . He probably thinks I am dead.

And well I might be—dead of shock! How do people *live* without music? That's the one art form I think I couldn't survive without, and that's with writing and clothing up there as competition.

Granted, when I type music and when you read music, we are thinking different things. *I* couldn't possibly name two of the six artists on the radio right now, and it was a miracle I remembered enough lyrics for the last few post titles (the ones that were song references, anyway). Rock and pop and jazz and all that is nice as far as background noise goes, but what I'm really thinking of here is *classical* music.

I know, I know. This is where I've lost you. Much like classic lit, classical music is just too dry and wandering and *required* for most people, and I get it. I think it's those things—well, the wandering thing, anyway—that I actually like, though. I love music I can get lost in.

Speaking of . . .

* * *

The man, Richard learned, was named Orpheus. His form was hazy, ill-defined, fading behind the bright lyre he held. But the name was familiar.

"Oh!" Richard beamed, relief overtaking his usual sense. "I've heard of you. Andromeda mentioned you. See, we were talking about her and Perseus and how they have to visit each other but it's really not as bad as it could be because—oh. Ergggh . . ."

Orpheus held his lyre closer. The effect of the starlit instrument shadowed his eyes, making his expression difficult to read. But something resonated around him, and Richard thought he could *feel* it. He apologized at once for reminding the musician of his lost love, Eurydice.

"It doesn't matter," Orpheus told him—a sentiment which, in a melancholy tone, was not exactly reassuring. "Andromeda was right."

"Yes, well, I'm very sorry," Richard said again. He hesitated. "I guess you might be wondering why I am here, and why I interrupted you. I really didn't mean to. I thought—"

But that certainly wasn't the right thing to say, either. Richard gulped. Orpheus tilted his head, watching him carefully. The night sifted in and out of his form as he strummed a few notes on the lyre—just a few short notes, and Richard was suddenly at ease.

"The thing is," he found himself explaining, "I've made a mistake. I don't know where I'm going. Somehow I have to get back home, but I don't know how; and at the same time, I have to find Ava and make sure *she* gets home too—if she wants to. I really don't know and it seems like the longer I am here the less I know about anything. I'm afraid that if I stay too much longer I'll forget what I have to do."

"You won't forget," Orpheus said, quietly.

"But what if I do? I wouldn't even know. And if I *did* know I had—wouldn't that be worse?"

The music became louder. Orpheus expanded. "Do you want help?"

"I don't know what help to ask for. Where I was going might not be the answer anyway. But I can't stay here."

"Then listen," whispered the music. "Listen, and you won't forget."

72

Liberty!

July 3, 2019

I'm not very political—it feels like almost a crime to admit it. But I have told you all before—as "fiery" as you think the blog might be sometimes, it's different in real life. *I'm* different in real life. And politics is too much like real life—or maybe not enough like it. Sometimes I just really, really, wish that politicians led actual lives around the actual people that they are affecting. But the horrible irony about politics is that anyone who would want to be a politician enough to run for office and cough up all that dough is 90% likely to be someone you would never actually want in a position of power.

(So clearly, me saying "I'm not political" doesn't mean "I don't have feelings about politics.")

But all this has been said before, hasn't it? In this day and age, it seems like everybody is saying anything to the point where everything has been said, including a bunch of things that never ever ought to have an audience.

But on to talk about fireworks and stars, because that's what we want on a national holiday—not commentary on the nation. You know who *is* political? Ava. Which is funny because I was not a "change the world" kid—not even a "run for school government" kid, not in the slightest. But I think I always liked thinking about the ideas *behind* politics, if not the sordid, minute details.

Idealists—both Ava, and me. And now angry to boot! Shocker! Jokes aside, I know people like to look down on idealists, but I've been thinking about it all day and there's something freeing about being an idealist, too. Because you can see how things *can* be better, which means you aren't confined to looking at drudgery *all* the time. Just sometimes, when seeing the difference between the ideal and the real, you do get angry. So . . . If you'll excuse me, I'm going to go watch things get blown up!

* * *

Ava touched her face. Was she crying? There was a sound all around her like tears, but she didn't remember where it came from. Everything was so alien, and it seemed so familiar; she stepped into it—followed it down the path, somehow knowing she was getting closer, even though it remained all around.

She didn't realize what she might be getting closer *to* until she noticed that the world was brighter. It happened all at once: there was a path joining hers as if from nowhere, and shapes shifting restlessly over it, back and forth. Not until the sound faded did she understand that the shapes shifted as she did, and she was the one who had been moving the entire time.

Slowly the sorrow drained away, and Ava's thoughts shaped themselves into words once more. Like wreckage out of floodwaters they emerged, one at a time, as the lights settled into recognizable forms.

"Richard!"

Richard blinked at Ava as she reached out to him. She had his hand before he could move: she always had been the faster one.

"What happened?" she was asking.

"I—" but he couldn't say he didn't know. It had been Orpheus. "Someone took pity on me, I think. But I don't know how—"

"*Goodbye,*" said the music.

Ava turned. "What?"

"But—" Richard twisted.

"Hello." the voice came from the opposite side—from behind them, where the two paths converged and continued as one. At this intersection, a stately form stood.

"Oh dear," said Ava. "Not *another* bird."

73

Modern Magic

July 10, 2019

Anyone with tumblr—or at least, anyone with a tumblr like mine (and who wouldn't want to be like me? Har har)—has seen them. The posts about 'new fantasy' or 'reimagined myths' or commonplace, everyday magic: not "and then I used a spell to take away his wand!" magic, but "I never lose socks in the dryer" magic.

And even if you aren't plugged into the internet (although if you aren't, how are you here with me?) you will have noticed that 'modern magic' is going strong in children's and young adult lit. I never realized when I was a kid that the Ibbotsen and Pierce I loved were in fact destined to be *my* editions of what has always been, stories of kids who fall into other worlds, or—as they get older—fall in love with darkness. We've had those stories since MacDonald and Radcliffe and even before.

But in any case. There's a feeling out there that the

modern world—technology in large part, but I think mostly skepticism—has driven the magic out of life. And then there's a bunch of people who want to pull the magic back in, mostly by making posts like those described above, writing novels, or buying 'do-it-yourself wicca' kits off Amazon.

And I'm not bashing any of it. But I am saying I think magic is still a thing. Magic was really just a tool of metaphor, a channel to let the story flow, a shortcut to wonder. We still have that—or at least I do, maybe because I am crazy. It might very well look different to most people but to me it looks like music—classical music in particular, as you well know (see previous post). And that, friends, is why I gave Orpheus such power.

I have always loved that guy.

* * *

The giant eagle regarded them with its head to one side, unamused. "I am Aquila."

"Oh!" Richard and Ava realized it at once. "You are the one we were supposed to find!"

"Yes."

"Could you—wait." Ava paused in asking the question. "How did you know we were looking for you?"

The beak tipped down as the fierce eyes bored into her face. "I am one many seek."

"It didn't actually know," Richard confided to Ava, just as she glanced at him with a roll of her eyes. Between the two of them, they laughed.

"I am so done here," Ava admitted, half jest, half sigh of relief.

"I completely understand," Richard agreed, smiling.

"I can hear you," Aquila reminded them.

"Sorry." Ava stepped forward and, in so doing, realized she had still been holding Richard's hand. Dropping it with a blush, she continued, "This is Richard, and my name is Yavalinra. We came here by accident . . ."

Richard listened as Ava summarized their journey, content to wait and chip in as needed. To him she sounded resolved, and yet at the same time more modest than he remembered; he admired her for it.

He could only have guessed the way her heart faltered as Aquila agreed to help them—provided they leave at once, and not waste too much of its regal time.

It wasn't that she regretted leaving—not at all, Ava decided. Once she had thought she might stay forever in this mysterious, timeless place, the one place truly Blessed to her people. But it did not have that shine of the unknown to it any more, and it seemed now she could hardly think of a place less fitting for her to be. And yet . . .

To think that *was the last thing I said to him.* Ava faltered as she followed Richard toward Aquila. The regret mingled with other thoughts—*it's not like I was wrong!* and *he probably has forgotten now anyway*—before finally settling into a determination to do better next time.

It was the only thing she could do.

74

Welkin

n: sky, especially night sky

July 17, 2019

That's right, I've been hanging on to this one 'til the end. Honestly I did have it in mind for the earlier posts, but I think I was busy venting about work or boys or something when Ava and Richard first went up. Then afterward it seemed awkward to sneak it in halfway through, so here we are.

You'd be surprised how often my overwhelming sense of what is awkward leads me to do things like this . . .

For instance: the other day, my mom called me up and I let her get halfway through telling me about how excited she was for her "daughter date" with Sabrina before the screaming kids in the background finally reminded her I was at work. (For the record they were NOT screaming because Tots Tinkering Time is torture. One stepped on another's toe.)

On a more related note, you should make a date of your own to go see the meteor shower coming up. I myself will not be making it a date, but I do think I'll go out and see it. It's been too long since I scrambled through the dark looking for a special light—literally, anyway.

And hey, while you're there, make believe Ava and Richard are coming down to their earth on one of those special lights, now that they've made their way across the Milky Way, just like Orion said. Or were they only able to fly home because Ava finally learned *not* to listen to Orion? Such is the difficulty in dealing with magic beings. Are they trying to help you or abduct you? We may never know! But we do know that our hero and heroine get to go home . . .

Goshdarn eagles making everything so easy.

* * *

As soon as they climbed onto Aquila's back, the world which had no time seemed to pick up speed. There was hardly a chance to feel sad or conflicted before the giant bird was plummeting through the air, not down exactly, but through a series of lights and sounds.

Richard wanted to speak to Ava, seated behind him, but he couldn't find his voice. Wind seemed to whip past them too fast for noise—but perhaps that was his imagination, for he found he could breathe freely. Riding Aquila was much like being in the moon—there was a barrier of lightness around him and he could see nothing up close, but he could see the night sky turning and fading far away.

But it was also nothing like being in the moon. The farther they traveled, the more *real* Aquila felt. And the entire time, there was Ava at his back.

For her part Ava had nothing to compare the experience to. It was nothing like riding a horse, nor even like walking along the starry path. One moment she was stuck in the sky with her many regrets, and another she was nowhere, apart from it all. She clung to Richard for her life, even though she wasn't exactly sure she was living any more. It was all so incredibly *changeable.*

The colors around them flapped and soared, dark blues and purples giving way to muted greens and gray. The further they went the more colors crept in, streaks of yellow and orange and bright waving teal, and they could not hear but instead *felt* Aquila's presence in their minds, probing for further direction.

Where was home?

75

Stereofree

July 24, 2019

A friendly note from your local interdisciplinary summer camp coordinator:

I am not a detail-oriented person. I write detailed lists, sure, but that's just to calm my anxiety about being the kind of person who remembers emotions and forgets names, can't remember numbers or dates—

And if I can't remember names, you ask, why do I like stories? If I can't remember dates, why do I like history? Well, I ask you right back: what are literature and history? Don't give me the PC answer you think I want. Tell me the worst thing you know about them. They're boring? Really? What about those lives of dead irrelevant people that inspired GoT—are they boring too? It's about names and dates? Ha! You think people are out there writing books and articles about just names and dates? You think they don't need all their notes and their books and their speech outlines in order to remember them?

I'm not here to make you love history, or art, or even reading. I'm not telling you anything other than what you already know. I'm only confirming what you already expected—that nothing is exactly the way you've been told it is, or the way you think it is. Science is not just atoms and outer space. Art is not just ditzyness and emotions. Math is not irrelevant and it doesn't even need to be hard. History is not about names and dates.

But you already knew this, didn't you? Of course you did—somewhere, maybe deep inside, you doubted. So maybe that's why I'm here: to tell you to believe in yourself. Believe in your doubts, and search for the truth. Because no stereotype is always true.

And similarly, no homecoming is exactly what you expected . . .

* * *

"Uh." Richard looked around, up at the sky, and back down to Ava. "I guess Orion was right."

But Ava didn't want to talk about that. "Couldn't it have picked a better place to set us down?"

Richard looked around. He and Ava were standing in a snowy clearing at the edge of a forest, in the dark of night and entirely alone.

"To be fair," he began, "it probably looked like some sort of comet was coming down, so maybe Aquila wanted to avoid any—"

"Sure," interrupted Ava. "But what do we do now?"

For a moment they just looked at each other. Their minds

struggled to make sense of what they had done, much less what they should do—though neither wanted to admit as much.

"Everyone's going to be worried about us," Richard said finally. His voice fell flat in the cold air, and suddenly he had the uncomfortable feeling of being ravenous, and very, very tired.

"If everyone is even still alive. Who knows what could have happened." Ava sounded miserable rather than combative, and Richard reached out to her shoulder.

"Hey," he said. "Let's at least go back and see, okay? And if there's no one left—at least we still have each other."

"But where do we go back to?"

"What do you mean?"

"I mean . . . you can't come home with me, not yet. And I probably shouldn't go to Runn . . ."

Ava paused, and in that pause, Richard felt for her. "Why don't we both go back to our own courts—just for now. And we can—we can promise to meet back here. How about when the moon is full?"

Looking up at the sky, Ava realized the moon was just a sliver. The sight of it sent an unpleasant ripple down her spine. *This has been crazy,* she realized all at once. *I wasn't ready for this.*

She looked at Richard, grateful he was still thinking clearly at least. If that ever changes, then we'll really be in trouble. Shaking off the exhaustion and the confusion for just a moment, she leaned in and kissed his cheek.

"All right," she said aloud. "Here goes nothing."

76

The Village

July 31, 2019

So I was out with my friend, right. We went to this local art fair and there were about a million kids. Now, as you might have guessed from last week's post, I'm in full summer camp mode and kids have been my life for the past forever (at least that's what it feels like), so I mentioned something. Something like it's great they're out and about or whatnot. Classic kids-these-days sort of thing to say.

"It's terrible," she said. I kid you not, that is the exact word she used. "Just look at that one. Is his mom *ever* going to make him shut up? Why even have kids if you're not going to pay attention to them? People like that should not be allowed to breed."

Now, in all fairness, the kid was *the* definition of a spoiled screaming brat and his mom could *not* have been less interested. His dad (if that's who it was) wore a wifebeater and a scowl and basically looked like he was going to be called to court on domestic violence charges in about a year's time.

But still, what my friend said seemed harsh to me. I think I've shared on here before that I personally am not going to have children, and I stand by that. But—and working in public programming has only strengthened my belief here—even in today's society, it's true that a kid is really raised by a village. There's a whole network of adults who can affect that kid's life. So even if the parent probably shouldn't have had kids, someone can step in to help.

Of course when I mentioned that, she shot back the good ol' "the child who is not embraced by the village will burn it down to feel its warmth." That's friends for you—always good for a cheerful bonfire maxim.

What it boils down to as far as I'm concerned is there are too many opinions out there regarding kids, and the act of making them. I'm retreating back into my fictional world, where of course every child gets the love and care they deserve . . .

* * *

Richard's plan had been a good one, and despite the sudden heaviness in her feet, Ava carried it out perfectly. But it wasn't the kind of journey she had become used to.

"Ow!" A startled owl leapt from the nearest tree as Ava banged her toe on yet another snow-covered rock, nearly adding a heart attack to her other ailments.

The pressure of hunger, failing energy, tender feet, and a freezing nose—the pressure of caring for herself—weighed heavily on Ava. These weren't the sorts of things that were supposed to matter—especially not on a journey *home.* Alone on the snowy plain and aggravated enough to continue talking aloud, she said to nothing in particular, "The end of the mystic journey is supposed to jump to the homecoming and the happily ever after. It's not supposed to drag on like this!"

Of course, they had very nearly done that. Aquila had flown them through worlds of space and time and story in what felt like an instant. "But of course we couldn't get all the way home," Ava continued through gritted teeth. "Because everything had to fall just *short* of a true fairy tale, now, didn't it?"

If Richard had been there, she could have blamed it on him, for he was undoubtedly lacking so far as strong and handsome princes went. But as a friend and a strategian he excelled, and she found she couldn't say anything else about him.

In a stubborn, sullen silence, then, Princess Yavalinra straggled up the monstrous cliff to the front gates of the castle of the Blessed Land Under the Sky.

77

Gamify

August 7, 2019

Okay folks listen up, I just found out the coolest thing. There is a batman version of D&D!

"No, Ashley," you say. "That's not cool, it's nerdy."

But wait! There's more! There's also a pokemon version. And steampunk and cyberpunk too. And of course there's harry potter and buffy the vampire slayer varieties. There's everything! Roleplay world!

Normally I'm suspicious of this trend of *gamifying,* as a lot of educators are. For those not in the know, gamifying usually means turning learning into a game, not necessarily fandoms. But still I instantly thought of it when our DM casually mentioned he was taking part in a pokemon rpg one-shot. Games might cheapen literature or academic spaces sometimes, but since pokemon was already a game, what's the harm?

And this begs the question, what *else* can we turn into a

role-playing game?

. . . there's Suburbs and SUVs, a popular one on tumblr . . .

Office Space could totally be one . . .

But consider: Terror in the Aisles—the grocery shopper rpg!

Can exercise be an rpg? Please?

Naturally, Awkward Family Situations would be a staple . . . the one everyone hates to pull out at parties, and yet it always makes an appearance anyway.

* * *

Richard's return home was slightly less arduous than Ava's, as he moved north into a more snow-free climate. By his own estimation, Aquila had dropped them squarely on the border between their two lands, at a place where the river was merely a frozen trickle during this time of year. He wondered how the giant star-bird could have possibly known to do this: had it read their minds? The possibility did not surprise him. He felt as though nothing could surprise him any more.

That feeling survived unbroken when Ben, on watch at the wall, welcomed him like a long-lost love. It cracked a little when his father seemed to actually be shedding a tear at his return—but then instantly mended when his three younger brothers waved instead of joining the family hug, and promptly took the distraction as an opportunity to run toward the stables.

"But where have you *been?*" his mother kept saying.

"I *knew* you would return," his father whispered.

That one *was* a surprise.

Richard's guilt and sudden warmth was interrupted,

though, by Ben's exuberant,
  "Just *wait* til you hear what we have planned!"

78

Surround Sound

August 14, 2019

I have horrible news for you folks. It isn't just Squirrel that's started to sound like the Old One.

I was having a conversation with Brent the other day and it was the weirdest thing. It was only him and me, but I could still hear the Old One in the room. This isn't hard: lately in conversations all she does is say the same thing I say, just a little bit later and louder.

But when it was just me talking, I could hear the echo in my mind still, and it made me doubt.

I say things like 'better luck next time!' and 'sometimes, you're no better safe than sorry.'

Does *she* say them because we're similar people, or because she is copying my personality?

Heaven forbid I'm taking on *her* personality . . .

It is a sad, sad historical truth that we often become the people we hate. I know that. But I *have* my own personality and I will *never* be as petty as she is. (If I ever become that way, push me off a cliff. No joke. Somewhere inside, my actual me will be screaming in agony as it watches the horrific descent of my sanity.) Even if I go senile though I don't think it will be the same because I was NEVER the degree of selfish bitch that she is. It just isn't in me.

And I really don't want it to be, ever, which is why the idea of conversational contamination makes me want to wash my mouth out with soap.

Truthfully I do think it is that she is copying me, because I have noticed her personality changes drastically depending on who she is talking to/who in the room is getting the most attention. She probably doesn't even do it on purpose. It's still disgusting though, and it's still true that you can be dragged down by the company you keep . . . as Ava, having been away a little longer than she expected, is about to realize when she looks at her home with fresh eyes.

Straight up, you guys, I don't even know what's real any more. If I were Ava, I'd probably still be stuck on the Milky Way!

* * *

"May I next present Princess Yavalinra, who was recently kidnapped for the span of one full month and held captive by—"

"No, no no!" Ava pushed her way past her mother's secretary, nearly knocking the officious man over. She took her stand in the middle of the grand courtroom, looking defiantly at the courtiers gathered around the edges—and most of all, at her mother, who sat on the dias in the middle of the main wall. "I was *not* kidnapped, and I wasn't held captive."

"But you *were* gone," a voice pointed out. Any of the courtiers were allowed to question the person in the middle of the room, and since most of them hid behind screens, it was difficult to say exactly *who* was making Ava's life difficult at any given moment.

"Yes, I was gone, because I—" Ava paused, and tried to compose herself. "My friend needed help, and I tried to help him using magic. But the magic backfired and it took us this long to get home again."

"And where is your friend?"

"But the princess can't even *use* magic!"

"She's just covering for those terrible barbarians in Runn!"

"I am not!" Ava's voice rang out loudly, and everyone shushed once more. "My friend had to go home too. No doubt *his* parents were worried about him." She glared at her mother again, trying not to wince as she realized she'd slipped in admitting Richard's gender. So what if he was a man, and she had been gone alone with him? Why should any of *them* care? After all in pure probability terms it was 50/50 who she'd get stuck with and—

Shaking some more relevant thoughts into her head, Ava continued. "I don't see why you can't just accept the fact that I have returned, and I'm okay. There's no one to put on trial or be mad at. Everything turned out fine. I mean, if you want to be mad at someone, you could investigate the amount of wanton magic that's being done around here, because that's what caused this whole accident in—"

"Accident?" The laugh was one Ava recognized: her sister. She watched warily as Ylandria stepped up near the dias. "Are you sure you weren't just trying to run away, little sister? We all know you aren't happy here, despite everything Mother has done."

"And if I *did* run away, you'd be the first to celebrate," Ava retorted. "Sorry to break up your party. But no, the entire thing was an accident, and no one is to blame."

"Then I wonder," said Ylandria, looking at her nails, "why you won't tell us the name of your little friend? The one who needed help?"

The courtiers erupted into gossip and questions. In amongst the speculation and demands, Ava could hear Liam agreeing with his betrothed. "It is very suspicious indeed!"

The words went right through her heart and she broke. "All right! Fine. You'll have heard about it anyway, if your spies are worth anything, *Mother.* The other person who got lost is Richard."

For a moment there was no reaction, and Ava sighed, recognizing why. "The Elder Prince of Runn."

79

Vilipend

v: to despise or regard as worthless; to vilify

August 21, 2019

This is an oldie, but a goodie. I love those lists of old put-downs and comebacks.

And it goes along well with something else I've been thinking about, something that Ava's about to be thinking about too. There are different ways to treat someone like a *person*—you can treat them like a person you like, or a person you don't respect at all. To ask to be treated like a person is really not to ask for anything.

Because what you want when you ask that is respect, right? I read a thing on the internet once that put it this way: you can respect someone by treating them like a fellow human, or you can respect someone by treating them as an authority. And sometimes people get those mixed up. Instead of treating you like a fellow human in return for you doing the same, they expect to be treated like an authority and so they'll automatically be offended and all mutual respect rules will fly out the window.

Idealism aside (we talked about that in a July post), Ava has a fascination with rights that I'll never really have. (That character trait emerged out of an AP Euro class, if I remember right, and at first it was just a quirk.) Maybe it's my depressive, distrustful nature, but I just can't work myself up to thinking I'm *entitled* to anything. I always expect the worst, especially from other people around me, even if they are people I like. It's weird, but anyway my point is I'm not sure how much about *rights* and *respect* and *entitlement* is fundamentally true, and how much is societal (not that that's a bad thing). But I do know that this is what bugs me about the Old One: she never respects anyone else's social cues.

* * *

The gasps and accusations following this statement were unbearable. When Ava finally shouted and shocked them all into silence, it was the Queen who took advantage of the silence.

"To kidnap any member of the royal family is an act of war," she decreed.

"Then *you* started it," Ava returned with no small amount of vindictiveness. "Because he only needed help because your witch stuck him in some magical prison and left him there to rot."

"What the witch does is none of your business," Ylandria reminded Ava.

"Why was the witch dealing with him in the first place?" The voice of her brother, Vanderlin.

Ava fumed. She had known Ylandria would be difficult and she had never expected the eldest sister, Ria, to intervene—it wasn't only Ava who considered the eldest princess to be a flake—but she had thought she might at least count on Van.

"You know what *I* want to know?" she cried, furious. "I want to know why everyone here is treating everyone else like they're guilty of a crime. Richard has a right to defend himself before you decide he was doing something terrible."

"The people of Runn have no rights when they wrongfully enter this land," said the Queen. She sounded bored, and well she might have been, because the conversation was edging into a common theme for Ava.

"Then *I* at least should have a right to be listened to!" Ava stared down everyone in the room. "Have *I* wrongfully entered the country? Do *I* deserve to be treated this way? Why did you even ask me to appear in court if you didn't want to hear what I have to say? And while we're on the topic, why did I have to make an appointment with a *secretary* in order to talk to my mother—and why do I have to do so in a room full of people? I am not a criminal. I am not a royal puppet. I am a person and I demand to be treated like one!"

"You want to be treated like a person, and not a princess?" a sister mocked.

"Yavalinra always was the *special* one, wasn't she?"

"You don't even care that I am back!" Ava cried, angry beyond words to find she was in tears. "You're just a warmonger, that's all you are. That's all you've ever been, since Dad died."

80

Dog Days

August 28, 2019

So as you may have guessed, it was a stressful camp season, and I had had enough of certain coworkers. I booked it out of the gallery as soon as the last camp was done—and, having nowhere else to go, made a visit home.

Mistake!

You know that feeling where a family member wants to sit down and talk but all you want to do is get lost in a book and not think about the drama for once?

Or how about the one where *you* have changed but nothing *else* has and so you're walking around old streets and the old house and you keep getting flashbacks of when you were younger, like you're haunted by the Past And Future That Would Have Been?

Or most of all, the one where everyone else is like 'it's all totally fine come sing kum ba yah with us,' and you're about to bust your top from not screaming *'of course this isn't fine how can you have forgotten?'*

My family excels at all of those. I just a vacation with the trifecta. Maybe if I write it down it'll help me remember so I never ever go back again.

And the fact that no one is as surprised about this as my sister really needles me, you know? Like don't come at me with that 'Ashley are you okay?' crap when the reason I'm not okay is you suck at handling your own feelings. To be fair, she *did* apologize about running away all those years ago. But it didn't have the effect it should have. You're supposed to forgive when someone apologizes, right, like my parents clearly did (probably desperate to have a daughter who doesn't spend all her time on the computer . . .) but for me it just brought up everything all over again. 'Oh, you're going to bring up that thing I was trying not to think about? Well guess what, it *did* mess up my life and you *did* hurt me and as far as I'm concerned you can go crawl in a hole and stay there with your apology, how's that?'

Really, the apology just made me angrier. It just made everything more raw. As if that were even possible . . .

* * *

"RichardRobertRonaldCrownPrinceGreatHonorofRunn."

Richard winced. His father used his full name and title not as a series of words, but as one long whip of sound.

"You expect me to believe you had *no* way of telling your mother and me that you were safe that *whole time?* And another thing! What son of mine would go *back* to a cursed *witch's tower* when it was that tower in the *first* place that started this mess?"

"Um," Richard tried to think. "You see, Ava had this idea that—"

"Don't you *dare* bring *her* into this mess!" King Verity thundered—and then all at once the storm broke and he smiled at his wife, Queen Valor. "You'd have loved her, Julie. *There's* a girl with a head on her shoulders."

"But—" Richard floundered, exasperated. He didn't feel like fighting with his dad about Ava, but he didn't feel like being the only irresponsible one, either.

"She'd have to have, to have survived a journey like that, hm?" The Queen smiled at Richard. She had never been anything but warm—and often amused—when it came to him, and his struggles with his father. "No one doubts your story, of course," she continued to Richard—with a wise glance at the King. "A Crown Prince of Runn would never lie."

King Verity may have choke a little. "Of course. But I'm just saying—"

"We were worried about you," Queen Valor finished for him.

Richard flushed. "I was too. Worried about you, I mean. And—a bit worried about me, too. If I had known any way to contact you, I would have, I promise."

"And yet where did he go first when he found himself stuck in the moon?" King Verity muttered, knowing he had already been defeated.

"That is a different matter, and one which the Prince has already heard plenty about, I imagine." Queen Valor smiled again at Richard, who could only agree. He could still hear Ava shouting at him as though she was only an arm's length away.

Struck by a sudden pang, not for being yelled at but for

Ava and her own family struggles, Richard didn't pay full attention as his father strode off to brood.

"He'll get over it," the Queen assured Richard. Though shorter than her husband, she was undoubtedly the more sturdy of the two, and everyone knew her word ruled. She now considered her stepson with clear, kind eyes. "But there have been others who have missed you very much too, Richard, and you had better make your peace with them."

81

Christmas Comes Early

September 4, 2019

Since Richard's thinking about Draco this entry, and I'm thinking about stuff no one wants to hear, let's take a step back shall we?

It's actually really neat. The first time I wrote this story, I had obviously just done a lot of 'research' (I put it in quotations because it was actually just nerdy me reading books I found interesting) into Greek mythology and our current constellations. The whole idea of 'intrusions' is something I fleshed out this time round—it was there before, but not in as much detail. So over the spring and summer I did a lot of *actual* research into different cultures' constellations.

Go check it out! Literally. Go to your local library and look up astronomy and mythology books . . . it can be a little hard to find them, I grant you, but it's worth it when you do. And anyway that's what librarians are there for (and they'll probably like a request about archaeoastronomy more than some of the *other* requests we get . . .).

One of the really mind-blowing things I found was that in some Native American cultures, it's taboo to tell certain stories at certain times of the year. Like they have one set of lore for when there's snow on the ground, and one for when there's not. At first this seemed totally novel to me, but then I realized it's essentially what we do with Christmas stories. There is a very specific time of year we want to hear those, and if they come early, the teller might be run out of town on a rail.

Okay maybe not that intense, but stores that sell Christmas stuff before Halloween should definitely be boycotted.

Anyway, there's just no end to the world of mythology. It's an excellent place to get lost in.

* * *

Richard knew who the Queen meant, of course. And he knew, too, that he *did* have to talk to her.

The thought was about as appealing as facing Draco again.

Still, a Crown Prince knew when to be dutiful. Richard's feet carried him through the fort. The world behind the tall, pointed timber walls was bustling—everyone was preparing for the summer move. Soon, they'd say goodbye to life at the edge of the tundra and instead would be on the coast. Instead of the frozen river, there would be the lapping sea; instead of peaks of rocks and ice, the horizon would be filled with rounded islands.

He hadn't realized how soon the move would be. As he thought about it, Richard was surprised to find that most of his anxiety was not about the conversation he was about to have — it was about the promise he'd made to Ava. *If I have to ride back on my own, then so be it,* he decided. But he still worried over it, because—well, because he had hoped a brief meeting wouldn't be the end of it.

Paying more attention to his thoughts than to his travels, Richard didn't realize he was passing the practice field until the noise hit him.

"Prince! Good to see you back!"

"Ey, Crown Prince Richard! Had us worried, you did!"

"And just where was it you've been?"

"Been afraid of practice, lad?"

"Don't listen to them." Ben's voice was loud in his ear. The knight had bounded over the fence and now hung from his shoulders, one arm slung over Richard's neck. "Gods, it's good to have you back though, Richard."

Richard paused, and smiled. "Thanks, Ben. I've just had to give Father the whole story, so I'm sure you'll all be hearing it."

"Aye, what's the excuse this time?"

"You're just jealous," Ben yelled back at the jeering knights in the ring, comfortably. With the pike in his free hand, he flicked mud from the trampled courtyard in their direction. The brown of the dirt, of the leather armor, of the wooden fortress and walls beyond, struck Richard suddenly as very strange. Was the recent blueness a dream, or was this?

"Anyway," Ben said to him in confidential tones, "everyone's really glad you're back. Want to join us? We haven't started drills yet."

"Thanks, Ben," Richard repeated. "I'll come and practice later, I promise. I have . . . I have some things to do." He shook off Ben's hold, and continued moving, on to the stables.

The stables here were low, set into the wall. The stables at the seaside—those were always better. That was where they had met. Or, not met exactly; Richard had always known her, and the other boisterous members of court. But that was where they'd been alone for the first time, and he had realized she was different.

82

Disappoint

September 11, 2019

I am disappoint.

And yeah, I know my bit last week about mythology wasn't fooling anyone. I did mean it, I just didn't want to keep harping on my personal life—but then my personal life snuck in.

It's just, I'm never sure who to tell things like this to. You're not supposed to be mad at your family—not unless they're abusers or murderers or whatever. And not unless you're fourteen. Or my sister Selene. But I never had that phase growing up—I guess I'm having it now.

But I really don't want to, folks. I don't want to feel this way. I don't want to be angry. It feels like it's literally eating up my soul. How are you supposed to get rid of a feeling like that? Go back again, and give everyone a hug? Write it all out and forget about it?

I'm just so disappointed in myself because I used to be able to do that. But then I think that me doing that was just part of a huge lie, a huge denial about what I felt, and that makes me even more disappointed.

* * *

"Oh, look who's here." Louisa stood and turned, speaking before Richard had a chance. She always beat him to the punch. She was quick like that—quick like Ava.

But that, Richard decided, was where the resemblance ended. Louisa was small, beautiful, though her hands were sharp from dealing with thick leather and her voice was high, sometimes hard in ways that he never expected. This time he wasn't caught off guard but he had no idea what to say.

Can you just say it right out? Richard wondered. *Do you have to say something else first?*

"No one thought you were coming back, you know. They all thought I was crazy."

"I—I'm sorry, Louisa," Richard replied. He got the unsettling feeling he was beginning at the end.

The young leatherworker sniffed and tossed her head. "No, it's fine. They were right, you know? It was crazy of me to follow you around all those years and always try to make everything all right. I wasn't ever going to be what you wanted, you know?"

"No—what?" Richard paused. It wasn't that they were starting at the end of the conversation, he realized: no, the tables were being turned on him. She *had* beaten him to it.

Relief washed over him, but he was still confused. He had thought they were just friends—or, okay, hopefully more than friends. He hadn't thought she was trying to do anything other than be.

"Of course you don't," Louisa continued impatiently. She reminded him a little of one of the nearby horses when she sounded so huffy. "You're so blind, Richard. You don't even think you've done anything wrong, do you?"

"I mean, I kind of have?" Despite lingering confusion Richard saw his chance and took it. "But not really. It's not like we were promised or anything, Louisa. I really have no idea what you're talking about. I am sorry you feel that way, though. But the truth is I met someone—"

Louisa laughed—a jagged sound that made Richard wonder what they had ever seen in each other. "Met someone? Oh, of course you have. You're just saying that because you heard about me and Andrew, aren't you? You know you really don't have to keep copying me or following me around."

"I thought *you* were following *me* around?" Richard's voice was shallow. *Which Andrew?*

"Not any more." Louis picked up the saddle she'd been working on, and smirked at him as she started to walk away. "Even being a prince is no excuse for breaking people's hearts."

83

Love is Messy

September 18, 2019

. . . But not in stories. You know? Just take Richard—who is by no means a Casanova—tidily finishing up one relationship before sallying forth to consider another. Now to be fair I suppose he was 'considering' Ava in that way even before, when he still felt some responsibility to Louisa, but still. He made a decision and he carried through.

And I think that is the reason my characters will always be better at love than me. They have this intuition, this *knowledge* of what they want, which is *so* very Idealized Teen Romance. That's not to say it's all clear sailing, and yeah, Richard and Ava are both still awkward young adults who aren't entirely sure how to handle whatever situation comes up, but when it comes down to it—in the times that really matter—they have this emotional clarity that I truly envy.

Because that's what we think love is like, right? "You just know." But that has never been my experience. Now you could say "oh but Ashley you just haven't found The One," which may or may not be true. But the older I get and the more I date, the more I think love is about making choices—hard ones. And I suck at making choices sometimes.

Like, Richard has a pretty straightforward set of choices. Break it off with Louisa and go woo Ava, break it off and be alone, or beg Louisa to come back. He makes Step One of the choice with no regrets. But to me, that would be anything *but* straightforward. I'd be sitting in that stable over-analyzing everything: 'but do I really like Ava? Do I really like Louisa? Why'd I ever get involved in the first place? Is it even likely she'd take me back? Is it even likely Ava will take me at all? Should I just be alone for a while? What is for the best in the long run? Am I hungry right now?' . . . you get the idea. Honestly most relationships I've been in, it was because the *other* person made a choice first. Seems the one decision I can make with clarity is when it comes to ending things, but that's a conversation for another day.

Anyway I think a good antidote to the 'love should be easy' mantra is to *show* characters making decisions. Maybe that's just me liking to know how people think? I didn't really do it for this story, not in depth, but I also wrote most of this when I was a Hopeless Romantic Teen.

* * *

The trouble, Ava decided, with royal possessions is that artisans inevitably went to great lengths to make them appear *royal.* This was the case with everything Blessed, at least, which meant everything in her room. What she wouldn't have given for a nice sturdy bag, like the one Richard had had hanging from his belt!

She surveyed her collection with her hands on her hips. Silken bedsheets, huge aquamarine robes, the softest towels money could buy. Which would make the best carry-all for the few possessions she had fit to travel?

"Leaving, are you?"

Ava startled: she hadn't heard the door open. She hadn't *expected* the door to open. She whirled at once even though she already recognized the voice: her older brother, Van.

He grinned at her from the doorway. "Or are you going to try to tell me you're just making an inventory of everything in your room, in case Ylandria took anything while you were gone?"

"She probably did," Ava muttered, scowling. "And I don't suppose *you* would have stopped her."

"Come on, Ava." Taking her antagonism as an invitation, Van strode in and sat down on the chair at her unused writing desk. "There's only so much I can do, there's so many of them. You know that."

"Sure. I had them all staring at me for the first time in forever while I stood in the middle of the courtroom *alone,*" Ava reminded him. She jerked the hem of her cast-off robe this way and that as though to test its strength.

To her annoyance, Van agreed. "That was awful. I had no idea they were going to be like that. I had hoped—well, I thought they might be as happy to see you as I was."

His sigh sounded genuine—Ava risked glancing at him. "Oh, so you were, then?"

"Of course I was. But I was also worried about you, Ava. I've heard only terrible things about Runn and its princes. I'm *still* worried about you. That's why I'm coming with you."

At first Ava heard only the first part of her brother's statement. "But that's just the point. Of *course* you've only heard terrible things, because *they* only want to *hear* terrible things. That way they don't have to feel bad ordering another war. Don't think I don't know what the Queen is planning. That's why I have to—"

She paused, her ears finally catching up with her mouth. "How do you know where I'm going?"

"Because I know you." Van grinned. "If I promise to get you a bag that will actually hold things, will you promise not to complain too much?"

84

Heuristic

*adj. encouraging learning through trial and error; enabling
someone to learn for themselves*

September 25, 2019

Guess what? It's school time again!

I mean, it has been for a while. Let's face it, it always is.
And even though I couldn't possibly be a school teacher, I do
love learning. And I love all the kids coming in with their
adorable little school groups!

No lie though, I really do. I know you all think I'm some
bitter shriveled shrew by now, but I really do never get tired
of helping kids make connections with art. As long as they
go home at the end of the day, am I right?

Honestly the only time learning is frustrating is when the
people around me *won't* do it. This usually is adults, not
kids. But I think I even feel a little better about that—for

the moment—because I was talking with an educator at a different museum today (he comes around once a month or so for programs, we collaborated on camp, that kind of thing) and he mentioned this coworker he used to have and went on a mini rant. "When I have to redo everything that you do and we both know it, you can help by not helping!" And folks, the vindication was real. "That is exactly how I feel!" I think I even squealed.

And that is example A of how you can learn in social situations, not just academic ones. For example B:

* * *

King Verity was uncertain about his son. There was the disappearance, of course, and the story about people in the sky. Not to mention before that the late night reconnaissance mission—not unusual for a pair of boys having fun, of course, but for a boy of *his* to get caught was disturbing. Now there was the strange matter of the boy's lack of heartbreak over the leatherworking maid, and on top of that, his insistence that they should finish marking the border along the way.

"But the route's all set," the King told Richard. Nearly everyone else had stumbled out of the dining hall and into the sleeping hall below. "We go north, like always."

"But we didn't finish the marking," Richard pointed out.

"No, we didn't, because we were worried about you!"

"But you're *also* worried about the Blessed Kingdom, right?"

"Aye." The King gritted his teeth. "All the more reason to get out of here, before they can pull another trick like *that* again."

"I already told you it wasn't them," Richard protested. "At

least, not the royal family. Not on purpose. Why would they do that to their own princess?"

"But you know how they feel about the sky," riposted King Verity. "And from talking to Ava it was clear they don't value the girl the way they should!"

Richard hesitated, visibly. "That's neither here nor there," he decided finally. "The fact is, we've known for a long time they could be plotting something, and you're worried about them expanding. And if you mark the border *now*, then you'll have a stronger argument *later* if they cross the line while we're away."

Pushing back from the table, from his empty plate and cup, King Verity thought. He considered himself nothing if not fair—and the boy *did* have a point. "But it's a delay," he said, not for the first time. "By the time we make it to the coast, we'll have missed the first days of the fish run."

"You can send some people ahead if you want to," the boy pointed out, exasperation evident in his voice. He never really had cared for fish.

"Glad we're in agreement. You can lead them."

"Me?"

"Listen, son, you need a change of scene." King Verity leaned forward once more. "I'm only trying to help you, Richard."

The Prince's face blurred, then softened. "Just trust me, Father. I know what I'm doing."

85

Wide, Wide World

October 2, 2019

It's time for light heartedness, yes? Especially as our two fictional countries prepare for war.

We had the most fun time at TEA last week (too much fun to care about grammar, if you can believe it). No one liked the book of the month, so we ended up just talking about the weirdest books we'd ever read or come across. Some gems:

—a tome on "mushrooms, Russia, and history"

—not one but several books on mortuary practices, including a youtube channel

—any Star Wars spin off

—a book that actually was about the history of tea!

—someone actually read one of those Barnes and Noble novelty books about poop.

—a dissertation from 1973

—politically correct bedtime stories (this was my contribution, and a total hoot)

—okay yes the dissertation was my contribution too.

* * *

Even days later, the feeling of winning an argument with his father was a strange one. Richard couldn't help but suspect that the Queen had had something to do with it—and he was grateful. Grateful to be packing up with the knights and the leftover timbers and even his younger brothers.

Queen Valor had left the day before with the fishers and the builders. With any luck, they'd have a home ready for the King, the Princes, and the knights by the time they'd planted the last post along the border.

While his brothers tore around the party like three whirling tornadoes, Richard let his horse step into place with Ben's. They had rear guard duty, watching over the back of the caravan that his father led.

"We're never going to sleep," Ben observed, watching the younger princes.

"Of course we will," said Richard. "After all, they have to."

"Yeah, in half-day stretches, while *we'll* have to be up making them dinner!" But Ben laughed along with Richard, his face bright. "Still, it's got to be hardest on you, right? You weren't even home a moon before we set out again."

Richard shrugged. "It's not like anyone planned it that way."

"Sure." Ben watched his friend closely for a moment. His smile became ever so slightly more calculating. "Say, whatever happened to the princess?"

"What princess?"

Ben reached over from the saddle, catching Richard's shoulder with the back of his glove, and making the Crown

Prince jump. "Yeah, sure, 'what princess.'" Ben laughed again. "You know, the princess you just went on a grand adventure with? Who even came over to Runn to speak for you?"

"Please, Ben. It's not like she really had a choice in the matter."

"But she would've."

"Would not," Richard replied, feeling ten years old. "You *know* how they feel about us over there. They think we're all barbarians."

"Eh, not wrong, are they?" Ben sat straight again, cheerful. "So what about her then?"

"I don't know," Richard admitted. "But . . . hopefully we're going to find out."

Ben read the expression on his face and joked, "As long as the civilized lords and ladies of the Blessed Kingdom don't conquer us first."

86

Wordy Little Secret

October 9, 2019

Most of you have properly diagnosed my taste in music as "old." So there I was, happily listening to the All-American Rejects' "Dirty Little Secret" whilst cleaning yesterday (much as I love classical, it's not quite the right vibe for fighting grime), and for the first time ever it hit me.

The 'best way we survive' is lying? Really?

Don't get me wrong—I'm not indignant because I believe in honesty as the best policy. We all know about white lies and how some questions *do* have a right answer. But that line caught me right in the word-loving heart yesterday. We have this great language, and the best way we can think of to survive in society is abusing it?

. . . Of course, now that I type it out, it makes total sense. Because lying isn't necessarily an abuse of language; honestly our language is set up for it. What's the difference between 'girlfriend' and 'girl friend'? Between 'hang out' and literally anything, because anything is a euphemism for sex? Between 'seeing someone' and just 'seeing' them? Between 'villain' and 'antagonist'? There absolutely is one, because our language gives us places to hide.

And one of those most common places in english is the fact that we have no plural 'you'. 'Y'all' doesn't count, not yet at least. Sure, *you* can come along . . .

* * *

"I thought just *you* were coming," Ava muttered to her brother as they made their way down from the castle plateau under cover of a particularly cloudy night. "I didn't know you needed to bring twenty of your *closest friends.*"

"And *I* thought you weren't going to complain since I got you a rucksack," Van returned cheerfully. "Look at us, hardly out the gates and already learning things on our journey."

Ava swatted him. "No one likes a know-it-all, Van."

"Too bad you're stuck with me," Van laughed. There was no need to be quiet: none of the castle guards would gainsay the prince when he said he needed to leave, and he needed the news to be secret until morning. "Anyway, Ava, it's a half dozen people at most, and we need them. Or were you planning to do all your own hunting and cooking?"

"It isn't that far," Ava protested. "I managed to get back from there, anyway."

"Speaking of," Van said with a glance behind them at their retinue, "where exactly are we going, and how do you know how to get there?"

"I just do, okay? It's—it's where the sky guardian dropped us off."

"I suppose you wouldn't forget something like that." Van was silent after that, and Ava appreciated it. She knew he believed her—he was one of the few who did, of the few she had told the whole story. He would always believe her, no matter what happened.

They moved across the tundra slowly, sporadic moonlight giving the landscape an eerie and shifting feeling. Ava found it far more unsettling than sky travel had been, and paid little attention to anything other than the horizon. She took no notice of the people behind her—though they certainly did of her. One in particular, an elderly, bent woman who barely kept up with the small company of guards, kept her gaze constantly on the princess. She had been brought along, perhaps, for her culinary skill; but her powers of observation were much sharper than her shrouded appearance indicated.

87

Nemesism

n. frustration and anger directed inward, at oneself

October 16, 2019

I just figured it was time to admit it. Officially. This is like my coming out post, when all along you folks saw me wearing rainbow scarves: not necessary for anyone, except for me, just so I can feel like I'm moving along the prescribed path.

Because you know all of the anger you've read here, no matter who it was about at the time—the Old One (whom I still hate, by the way, even though it's entirely irrational and she's at the point now where she can't even remember from day to day that I hate her), some stupid guy, The Break Up, The Family, The Public, any number of capital letters—all of that pales in comparison to what I feel about myself.

It's one of those things that deceptively difficult to talk about. Our society is so high-stress and so tumultuous right now that we're used to things like self-mutilation and suicidal thoughts. So you can say 'hey guys, I really hate myself,' and everyone else is like 'yeah me too.' Then you're like 'no but really though,' and you can see them thinking, 'well, she doesn't have scars on her wrist or a knife in her hand, so it can't be too bad.'

And I'm not trying to complain—really I'm not. I don't even *want* any of you to worry, because what would you do about it? Call a hotline? No thanks. If anything's going to push my self-hate over the edge, it's being watched and prodded and clucked over by strangers whose time I am wasting with things I'd rather keep hidden.

It's just weird, you know? I just want someone to understand. And not in a 'yeah I can't BELIEVE I ate a whole family size bag of doritos and twenty chicken nuggets yesterday, I am the worst' sort of way. Our societal self-hate, the kind you find around the internet, that's like waving around a bubble sword, you know? Potentially a little bit harmful, yeah, but also fun. But the 'I've been lying to myself and everyone for years trying to make things better and I never even succeeded and now no one knows who I am and it's all my fault why did I choose this,' that kind of self-hate, that shit doesn't mess around with bubbles. That is a yawning abyss edged with a million katana. And sometimes I think it'll bleed me out even if I never cut myself physically.

And sometimes, like last week, I think about *language* and *lying* and creating entire worlds in your head and characters that go on to feel real and affect your *life,* and I wonder if the pen really is mightier than the sword somehow.

* * *

Ava and her little group made camp near the frozen river, snug at the base of a row rise that gave some shelter from the wind. They had stopped early, just short of their goal, after walking through much of the night before. As a group they moved slower than one person alone but, Ava decided as she sat by the fire munching freshly cooked food, perhaps that wasn't a terrible price to pay.

Van waited until the others had retreated before speaking to his sister. He didn't notice that one of the guards had not returned from the hunting party yet. Instead, in the light and wind-chilled evening, he thought of other things.

"Ava. Are you *sure* you can trust this prince?"

"His name is Richard," Ava said stubbornly, as though this was answer in itself.

"I don't care what his name is. He could be Honesty himself for all I know. Can you really trust him?"

Ava paused. Richard *did* have something of the schemer about him. But of course, she told herself, he was a little too—well, un-Runnlike—to scheme things like violence and betrayal. "Of course I can. The real question is can *he* trust *us*," she added darkly, thinking of the guards they'd brought with them—not so unlike her mother's troops.

"Well I can tell you're still worked up about it," Van grinned.

"Am not!"

"Are too. Whenever you get worked up you start *talking* like *this*."

"I *am not*—" Ava stopped dead, and all at once she laughed. It was true. And after all, if things *did* go wrong the next day, she didn't want her last conversation with Van to be a childish fight.

Not like Orion.

"Don't worry, I get it," Van was saying. "It's important. But relax a little, okay? If he really is your friend, then what's the worst that could happen tomorrow?"

88

Call off the Hunt

October 23, 2019

Okay, people, call off the dogs and cancel the witch hunt!

(You don't know yet, but it's funny because we'll talk about a witch later.)

It's actually not funny right now though. Would you folks calm your shit down, please?

That is to say, look, I appreciate the sympathy. I did read all the comments on the post last week—some meant more than others, but that's life. I love the written word, but sometimes it's a cold comfort. What I *especially* don't love, though, is you people taking my admission and turning it into a victimization.

I'll say this very slowly, okay? I. Do. Not. Expect. Anything. From. Anyone. And. No. One. Has. To. Stop. Saying. They. Hate. Themselves. To. Make. Me. Feel. Better.

Some of you clearly feel victimized yourselves, in your own lives, and that's why you responded to my essay like it was an opinion piece on The Latest And Most Insensitive Shit Americans Are Saying Wrong. If that kind of struggle is your thing, then have at it—but it isn't mine. I'm not starting a movement. I don't care if kids keep joking about suicide. My experience is *not* an example of how I feel bullied by society, damn it. It's an example of how I bully myself, and I didn't tell you because I wanted you to write up a petition. I was just trying to make sure I saw what was going on inside myself.

I get that you thought you were helping, but honestly it just made me mad. I almost took down that post entirely, thinking I'd made a mistake in sharing it. It's no good saying to kids "you can't talk about hating yourself because someone else hates themselves more"—I mean that's basically what I was saying makes it tough in the first place. Anyone who has any amount of self-hate is going to have a rough time sometimes, and why shouldn't they joke about it? I just needed to be able to voice the difference, that's all.

Okay, rant over. Now on to actual witches:

* * *

Bess, the old and cow-obsessed witch, Head of Magics to the Blessed Court, would never have done this.

Bess couldn't cast a glamor spell to save her life—and she especially couldn't keep up a disguise as a guard, nor slip away without leaving a trace.

Bess wouldn't have thought to use her cauldron for summoning, rather than for cheese.

Bess couldn't even have imprisoned someone in the moon—not without help.

And Bess wouldn't have braved the elements alone.

Bess never would have made a potion without using milk, probably never even read her books about monsters (not the bovine kind), and never dabbled in magic that might involve blood.

Bess never realized that a true witch's greatest opportunity to shine, to be *needed,* to be *recognized* was war.

But her apprentice Bertha did.

89

All Hail

October 30, 2019

Happy Halloween! It's our second Halloween together—isn't that cute?

More like scary, muahahaa.

This year's Halloween is infinitely better than last year's, because this year I celebrated it properly: by summoning **ahem: FIGHTING** a demon in D&D!

So we got down to the end, right. The party is stuck in a mine filled with zombies ruled loosely by this female demon who's got about half her health left, and we're one healer down. We all had rolled special characters for this one-shot, so I wasn't my adorable paladin ball of annoyingness: I was a thief/druid combo, and someone *else* was the paladin. I just wanted to make that clear. With that in mind, consider the following:

Warlock: shit, no spells left . . . I throw my net!

DM (preparing to cackle): roll!

Warlock: shitshitshit . . . 20!!

DM (crestfallen): Okay, fine. She's in a net.

Me (because druids do things other than be animals!): Also she is still slowed!

DM: Yes. Also slowed.

Paladin, rubbing hands together: excellent. My turn. IC: "Help me out, guys! I'm going to consecrate her!"

DM, gone pale: You're going to *what?*

Paladin: Consecrate. Make holy. You know, like, she won't die, but she'll be tortured constantly by her own fellow demons now that she's turned against her will . . . "Ready?"

DM: Aaaaand, hearing that, she pulls out a ceremonial dagger and kills herself.

Party: . . . We win!!

DM: You guys suck.

* * *

It came all at once—not like a thunderclap, but like an anachronism, that jarring sensation that makes you take a good look around the story. *Is this really the genre I thought I was living in?*

Richard reeled, wondering if his adventures in the sky were going to catch up to him in the worst way possible.

Ava simply didn't believe it at first.

They stood in their separate camps across a stretch of gleaming ice. Neither side had been aware of the other and even now, neither noticed what was happening on the opposite bank; but both were very quick to put two and two together.

"It's a war beast of that cursed Blessed country!" cried the

King of Runn.

"It's a Runn trap!" declared the Blessed Prince.

It hung in the space between the statements, huge, breathing, slicing the rays of the morning sun. It was larger than any animal anyone had seen in this world. It was flying. And its dark, dark eyes did not look happy to see this particular setting.

It was, in fact, a dragon.

90

True Grit

November 6, 2019

So one of my coworkers is pretty cool. She's part-time here and part-time at a counseling center, so when she asked about my blog I figured she's seen worse than this—why not?

Heh. Heh. She comes in the following Friday like "Wow Ashley, that was way darker than expected."

And I know it has been, lately, and that isn't what I planned. So I get that she had that impression and that she was surprised but on the *other* hand, I wanted to say,

Well it's not like people are getting tortured or having sex with their siblings or murdering people for thrones!

But that's the thing, isn't it? Violence and rape don't necessarily make a story dark. Heck, if you throw too *much* of them in you get the opposite effect, where people get bored and think you're some kind of poser as an author (coughcough *teen lit* coughcough). I'm more of a light fantasy person, so I had never thought about it before, but I guess what makes a story *actually* dark is hatred. And frustration. Futility. That's where true grittiness comes from.

But I didn't have this conversation with her, of course, because I'm way too awkward. Instead I think I apologized, actually. (Always a safe bet where I'm concerned.)

As she was leaving for the day, though, she said to me, "Having those feelings and still coming to work every day and smiling like you do is a real strength, you know."

Yeah, I know. I mean, we've all heard that. The saddest people have the biggest smiles, and whatnot. But I don't like to think of that as *strength* any more. It's a lie, and lying can be so easy. Much easier than admitting you're broken.

Real strength is looking at a dragon and thinking to yourself, *Eh!*

* * *

Eh, thought Ava, looking up at the two-story-tall brilliant green beast. *I've seen worse.*

And she *knew* that what her brother said was wrong. Behind her, in the hollow of the hill, he was marshaling his few troops—

"You, get over here! Weapons ready! Why—are we missing someone? No time for it now! You, stay here and guard the cook!"

"Van really," Ava began over her shoulder, "this isn't—"

But her words were drowned out as the dragons screamed and, with two ferocious beats of its scaly wings, dove at their hill.

"You were saying?" Van huffed as they scrunched under an outcropping for cover.

"But it *isn't,*" said Ava. "they would never think to do this. They'd rather fight you themselves. Anyway if it is you'll still never have any luck fighting it with yourself and four guards. And—look!"

"It's five!" Van snapped. He was too slow to add, *don't stick your head back out there where it could get snapped off.* Since she was already doing that, and pointing too, he decided he had no choice but to follow suit. As he peered around the rock, he saw what she meant: the dragon was now attacking a contingent of Runn knights on the other side.

"That's what they get for summoning a dragon," said Van stubbornly. "It turned on them."

"It did not. I mean, why would they summon a dragon if it could turn on them?" Ava paused—for a moment it seemed she heard something, a faint cackling, on the wind. "I'm going to find Richard."

"You are *not* going out there!"

"I am!" Ava stood up, ready to run. "If you want to be helpful, then make a distraction!"

91

Retrodict

v. to explain something in the past with a modern inference or assumption

November 13, 2019

This is a fallacy, by the way. Our DM talks about this sometimes (guys it is a ride having a history major for a DM, let me tell you). To look back at a historic figure and diagnose them with some condition only recognized by the modern world might be interesting, but it's not academic, and you shouldn't believe anyone (ahem, *media*) who says things like "Napoleon had an inferiority complex" without immediately qualifying that. As far as I can tell, research is all about qualifications—just not the kind you put on your resume.

But anyway, in our own personal lives, retrodiction is fun, isn't it? Looking back and having a sudden revelation where now, as an adult, you suddenly understand what was probably going on. I think it works a lot better with emotions than with facts. I guess it's probably not fair to take your modern assumption and go on a tirade against your sibling, though . . . okay yes fine that is happening . . . but I'm not the tirading sibling this time!

Ugh, whatever. Have some knights tirading instead!

***

For all the practicing and posturing of Runn's knights, they didn't actually battle all that often. Richard himself had been in only, say, a battle or two a year. And all of those had been dealing with other hunters—maybe an enemy ship—but *never* with monstrous, magical beasts.

Still, he thought, the knights were doing pretty well.

"Stick together!"

"Remember the training!"

"Hit it in the armpit!"

"Gahhhh!"

"Watch out for the claws!"

Although, Richard added to himself, panting under the weight of his spear, *'pretty well' doesn't seem to make much difference to a dragon like this.*

Though he would not leave his camarades, Richard spared a look around. In one large body, the men and women of Runn made a group nearly as large as the dragon—but they were caught against the river's edge, and the dragon could simply rear up and fly away if it looked like they might score a hit. There was his father, and even his little brothers, fighting bravely; but what could what they do when *they* were the ones trapped? Richard racked his brain. He wished he could remember something, something from fighting Draco perhaps—if only he hadn't been so useless then—

"*Richard!*"

Richard shook his head. This was hardly the time to be remembering *Ava.*

"*RICHARD!*"

But we did agree to meet here, he remembered suddenly. How could he have forgotten?

Richard broke for the nearest hill in order to see more clearly. The dragon wheeled up and around, following some clamor on the other side of the river, and the knights streamed after it, his father's shouts reining them in. *Where is she? Surely she would have the sense not to—*

"Oof!"

Richard wasn't sure which one of them spoke as he collided with Ava head-on and they both toppled to the ground.

"Finally," Ava said. But she grinned as she looked up at him.

Richard ignored the warmth in his chest. "Ava, this isn't the time for—"

"Come on," she urged him, standing up without any other preamble. "I know who's doing this. At least, I think I do. We're going to find her."

"'Her'?" Richard checked the knights: they would hold for a little while. He ran after Ava, who shouted back,

"An old friend of yours!"

92

Mirror, Mirror

November 20, 2019

Okay this is perfect, especially with what we were just talking about last week. LADIES AND GENTLEMEN, AND EVERYONE ELSE. I have figured it out!

I was sitting there earlier today and emailing that one coworker, the guy who works at another museum, about how I gave up having meetings just with the Children's Gallery because The Old One flatly refuses to contribute, and I couldn't quite figure out how to explain it. Just like I can't explain anything in my life right now, as you folks know well. BUT THEN.

It was innocuous at first. "Well I think they never had meetings, and my predecessor just had her plan everything," I wrote. Which is true by the way, all my predecessor wanted to do was paint with kids, not all this running part of the museum nonsense. Anyway, I added, "then I came in and when I didn't fall in line immediately, [The Old One] was like 'fine! This is your job now!' and has refused to take any interest in any program ever since."

Which is actually . . . true. Except she never said that verbatim, of course, and it wasn't that *I* didn't fall in line right away (we actually got along for a little bit, as you might remember); it was that our boss had told her point-blank that scheduling was going to be *my* job (like it always was, only my predecessor didn't do it) and that she'd have to get used to the change.

The Old One hates change.

The Old One hates *me.*

Oh my god, folks! Mind blown!

I realize this might not make a lot of sense if you're not inside my head. The thing is, this whole time I have felt *so bad,* and just *so confused,* wondering why the heck I hated this old bat so much that I couldn't even look her in the eye. I'm not the type to take a dislike to anyone. But! I *am* the type to take whatever someone feels for me and reflect it right back at them . . . even without knowing what I'm doing. This whole time since The Break Up (and even before it) has just been me being interested in people because they were interested in *me* first. I think it's something we all do, whether we're conscious of it or not, but when I look at my relationships I know it's something I've been doing to the max ever since I was little, because I wasn't really sure what else to do and I wanted everyone to just be comfortable.

So then this selfish lady comes along and, even if she doesn't want to, she definitely hates me. I'm the new upstart that everyone else likes better than her. And without even realizing that this all started even *before I got there,* I took that undercurrent of hate and was like, 'oh, we're playing this game? I've never played *this* game before!' and along with reflecting *her* feelings, I added in a good dose of my own pent-up hatred that until now I had never let loose.

And if you think it's funny that until now no one has apparently hated me much, remember, I've been bland vanilla 'how can i help everyone else?' girl forever. Anything that was substance enough to hate, I've been hiding for ages and ages.

But it totally makes sense now when I look back on the early days. Every time I came home from work going, "but how could she *think* that of me? Why would she think I would *do* that?" it was because she hated me. Maybe she didn't even know it herself. But people will believe absolutely anything about people they hate. "Oh, Greg eats babies and blows up bridges? Well that explains it, that guy has always gotten on my nerves." That's the thing about hate—it destroys the other person's humanity.

This has changed my world, folks. I can't say it's made everything better, because honestly it still sucks that there's hate in the workplace at all. And I still think she's stupid, though now I mostly feel sorry for her rather than disgusted by that. And I still need an assistant of any age who can actually use Word. But . . . if it is a game, it's one I've won just by being here still. And it's one she's going to lose no matter what, because she'll never not be hateful at this point, and she'll never get things back the way they were. All she can do is lose a little less by seeing me be bitter too.

* * *

How Ava knew to run to the hillside of the island in the river,

Richard never did figure out. At the time he supposed it was only logical; it was the midway point between the two camps, directly under the spot the dragon had appeared. It had only a few of the tall evergreens which dominated the northern side of the river, and much of the snow which dominated the south: between the barren landscape and telltale footprints, they had very soon found whom they were looking for.

"Oh," said Richard, skidding to a halt just behind Ava, and looking around her at the witch's cauldron—and the witch's apprentice. "That was easy."

Bertha turned and saw them over her shoulder. She had tucked herself and her conjury into a sort of ravine on the northern edge of the hill, but the smoke from her glowing cauldron rose up and up, past the frosty cover. When she saw the prince and princess, she too seemed to glow.

"*Easy,* you say? This is *too easy* for you?"

"You know, Richard," Ava muttered under her breath, "I really would have taken you for the 'let's sit around the corner and plan about this' type. *Not* the 'let's bump Ava into plain view and tell the witch she's easy' type . . ."

Richard protested. "I didn't realize she was *right there!*"

"Enough! That's enough scheming from you two!" Bertha rose. It wasn't a very dramatic effect, however, as she wasn't very tall: she was only a young woman, after all.

"That was hardly scheming," Ava commented to Richard, undaunted.

"True. Do you think we should just leap at her, then?"

"Isn't that what got you put in the moon last time?"

"Technically, last time we got put in the stars—"

"SHUT UP!" Bertha put her arms out and for a moment Ava thought she might grab them—fear struck her, fast and bright—but instead the apprentice began muttering furiously, waving her hands over her cauldron. Above their heads, the dragon roared.

93

Many Happy Returns

November 27, 2019

Happy second Thanksgiving! This year, I'm gonna put out a list of things I'm grateful for:

—music (but NOT a certain STILL-OVERPLAYED but related Ariana Grande song)

—the stars (cheesy, I know, but . . . seriously, where would I be without the inspiration for this story?)

—the fact that we still have records of stories people thousands of years ago told! Is that not the weirdest and neatest thing when you really think about it?

—similarly, the fact that kids read, and get to share in those stories too. I know everyone's like 'kids these days don't even know the alphabet' but that's not true, and I'm grateful for those that do.

—patrons who actually read signs

—Winnie the Pooh, which is where the title for this post came from. I know it's actually for birthdays, but it seemed appropriate for a holiday about gratitude too.

—food, because of course

And finally . . .

—lists on blogs (easiest post ever!)

* * *

"Well she can't have it come get us here," Richard said reasonably, pushing an uncomfortable Ava further into the ravine.

"Yeah but she can do other things, remember?"

"Ava, why weren't you having these thoughts *before* we found her?"

"Well I didn't realize she looked so—desperate!"

"STOP TRYING TO BREAK MY CONCENTRATION!"

" . . . Oh, is that what we're doing, then?"

"YOU ALWAYS RUIN EVERYTHING!" Bertha stomped, and Ava felt her fear ebb. "Coming in and ruining my experiments and asking stupid questions and trying to stop me from becoming what I'm meant to be! You're just jealous! And *then* you had to go and get *lost* and I didn't have anything to show Bess for my project and so—"

"Wait," Richard thought aloud. "You *lost* us? You were doing a project?"

"That explains a lot." Ava made her decision all at once. She leapt forward and with one sturdy boot knocked a log from the fire. The bubbling cauldron tipped over toward her, and she and Richard had to leap to the icy edge to avoid steaming, green-yellow sludge as it seethed and hissed over the ground. With the cauldron tipped and rolling sideways, the fire leapt up in its place, right into Bertha's face.

"Nooooo! I'm meeellllttinggg!"

"You are not," Ava said matter-of-factly. "It's just hot. Richard, did that get rid of the dragon?"

"Um . . ." Richard peered out behind them. The land was eerily quiet. "I think so. Are you sure she's okay?"

Ava kicked the cauldron for good measure, barely looking at the sobbing witch's apprentice. "She's fine. She's not actually hurt, she's just not used to the heat. They keep it cold in the witch's tower, you know—for the cheese."

"Always Bess! Always cheese!" Behind her hands, Bertha moaned bitterly. But she never had been a very quick thinker, and she let herself be led away for lack of anything else to do.

94

Hiraeth

n. a longing for home akin to nostalgia

December 4, 2019

It's kind of the Welsh version of homesickness. I didn't feel anything like homesickness last year, at least not that I remember; probably I was too busy setting up the holiday programs and avoiding The Old One to notice anything I was actually feeling. I do that a lot.

You wouldn't think I'd be homesick this year, not with The Great Family Feud and all. It's patched up for now, but not really. I'm still mad that anything like any of it ever happened in the first place. Although at this point it's hardly anyone's fault, either, so I don't even know what to do with my anger.

And so it's sad but when I get homesick it's not for my sister or my parents really. It's more for . . . who I used to be.

I have this constant feeling, especially this year since I've been angry, that I'm losing part of myself. The better part of myself. It's obvious just in going back through this story that I have changed. As a concept, I actually like and embrace change, but in this case . . . it's hard.

* * *

Bertha was still scowling and muttering angrily about witches and cows much later that night, when everyone had convened in one bright and unsettled camp. Her eyes were still teary too, but she insisted that was from Ava's attempt to 'set her on fire.'

"For sky's sake," Ava said finally, setting down her dinner. She looked not at Bertha, but at the uneasy circle of knights, guards, royals, and cooks. Each face was lit not only by the campfire but by a multitude of torches: the Blessed folks' love of the night sky had been overruled by the more numerous—and, after a dragon attack, overly cautious—knights of Runn. "All I did was knock something over."

Beside her, Richard cleared his throat. "If you'll remember, that's all *I* did, way back in the beginning—"

"You were trespassing where you had no right to be!" Bertha flared from between two guards.

At the fire, the cook from Blessed nodded, her head still shrouded by her cloak. "Aye, what have you to say to that, Prince?"

The question was an unexpected one, strangely spoken. Ava and Richard looked at each other, equally taken aback.

"The Prince doesn't need to say anything about it," King Verity broke in. "He was collecting information, which is essential when your neighbors start shifting their borders and summoning bloody *dragons.*"

"Ah." Richard paused in the act of explaining himself and stared at his father, floored. He had never heard him refer to 'collecting information' as 'necessary' before.

"I'll admit we of the Blessed Court can not throw *too* many stones in that direction," said Van reasonably, with a glance at the cook. "I wonder if, now that we're all together—including the witch's apprentice—now is a good time, Ava, to hear your story again. Fully."

95

Book It

December 11, 2019

File this under Further Shit That Proves It Really Never Does Rain But It Pours.

I got an email from my ex the other day. No, not any of those other creeps—*the* Ex. He emailed me with a book recommendation. That's it.

And like . . . part of me really wants to reply, but just, not as me. You know? I wish I could write a reply that is perfect: wise, funny, calm, steady, firm . . .

But that's really not me, and that's why we broke up in the first place, isn't it? I don't really get why he messages me like this sometimes. Like I get that we had similar likes and we did *want* to stay friends, but I kind of figured that he thought I was crazy after everything that happened. *He* was the one putting passive aggressive stuff on facebook, after all, and *I* was the one who broke down and ran away with really no explanation to offer. Which of those two people would you expect to be the first to make contact again?

Truth is I have never really understood this guy. He was always out of my league, and a commitment-phobe on top of that. Just not as much of a commitment phobe as me, apparently.

What do you think, O Wise Denizens of the Internets? Should I even bother to reply?

* * *

Unable to contradict her brother when it really mattered, Ava set about telling the story—again. King Verity listened absently, poking at the fire; he had heard it before, parts of it twice. The knights of Runn were a great deal more interested (*wanting gossip for later,* Richard decided), as were the Blessed guards.

The story progressed slowly, for there were many interruptions.

Richard: "I was *not* trying to be a creep! I needed help!"

Bertha: "I TOLD YOU NOT TO COME IN MY TOWER—"

Van: "It isn't your tower anyway. Did you *mean* to send them to the sky?"

Cook: "So that's *really* where they went, is it?"

King Verity: "I don't see how it's hard to believe. You people talk about the sky all the time."

Bertha: "—SUPPOSED TO BRING THE CURSE OF THE SKY UPON INTRUDERS—"

Richard: "Anyway, everyone we met up there was very kind. . . . Almost."

Van: "You *met* people? Ava didn't tell me that!"

Cook: "That queen doesn't sound very queenly to me."

King Verity: "They're all off their rocker up there, in my opinion. No offense meant, Blessed . . ."

Bertha: "—STILL DON'T UNDERSTAND HOW SOME-ONE LIKE *YOU* COULD—"

Richard, wounded: "What's that supposed to mean?"

Ava, finally, feeling this had gone on long enough: "Well anyway, so we did find Aquila and it carried us down. Then we each went home, as you already know, but we had arranged to meet just in case. And it turned out that was needed, because—King Verity, Richard," she turned and said in a rush, before Van could stop her, "the truth is you *are* in danger. The court at Blessed wouldn't listen to me, and they're going to turn this all into an excuse for war. Not with dragons—at least, not if *someone* wants to keep their mouth shut," she added, with a fierce look across the campfire at Bertha.

Bertha shook visibly.

"Oh, don't worry." The cook stood from where she too had been poking the fire, across from the King of Runn. "I think we can make sure there are no more dragons."

"*Mother?*"

96

No Fantasy

December 18, 2019

So I went to a holiday party or what have you the other day, and since I'm finally getting comfortable with these people—the friends, you know, whom I've now been around for almost two years—I was considering opening up about writing. About this blog. So I was asking some questions because I *know* some of them read, when all of a sudden one girl ups and says,

"I like all kinds of genres—just not fantasy."

Well, thought I, *shit.*

"I mean if I see it in a movie of a show, that's fine, but in a book I just can't make sense of it . . ."

Okay, okay, fair. If the world is super different from ours, then yeah, it can be hard to keep track of that all via text. But I mean . . .

Isn't that the point of reading?

To stretch your brain, make you see new worlds? I mean,

I kinda *like* flipping things around in fantasy. You may have noticed by now that in Ava and Richard's world, south is cold and north is warm. (Or maybe you didn't notice. Maybe you're only here for the rants?) And even that isn't super revolutionary. There are places in our very own world that are like that. It's just those places aren't the US or Britain, so it seems crazy exotic.

I don't know, guys. Sometimes I really do wonder, what is that point? Who am I transcribing this for, really? I had toyed with the idea of printing it, just the story, but if it has no audience then why bother? I mean obviously there's you guys reading this now. But now that I think of it, your comments *are* usually about the blog, not the story. Aren't they?

* * *

Prince Vanderlin grinned as he, too, rose. "Ladies and gentlemen, allow me to present the Blessed Queen."

"What?" Ava wasn't the only one outraged: King Verity leapt to his feet and Richard, caught between the two of them, decided he might as well stand too. Soon enough everyone around the circle was standing, either aghast or awkward, depending on which country they were from.

The Queen laughed—a sound that did not put Ava at ease, for she had not heard it for years. And yet as the cook straightened and shook back the cloak, it was impossible not to recognize her mother's perfect hair, hard eyes, and wide mouth.

"Be at ease," said the Queen. "Our intent was not to deceive you, but to deceive the Princess."

"Well *that's* a fine thing to say," Ava piped up at once. "First you don't listen to me and threaten war against my friends, and then you lie and follow me around like I'm some sort of toddler?"

"Ava," Van intervened, "she *did* listen to you. She listened to you right now."

Ava turned to her brother, speechless. Richard wondered exactly how long it was going to take his father to catch on to the 'war' bit, but the king stayed silent.

"This was my plan." If Van felt awkward or ashamed as he looked around the circle, he did not show it. "I knew the two of you weren't communicating very well, and then Ava you were so convinced that if we talked to the Prince of Runn then everything would end peacefully, so bringing her along—the Queen, I mean—it was two birds with one stone."

"And you agreed to come walk through the snow with us just for that." Ava's disbelief was plain as she stared down her mother.

"At the time, we did not realize there would be any danger of dragons," the Queen observed dryly, with a glance at a trembling Bertha. "If we had known, we would have brought more guards."

There was an uneasy chuckle around the circle, which grew and grew and broke the awkwardness as the Queen stepped forward and smiled.

"Yavalinra," she said, "you always were a strongly opinioned child. But you always were an honest one, too. I wanted to believe you. I am glad now that I can. And we would be glad," she added, turning to King Verity, "to take this unfortunate event, and make it grounds for peace."

97

Merry Holidays

December 25, 2019

This year for Christmas, enjoy twelve delightful malaphors! If you don't know what a malaphor is, go look it up, or catch on as we go; haven't I done enough explaining words on this blog? And yes, I know the title *technically* is not one, but I just had a bunch of eggnog and I do not care.

1. We'll burn that bridge when we get to it.
2. Don't judge a book before it's hatched.
3. Whatever turns your boat.
4. Like looking for a needle in a hayride . . .
5. It isn't rocket surgery!
6. It's as easy as falling off a piece of cake.
7. Get all your ducks on the same page.
8. You're the top of the crop!
9. Gotta get that elephant out in the open
10. Too many cooks in too many pies

11. The world is your oyster shell
12. Birds of a feather judge a book by its cover.

* * *

If you had asked Ava, she would have said war was in-evitable—if stupid—simply because both sides *wanted* it so much. Even her own people seemed to her to be bloodthirsty and cruel, especially after she had seen such behavior in others among the stars.

And yet with an alacrity that astounded her, the Blessed Queen and the King of Runn agreed to a new and complete peace. It was more parental than political, but perhaps that was for the best.

The next day, the two parties made haste to leave—neither being thrilled about the idea of camping on the ice any longer. Though the knights of Runn were jovial, the Blessed side of things remained frigid: it turned out that while Ava and her mother could listen on grand occasions, they had difficulty with day-to-day conversation.

"I *told* her to put out the fire," Ava was saying to Van, as Richard came up.

"If I remember, you just told her it had to be done. You need to be patient, Ava; she's a queen, not an adventurer like you are now."

"Then why'd she come along as the cook, if she can't even look after a fire?"

"I'm not saying you aren't right, but—" Van caught the barest whisper of a suggestion of Richard clearing his throat, and turned on the spot gratefully. "Oh look, it's the Prince of

Runn. Very good to have met you, by the way."

"Erm, you too," Richard said. His voice was earnest: secretly he respected what Van had done. But his eyes turned back to Ava, and Van saw that at once.

"Right, well, I'll leave you to it," he decided cheerfully, making his escape.

As Ava turned to Richard, she was still glowering—a familiar look, he thought. At least this time it wasn't at *him*. "I just don't understand why everything has to be so difficult," she said.

"At least it turned out all right, Ava."

"For now anyway." Ava sighed. "You're lucky. Everyone in Runn seems much more sensible. And you get to go and be by the coast . . ." her voice faltered—she hadn't thought that one through.

"Well, you know, Ava, you could—" Richard paused, and cleared his throat for real this time. "We could write letters? I could tell you all about it."

"Sure." Ava looked down and bit her lip, determined not to let her disappointment color this conversation. "I really hope you enjoy yourself, Richard. And—go easy on your family."

At this, Richard grinned. "Same to you."

Behind him his father called, and though there was more yet to be said, there was no time. In a moment it was over, and he was gone.

98

Auld Lang Syne

January 1, 2020

Instead of doing a year-in-review—because how well do those ever work out?—we're going to look back at the last *two* years. Well, almost two years. (Can you believe this is blog post #98? But then, who's keeping track?)

And we're just looking at the good stuff—the story. You've probably figured out we're headed for an ending. (Speaking of which, stop leaving pleas and threats regarding the end in the comments, or else the whole thing is going to conclude with a giant meteor strike!) So let's take a moment for a story recap:

—the prince of Runn goes out for some light spying with his bro, and like a total amateur, gets caught

—the princess Ava meets a stranger on her roof who has no body

—we spend a good deal of thought trying to get Richard out of the moon, even taking a detour to Runn for the purpose

(albeit accidentally)

—in a raid on the witch's tower, emotions run high, and "true love's kiss" backfires

—our heroes find themselves in a strange new world being accosted by a dude in a skirt

—we traverse the Milky Way, meeting many of the constellations and their various levels of dysfunction

—we traverse *back* along the Milky Way, because a crazy queen won't let us past without some bling

—we meet some adorable dogs

—Ava decides "f*** the bling" and instead everyone fights a dragon

—Richard and Ava disagree (basically the whole story)

—Ava wanders alone

—Richard meets Orpheus, probably the coolest guy up there

—Orpheus bends space (literally!) with his music, and gets them on their ride home

—things fall apart

—Blessed kinda sucks and Runn is kinda cool

—peace! . . . maybe?

* * *

If Ava dwelt on Richard's lackluster goodbye, it wasn't for long. The moment she and the others arrived back at court, she was met with a strange greeting—

"And there she is! The famous princess!"

Ava glanced around, confused. She was used to people knowing her; but usually they did it with a resigned grace, not with any sort of fervor. And yet now, entering the gates, she was greeted with even more comments than the Prince and even the Queen.

"What, did something happen when I was gone?" she asked no one in particular.

Van answered, smiling broadly. "I think you'll find it happened just *after* you were gone. The first time."

This cryptic remark remained unexplained until Ava finally made it through the gauntlet of bows and politely veiled questions to reach her room—and more specifically, her once-unused desk. Where before it had lay empty, some delivery person had taken it upon themselves to pile stack after stack of letters and scrolls.

"What in the heavens . . ." Ava picked the first few up and overturned them as she had never seen the written word before. Contrary to her first suspicion, they *were* all addressed to her, and not in the same hand, either, so it could hardly be a joke or some fresh new creep.

Dear Princess Ava,

I do hope it's okay to call you that. It's what everyone calls you in the market. We all heard yesterday how you had stood up in court and said such brave things and I just had to tell you I think you're grand . . .

To the Princess Yavalinra:

It's about time someone stood up to the Queen!

Princess Yavalinra,

We always knew you'd talk about rights but this is something different. Now we know you'll really stand up for us. Won't you help us . . .

"Oh. My." Ava sat heavily, letters scattering around her. And after a moment of thinking about it, she smiled. "Looks like people outside of court have a voice, after all."

99

Adomania

n. the depressing feeling that the future is coming too fast

January 8, 2020

This is actually a made-up word—a recently made-up one, that is, since all words are made up. It's an older project but in case you've never heard of it, definitely go check out the Dictionary of Obscure Sorrows. Super cool! . . . in a mellow, sad kind of way haha.

And I am embracing that feeling today because guess what, folks? This story is just about over. No, I'm not going to immediately begin something new, *or* devise some kind of sequel, and everyone who suggests that in the comments deserves a poke in the eye. (And maybe also a hug for being so interested.) I *do* still have some of the other stuff I wrote as a teenager, but it's mostly crap. And . . . after this, I'm going to need some time.

Because a lot of myself has gone into this, people. I don't think you realize that I'm not over here just baking cakes for you to consume. It feels more like I am creating from scratch my own recipe of a cake that is my soul. Or at least, my soul in the present moment. This was supposed to just be a project from my past, maybe reconnecting with my old self a little, and instead it's become my present self pasting itself over what I thought about the past and dictating where it goes in the future. And that future is only a week or so away.

* * *

As soon as they reached the northern shore, Richard sat down to write to Ava. Since he had been doing this nearly every other night during the entire journey, many of the knights ignored him—they had tired, finally, of making fun.

It would be his sixth letter to her, and he was surprised to find he wasn't running out of things to say. It wasn't that he had so much to express about his travels: after all, he'd traversed the same path between the shore and the river since he'd been born. It was, he decided, mostly writing about what *others* had said. And while that wasn't something he had any interest in as a rule, in this case he just couldn't get over it.

My father asked my opinion on the best place to put the new tower when we get there . . .

So then my father said why don't I arrange the watch . . .

It was decided that Ben and I should be the scouts, since we have a 'talent' for it, everyone says; and they reminded us not to get caught, but they must have been only joking since they were quite happy to let us go . . .

It had occurred to him that perhaps Ava was getting tired

of this story. But the feeling of being appreciated was still something so new, he could only marvel at it.

And Richard's fears were set to rest when, later that evening, his mother finally had the chance to give him Ava's letters in return. The usual caravan had come through two days ago, she said, bearing no less than three replies. It wasn't six, but Richard wasn't going to complain; not when he read Ava's description of her newfound role in court, and her own complaints of a sore quill hand . . .

Quietly, Richard smiled to himself. It would, he decided, be a very busy summer.

100

You Have Shoes on Your Feet

January 15, 2020

Okay, you folks were right, last week was kind of a downer. I don't get what you're so surprised about, though. Hasn't this whole blog—the blog part, not the story part—been that way? I feel like it's been a whirlwind of sad-mad-bad-glad-sad again, like some sort of inverse Seuss book.

You know, I had never thought a lot about Seuss until we did an event on him here at the gallery last year. He wasn't all jokes and smiles—in fact he had some racist tendencies that'd probably get him burned at the stake today, and don't think we didn't hear about that during our event!—but I can definitely identify with the whole "you have kids, I'll entertain them" philosophy. I think the one thing this blog proves, if it proves anything, is that I am nowhere near stable enough to have kids of my own or to be considered an actual adult.

And I think that's what makes this feel so weird, actually. The *story* story is coming to a close, but my *own* story, the blog part—there's no resolution to that for me to give you. I'm still single; I'm still awkward; my coworker still hates me; my family relationships are still strained. My cats are still cute, I still love books, I still have good friends who make me do stuff like D&D. So . . . it's not the proper hero arc and it's not a tragedy either. It's just one of those really annoying slice-of-life shows that doesn't really have an ending. And for me, it's like, well who am I going to rant to now?

I had this all planned out at one point, you know. I wanted to end with something clever, so that you'd feel like it was an ending, even though it isn't. But then I kind of got in my own way. I guess that's as good a moral to this story as any: in your own story you can be the hero and the villain, and you can even be both at once. But the weirdest part is that you're going to end up changing, no matter which role you choose.

* * *

Bertha had never received such a scolding in her life.

So she had thought, anyway, upon getting an earful from the Queen on the return journey. But then they'd arrived at court, and she'd gotten much worse from the witch Bess.

Scoldings didn't come much worse than those that smelled like cheese curds and brine. And to top it off, she was reduced to nothing—no spells, no books, no potions. Just scrubbing milk crud off cauldrons and wringing out endless reams of cheesecloth.

Really, it wasn't as though anyone had *died,* Bertha often thought to herself. Really, one person had got a really excellent view for a while, two people got a trip through the sky, a bunch of knights got to see a rare beast, and two kingdoms saved themselves the trouble of war.

They *ought* to have been thanking her.

But of course, they would never do that. Just like they would never understand. Bertha paused in her scrubbing, which had carried on late into the night because she paused often. She looked up at the sky—at the glowing, growing moon, at the trail of light amongst pinpoints of stars. Everyone else looked at the stars but she looked between them, at that varied darkness. She looked into that blue and black and purple, and longed to be anywhere else.

Perhaps this time, it would not be an accident.

The End . . .

101

What's My Age Again

February 5, 2020

Okay, okay! Uncle!!

I swear some of you have done nothing for the past two weeks but comment on this blog.

And ONCE AGAIN, Internet, Dear Reader, You Creeps, you're right.

. . . I changed the ending, okay?

Originally, yes, Ava and Richard ended up together. There was this very cute and very carefully-thought out scene where Ava snuck up on Richard by pretending to be someone else, a la Jane Eyre and Mr Rochester, and everyone declared their love and was very happy. Finally.

And NO, I didn't change it because I hate Ava. Or Richard. I adore Richard and I respect Ava but . . . this time around I just felt like they were too young, okay? I think *everyone* is too young in fiction like this, honestly. I swear, I turned 80 when I was 11, and stayed ancient right through until I hit

24, at which point I promptly began acting like I was eight. "Ewww romance? Boys are icky!"

Fine. It's because I'm bitter and taking it out on my characters! But . . . can you see where I'm coming from? I didn't rewrite it just to be mean. I legit thought that would make the story more realistic.

But maybe being angry changes what 'realistic' looks like. Anyway, the terrible vengeful goddess has relented, and I now present to you an addendum to what I *thought* was the end of my story.

I guess we can take this as an answer to all my "what's the point? What is *real?*" angst. The point and the reality is that you guys cared about these characters!

And yeah. I guess I did too. I just didn't want them to get hurt.

How's that for a soul-searching conclusion?

* * *

When Princess Yavalinra of the Blessed Land showed up at the gates of Runn, she realized quickly that sneaking in was not going to be an option. If she had thought that the knights of Runn could forget her in the span of a year, she was gravely mistaken: even before she had made it up the hill their fortress topped, they were yelling down from freshly risen walls:

"Oi, it's the Princess!"

"Ava! Hey, Ava!"

"Hail, Blessed dragon-slayer!"

Amid the noise, Ava could discern a voice she recognized—not the one she wanted, but she smiled all the same. Ben was upon her the moment she made it through the gate, saying, "Hey, I was just telling Richard, we ought to go visit you. For old times' sake."

"And he was too chicken?" Ava grinned and tried not to look around the circle of knights too obviously. Over their shoulders, the encampment bustled: the court of Runn had only just returned from their season by the sea. "Where *is* the Prince, then?"

"Oh, probably overseeing something or another, or plotting the next raid on the Blessed Lands. Kidding!" Ben stepped back with both hands up as the knights around them laughed.

"You'd better hope he isn't," Ava laughed along with them. She had always felt so much more at home in Runn than in her actual home country. "You're lucky I left my guard at home."

"You came all this way on foot, alone?"

Ava shrugged. "It's really not that far." And she had only been able to make it because she'd finally convinced Van to get her a pair of *real* shoes, but her audience didn't need to know that. Discretion, Ava had found, was a very large part of being a princess. "So how was the coast?"

"Perfect. You have to see it sometime," was the general consensus. As he led the chorus, Ben caught sight of something over Ava's shoulder. Disguising his nod at the signal, he continued, "The pirates really made a good run of it this year. You should've seen this one ship, they even went so far as to paint it green and—"

"Excuse me, miss," came a clear, officious voice from behind Ava. "Do you have the proper authorization to be here as a foreign dignitary?"

"The *what* now?" Ava whirled, with the unsettling feeling that her bureaucratic customs had followed her across the border. But when she saw who was standing there, her peevish bravado cracked.

Richard beamed at her. "You wouldn't want to be accused of being a creep, now, would you?"

102

Excuses

February 12, 2020

Well here we are, folks. *Officially* two years. *Officially* Valentine's Day. Raise a glass of wine!

And what do you people give me, otherwise alone and loveless, on Valentine's Day? A nasty online comment, naturally! "Being a writer is no excuse for being maladjusted."

Well, you know what, Anonymous? I agree with you. Being a writer is not my excuse for being maladjusted; in fact, being maladjusted is my reason for being a writer. However being a wormy creep too cowardly to leave their own name on a personal critique is no excuse for leaving your slimy trail on someone else's art, so put that in your pipe and smoke it!

Love and kisses!

But really, I'm not bitter or anything. It's all true stuff, and anyway something WAY better happened this past week: betrayal!

Of the best kind, though. Turns out one of my TEA

members (shout out, you know who you are!) has been reading this since like before Richard and Ava even liked each other (she stalked me online when I started at the museum, apparently; new employees beware, this really does happen, it's not your employers but your coworkers who will be going through your twitter and judging you!) and she even shared it with the other members. They all confronted me about it last week. Honestly I think they were planning it as an intervention—a Love Intervention—because they hadn't yet read the last blog post. But maybe it just came off that way because all their snacks and utensils were Valentine's themed. Either way, they got the happy ending they wanted, and it turned out to be a big celebration.

And really the happiest person there was me. Not because of Ava and Richard getting together in print; remember, Ava and Richard live in my brain, so I know tons of stuff about them that's not on the blog. There are some things it doesn't matter too much to me if you folks end up knowing or not. But jokes aside . . .

I love all you on the blog, I really do. You folks have gotten me through a really rough two years. And something about celebrating in person was even better. Now, this isn't a cozy mystery—it's not like one of the TEA members is secretly an editor or knows the head of a big publishing company and suddenly I'm going to be A Writer and I'll have time to solve murders with my cats. It's never really that easy, is it? But I don't mind that so much. I have this blog, and I have books. What more do I need?

Everything is only stories, anyway.

* * *

As the knights' delight settled down, Ava and Richard managed to break away, to stroll around the fort together. Richard held himself a little taller, and Ava wore her traveling clothes with a little more ease, but otherwise they found at once that they were the same as before. With each moment alone, their own delight grew.

"So listen," said Ava, as Richard steered them around a herd of uneasy horses. "Writing letters is great and all, but it's not like our countries trade all that often, to be carrying letters back and forth. I think we should do something more. We should set up an exchange system."

"You mean like ambassadors?" Richard looked ever so slightly up at Ava in surprise. The blue sky behind her highlighted her unusual hair.

"Sure, if you want to use the fancy word and all. But they have to be *real* ones, not crotchety old men who arrange abductions."

As their laughter faded, Richard couldn't help but ask. "So who would be the ambassador from the Blessed Lands?"

Ava's response was immediate. "Which of us can you stand?"

"Well, you know, *you* would make the obvious choice . . . you are already here, after all."

"Yeah, but I might be otherwise engaged."

"Oh." Richard nearly slipped in the mud and was glad of the chance to look at his feet. Ava's voice sounded so cavalier, cheerful even, and he wanted to be glad for her, but what did she *mean?*

"Richard," Ava laughed again, seeing this, "you're way too humble. I'd be mad at you if it wasn't one of the things I love about you the most."

Eyes wide, Richard looked back up. "What . . ." Then as his eyes narrowed thoughtfully, he grinned. "Are you saying you'll be 'otherwise engaged' because you're proposing to me, then?"

"Not a bad idea," Ava decided. "I hadn't thought about *how* it would happen, only that it should."

"Shall we call it a team effort, then?" Richard's gait stuttered, because he no longer walked on the ground. "Ava, you're just as bad as everyone else here, thinking up a thing that you want and then making *me* figure out how to get it."

"At least I know what I want," Ava grinned. More soberly, she added, "I'm not saying it needs to happen right away, though, or even that it'd be easy or whatever. I just figured that since we got out of the sky—"

"—and into it—"

"—together, we probably have a good shot at this."

"More than probably," Richard corrected, finally coming to a halt as they hit the end of the courtyard, "because I love you, Ava."

"I love you too, Richard. Now will you kiss me already, or do you plan to make me climb the walls first?"

"But what if we get somewhere even *more* fantastical this time?"

"Well, how about we find out?"

Book Club Exclusive: TEA's Interview and Questions for Further Discussion

TEA Question for Ashley: First things first! Now that we've finished this book, when will you begin work on the sequel, Ashley?

Answer: Um . . . Does 'never' count? Okay, okay, kidding! I really hadn't thought about it. If I ever do write a sequel, I'll have to take some time to let it really stew. After all, this story technically took me ten years. So give me a break!

Q: Okay, we'll work on that. Moving on . . . let's go back to the beginning. A lot of us were wondering, where did you get the idea for the name of your blog?

A: Oh, *Gallery of Myth,* you mean? It seemed fitting, since not only are Ava and Richard meeting myths, the whole story felt somewhat myth-like to me because it's so old. I mean, it *feels* old to me, since I wrote it forever ago. Okay, maybe that only makes sense to me! Actually, *Gallery* was my second choice—at first I was going to name it *The Pillowbook.*

Q: The "Pillow Book"?

A: Something like that. It's a reference to a text written by a Japanese courtier in — oh, I don't know — the Middle Ages? You folks know I'm bad at numbers. Anyway, it's called *The*

Pillow Book of Sei Shonagon, and it's basically her diary, but she doesn't write "today I ate fish and did my hair." Instead she lists things she likes or doesn't, stuff she's seen, things like that. It's all just loosely strung together, just random reflections of her world—and I really liked that. That's how this blog has felt to me. Plus, it seemed perfect because the story itself—Richard and Ava's story—is basically a bedtime story.

Q: Oh, we'll have to look that up! You should do a gallery program on that. Rose, write that down! Okay, now, next question . . . How about any other influences on the book?

A: Well, there's Greek mythology, of course. And mythology in general, since this time around I tried to incorporate more constellation stories. When I first wrote the story it was pretty heavily influenced by *Jane Eyre*—I think I mentioned that in the blog at some point—which is kinda funny, if you think about how I ended this version at first, if you've ever read *Villette.* Come to think of it, I may have talked about that in the blog too . . .

Q: It's clear Charlotte Bronte inspired you! We really love how everything turned out. In the *new* ending, that is.

A: The "new" ending, which is very much like the original ending teenage me wrote? [laughs] I have to admit, I agree with you. I really thought I was doing the right thing at first by leaving Ava and Richard separate, but . . . it does feel better ending things with them together. I never thought about how much of writing is actually *feeling,* you know?

Q: And reading, too! And speaking of feelings, how do you feel about how Ava turned out in this version? You mentioned in your blog that you changed her character a bit.

A: You mean, made her angrier? [laughs] It's kind of funny,

isn't it, given that I thought of this story as a light-hearted fantasy bedtime story type of thing. And it wasn't just Ava, either. Honestly one of the big themes of the whole project is probably anger. I guess you see it more in the blog than in the story.

Q: Do you feel like it gets resolved, in the story? Did you mean for it to?

A: In some ways, yeah. But I think for me, with anger, it doesn't resolve so much as change. That's probably because of my own shortcomings in how to deal with anger. Like, as a kid writing this the first time, I figured the right thing for Ava to do was hold all that anger in until it exploded in a meaningful, really poetic kind of way. I think in the first draft Ava had only one or two outbursts, and they were *perfectly* worded. Then later—like initially when I began the story—my thinking was just to hold that anger in and deny it existed until it leaked out in strange places, like on a blog on the internet.

Q: And now?

A: Now, well, I guess I *will* need that blog still . . . [laughs] kidding, kidding. I mean you obviously can't be letting it out everywhere all the time. You have to let it out in little pieces, somehow. That's the thing about me—and Ava, even though I didn't realize it when I wrote her. But I didn't realize it about myself either, so there you have it. We both have all this anger stored up—way more than you can let go of in just *one* outburst, or blog post.

Q: So do you think of Ava as yourself, then?

A: Oh, definitely not. No, I'm not nearly that plucky, you know? [laughs] But she *is* a part of me. We overlap—she came from a certain place inside me, even way back then, and then she grew in her own way. Same for all those characters . . . Except Bertha. She was just a laugh.

Q: How about the constellations? Did you have a favorite one?

A: Orpheus. What, you thought this was a hard question? Nope! [laughs] Although Aquila was pretty convenient from an author's point of view, I will admit. That's one point in favor of magical eagles.

Q: In a way, you treat all the constellations as magical. In the story, Ava—and Richard, too—wonders a lot about what they actually *are.* Did you mean for them to be pure magic, like spells?

A: I'm not sure "spells" is the right way to put it. But they do have an element of magic, for sure—most myths do, after all. It's a little hard to say exactly what I meant, because that was something that was actually in the story when I wrote it as a kid. I think I had this idea of the constellations kind of like fairies, or the fey: you know, impossibly beautiful, never aging, possibly helpful, but also really likely to abduct you if they get a chance. They have all this magic, but they're low-key obsessed with humans who have none. After all, Ava and Richard are the ones who can remember things, *feel* things, and find things—they're the ones who are really *alive.* And I think some of the constellations, like Orion and Cassiopeia, were really jealous of that on some level.

Q: I love that. Okay, last question: what's next for you? You said you don't have a sequel in mind, but have you thought of doing anything else?

A: I've thought about it a lot, but nothing has really struck me yet. I guess we'll have to see. It's all one big adventure, right?

Discussion Questions:

1. Which constellation is *your* favorite? How many did you know of before you read this story?
2. Do you think you fit in better in nomadic Runn, or the highly ordered Blessed Land?
3. Aside from anger, what emotions do you think drive this story? What does this story make of redemption?
4. Which character do you find most sympathetic?
5. If you could travel through any land, fictional or otherwise, what would it be? How do you think it would change you?
6. Where, in your opinion, is the line between what's real and what's fiction?

About the Author

Hi! I'm T.A. Page, and I write fantasy novels that are wacky, heartfelt, and maybe a little bit true. When not writing, I enjoy long walks, gazing at the stars, devouring mythology, and wondering over the power of words. Find me online at the links below!

You can connect with me on:
- https://authortapage.com
- https://twitter.com/AuthorTAPage
- https://www.facebook.com/authorTAPage